Summer 2005   Vol. XXV, no. 2
ISSN: 0276-0045   ISBN: 1-56478-440-1

THE REVIEW OF CONTEMPORARY FICTION

D1233600

Editor

JOHN O'BRIEN
Illinois State University

Senior Editor

ROBERT L. MCLAUGHLIN
Illinois State University

Associate Editor

IRVING MALIN

Book Review Editor

JEREMY M. DAVIES

Production & Design

N. J. FURL

Cover Photographs

MICHAEL EASTMAN (WILLIAM H. GASS)
PETER MARTIN (ROBERT LOWRY)
LARRY MERRILL (ROSS FELD)

The *Review of Contemporary Fiction* is published three times a year
(January, June, September) by the Center for Book Culture at
Illinois State University (ISU Campus Box 8905, Normal, IL 61790-8905).
ISSN 0276-0045. Subscription prices are as follows:

Single volume (three issues):
Individuals: $17.00; foreign, add $3.50;
Institutions: $26.00; foreign, add $3.50.

DISTRIBUTION. Bookstores should send orders to:

Review of Contemporary Fiction, ISU Campus Box 8905,
Normal, IL 61790-8905. Phone 309-438-7555; fax 309-438-7422.

This issue is partially supported by a grant from
the Illinois Arts Council, a state agency.

Indexed in *American Humanities Index, International Bibliography of
Periodical Literature, International Bibliography of Book
Reviews, MLA Bibliography*, and *Book Review Index*. Abstracted
in *Abstracts of English Studies*.

The *Review of Contemporary Fiction* is also available on 16mm
microfilm, 35mm microfilm, and 105mm microfiche from
University Microfilms International, 300 North Zeeb Road,
Ann Arbor, MI 48106-1346.

www.centerforbookculture.org

THE REVIEW OF CONTEMPORARY FICTION

BACK ISSUES AVAILABLE

Back issues are still available for the following numbers of the *Review of Contemporary Fiction* ($8 each unless otherwise noted):

DOUGLAS WOOLF / WALLACE MARKFIELD
WILLIAM EASTLAKE / AIDAN HIGGINS
CAMILO JOSÉ CELA
CHANDLER BROSSARD
SAMUEL BECKETT
CLAUDE OLLIER / CARLOS FUENTES
JOSEPH McELROY
JOHN BARTH / DAVID MARKSON
DONALD BARTHELME / TOBY OLSON
WILLIAM H. GASS / MANUEL PUIG
ROBERT WALSER
JOSÉ DONOSO / JEROME CHARYN
WILLIAM T. VOLLMANN / SUSAN DAITCH /
    DAVID FOSTER WALLACE
DJUNA BARNES
ANGELA CARTER / TADEUSZ KONWICKI
STANLEY ELKIN / ALASDAIR GRAY
BRIGID BROPHY / ROBERT CREELEY /
    OSMAN LINS
EDMUND WHITE / SAMUEL R. DELANY
MARIO VARGAS LLOSA / JOSEF ŠKVORECKÝ
WILSON HARRIS / ALAN BURNS
RAYMOND QUENEAU / CAROLE MASO
RICHARD POWERS / RIKKI DUCORNET
EDWARD SANDERS
WRITERS ON WRITING: THE BEST OF *THE REVIEW OF CONTEMPORARY FICTION*

BRADFORD MORROW
JEAN RHYS / JOHN HAWKES /
    PAUL BOWLES / MARGUERITE YOUNG
HENRY GREEN / JAMES KELMAN /
    ARIEL DORFMAN
JANICE GALLOWAY / THOMAS BERNHARD /
    ROBERT STEINER / ELIZABETH BOWEN
GILBERT SORRENTINO / WILLIAM GADDIS /
    MARY CAPONEGRO / MARGERY LATIMER
ITALO CALVINO / URSULE MOLINARO /
    B. S. JOHNSON
LOUIS ZUKOFSKY / NICHOLAS MOSLEY /
    COLEMAN DOWELL
CASEBOOK STUDY OF GILBERT
    SORRENTINO'S *IMAGINATIVE QUALITIES OF ACTUAL THINGS*
RICK MOODY / ANN QUIN /
    SILAS FLANNERY
DIANE WILLIAMS / AIDAN HIGGINS /
    PATRICIA EAKINS
DOUGLAS GLOVER / BLAISE CENDRARS /
    SEVERO SARDUY
ROBERT CREELEY / LOUIS-FERDINAND
    CÉLINE / JANET FRAME
WILLIAM H. GASS
GERT JONKE / KAZUO ISHIGURO /
    EMILY HOLMES COLEMAN

NOVELIST AS CRITIC: Essays by Garrett, Barth, Sorrentino, Wallace, Ollier, Brooke-Rose, Creeley, Mathews, Kelly, Abbott, West, McCourt, McGonigle, and McCarthy

NEW FINNISH FICTION: Fiction by Eskelinen, Jäntti, Kontio, Krohn, Paltto, Sairanen, Selo, Siekkinen, Sund, and Valkeapää

NEW ITALIAN FICTION: Interviews and fiction by Malerba, Tabucchi, Zanotto, Ferrucci, Busi, Corti, Rasy, Cherchi, Balduino, Ceresa, Capriolo, Carrera, Valesio, and Gramigna

GROVE PRESS NUMBER: Contributions by Allen, Beckett, Corso, Ferlinghetti, Jordan, McClure, Rechy, Rosset, Selby, Sorrentino, and others

NEW DANISH FICTION: Fiction by Brøgger, Høeg, Andersen, Grøndahl, Holst, Jensen, Thorup, Michael, Sibast, Ryum, Lynggaard, Grønfeldt, Willumsen, and Holm

NEW LATVIAN FICTION: Fiction by Ikstena, Bankovskis, Berelis, Kolmanis, Neiburga, Ziedonis, and others

THE FUTURE OF FICTION: Essays by Birkerts, Caponegro, Franzen, Galloway, Maso, Morrow, Vollmann, White, and others ($15)

NEW JAPANESE FICTION: Interviews and fiction by Ohara, Shimada, Shono, Takahashi, Tsutsui, McCaffery, Gregory, Kotani, Tatsumi, Koshikawa, and others

Individuals receive a 10% discount on orders of one issue and a 20% discount on orders of two or more issues. To place an order, use the form on the last page of this issue.

RCF Call for Contributors

www.centerforbookculture.org/review

The *Review of Contemporary Fiction* is seeking contributors to write overview essays on the following writers:

Felipe Alfau, Chandler Brossard, Gabrielle Burton, Jerome Charyn, Stanley Crawford, Eva Figes, Karen Elizabeth Gordon, Carol De Chellis Hill, Violette Leduc, Julián Ríos, Esther Tusquets.

The essays must:

- be fifty double-spaced pages;
- cover the subject's biography;
- summarize the critical reception of the subject's works;
- discuss the course of the subject's career, including each major work;
- provide interpretive strategies for new readers to apply to the subject's work;
- provide a bibliographic checklist of each of the subject's works (initial and latest printings) and the most important (no more than five) critical pieces about the subject;
- be written for a general, intelligent reader, who does not know the subject's work;
- avoid jargon, theoretical digressions, and excessive endnotes;
- be intelligent, interesting, and readable;
- be documented in MLA style.

Authors will be paid $250.00 when the essay is published. All essays will be subject to editorial review, and the editors reserve the right to request revisions and to reject unacceptable essays.

Applicants should send a CV and a brief writing sample. In your cover letter, be sure to address your qualifications.

Send applications to:

Robert L. McLaughlin
Review of Contemporary Fiction, ISU Campus Box 8905, Normal, IL 61790-8905

Inquiries: rmclaugh@ilstu.edu

Contents

William H. Gass

Stanley Fogel

> *"My lips are highly rated,*
> *and my fingers celebrated,*
> *as for my tongue it's equally fun,*
> *however it's rotated . . ."*
> —*Omensetter's Luck*

This limerick is uttered by Jethro Furber of *Omensetter's Luck*, one of William Gass's beleaguered but irrepressible and loquacious, even logorrheic narrators. Like the rest of them he acts tentatively, if at all, but produces a relentless, creative, Muhammad Ali-like patter. It is replete with sexual innuendo and linguistic exuberance. Indeed, limericks, usually bawdy and playful as well as somewhat sophomoric, broadcast their maker's delight in wordplay. They occur frequently in Gass's work, especially *Omensetter's Luck* and *The Tunnel*. This particular one, with its emphasis on the oral (lips and tongues) and the written (fingers) and their link to desire's prodding, could well stand as a summation of Gass's achievement (freed from the frantic context in which Furber fashions it).

Performance is the word that comes to mind when one thinks of Gass's oeuvre. Whether it is a monologue by obsessives such as Furber, *The Tunnel*'s Kohler, and the "Order of Insects" narrator-housewife or riffs in Gass's own voice such as in that dazzling bit of legerdemain *On Being Blue* and the celebration in "And" of that conjunction, what one remembers, the residue one is left with, is the flourish, the flamboyant sentence. Pithy or sprawling, it is always an architectonic marvel. Its impact is augmented, too, by the rhythmic, alliterative language that blurs the line between poetry and prose. Then there are the tropes that concretize and make vivid what would otherwise be abstract and arid philosophical discourses. Transmitted through a Gass sentence is the energy of the voice regardless of whether the topic is sex or something more sublime (both usually finding their way into the same lavishly created space, giving it amplitude and heft).

Here, above all, is a writer in the sense Roland Barthes gives that word in the title of one of his essays, "To Write: Intransitive Verb." Less important than the subject he chooses to write about is that Gass has written (about) it, and always with panache. In an interview jointly given by him and Stanley Elkin, an author with whom he shares a good many aesthetic values, Gass states, "As a writer I only have one responsibility, and that's to the language I'm using and the thing I'm trying to make" (qtd. in Duncan 53). A little further on in the interview Gass emphasizes this preoccupation of his: "I've always been interested in writing as writing. My interest in the various forms is dominated by an interest in style as such" (64).

Maxims are delivered breezily and assuredly (à la Barthes): "The soul, we must remember, is the philosopher's invention, as thrilling a creation as, for instance, Madame Bovary" (*Fiction* 5). Metaphors are fashioned that range from the ostentatious (". . . I came like an ad in the mail" (*Tunnel* 12)) to the outrageous (of victims of the Holocaust Gass wrote, "In groups of twenty, like smokes, they are directed to the other side by a man with a truncheon and a whip" (*Tunnel* 34)). He can be pithy and witty, categorizing trashy literature as "dick, prick, and booby books" (*Fiction* 271-72). He can also wax lyrical and tender as he does in the following paean to his ideal reader:

> [S/he] is skilled and generous with attention, for one thing, patient with longeurs, forgiving of every error and indulgence, avid for details . . . ah and a lover of lists, a twiddler of lines. Shall this reader be given occasionally to mouthing a word aloud or wanting to read to a companion in a piercing library whisper? yes; and shall this reader be one whose breathing changes with the tenses of verbs? yes; and shall every allusion be caught like a cold? no, eaten like a fish, yes; and shall there be eyes and eyebrows raised at rhymes? . . . oh a sort of slowpoke singer, finger tracer, then, mover of lips. . . . Let's imagine such a being. And begin. (*Heart* 31)

What Gass demands in this quotation (as well as elsewhere—he often makes pitches to his reader) is someone whose love of and sensuous engagement with language is commensurate with his own. In his urgings he sounds like Vladimir Nabokov, one of the writers he respects most and about whom he writes on occasion. About his famous novel *Lolita* (as well as other works), in which he teases the readers' avid desire for digestible information, Nabokov demanded that they "caress the details" (Wetzsteon 245). By this he meant the luxurious, intellectually febrile prose, the well-crafted sentences and the urbane diction, not the clichéd, flaccid plot in which an aging love-struck pederast cavorts with his stepchild. Certainly, Gass's stylish prose, not to mention the self-conscious use of limericks and other devices that signify artifice, overwhelms—in quantity as well as quality—whatever plot apparatuses appear in his fiction or theses in his nonfiction.

Willie Masters' Lonesome Wife, for instance, is less a novella than a compilation of typefaces, page colors and textures, photographs and, most important, prose constructions that dramatize the unrealistic elements of a book; it also tests the limits of how close to, yet separate from the world words and literary texts are. In *On Being Blue* Gass undertakes to exhaust the linguistic potential of the word *blue* in and out of literature; he revels in as well as examines the dilemma of making sentences sexual. Moreover, if much of Gass's work is a testament to his celebrated fingers (on the typewriter or later the word processor), many of his essays attest to the dexterous rotation of his tongue because they were originally delivered as lectures—to the Modern Language Association, say, or at faculty seminars and colloquia—before they were published.

William Gass is a significant figure in American letters not only for the legerdemain with which he handles language and experiments with literary forms but also for his influence on the literate public. As a featured reviewer of fiction and works of philosophy for such leading liberal journals of art, culture, and politics as the *New York Review of Books* and later *Harper's*, Gass has been, for a good many years, shaping the values of readers, cultivating a coherent theory of literature and a taste for certain writers whose work affirms and embodies that theory. With the kind of flair he shows in his fiction—with all the artfulness and flamboyance he devotes to giving the sentences in his novels their distinctiveness, Gass has articulated his criteria for a rich culture and civil society, generally, and incisive fiction, specifically; he has done this in venues other than the arcane journals of theory (and, often, deconstruction) in which such formulations are usually found.

As early as "Philosophy and the Form of Fiction," published in his first collection of essays, *Fiction and the Figures of Life*, Gass outlines the kind of writing he has consistently championed:

> There are metatheorems in mathematics and logic, ethics has its linguistic oversoul, everywhere lingos to converse about lingos are being contrived, and the case is no different in the novel. I don't mean merely those drearily predictable pieces about writers who are writing about what they are writing, but those, like some of the work of Borges, Barth, and Flann O'Brien, for example, in which the forms of fiction serve as the material upon which further forms can be imposed. Indeed, many of the so-called antinovels are really metafictions. (24-25)

Relentlessly, Gass has reviewed the books of and, concomitantly, promoted the works of such writers as John Barth, Robert Coover, and Donald Barthelme, all of whom interrogate the means by which they create fiction. Like Gass they reject the mechanical deployment of plot and narrative; in short, they, like him, write metafictions. Moreover, Gass champions precursors of metafiction, writers of antirealistic novels such as Nabokov, Jorge Luis Borges, Samuel Beckett, and Gertrude Stein. *Avant la lettre* (she is very fashionable now as a protofeminist and queer icon), Stein is revered by Gass not only as an iconoclast but also as a leading experimenter with the form and language of fiction. For Gass she is revolutionary because she shows how the language of the novel can be antireferential, can resist being a window that provides direct access onto the world.

Although Gass criticizes Barthelme for occasionally being too cerebral, for displaying an excessive amount of cleverness, he applauds the kinds of tactics Barthelme deployed to rupture a novel's verisimilitude, the texture of everyday life that for too many, according to Gass, is the novel's main virtue. This was the principal goad for his famous debate with the novelist John Gardner whose *On Moral Fiction* gives a sense of the opposition generated by a writer and critic for whom literature, specifically the novel, has a more immediate impact—hortatory and didactic—than Gass can accept.

While Gass shares the love of experimentation that the other writers of metafiction named above display, his fiction differs markedly from theirs. Barth, for instance, is enamored of the myths and folktales that he parodies and adulterates. Barthelme is a metafictional minimalist: one of the characters in *Snow White* drolly remarks that the "palinode" (13), or retraction, is his favorite form. Coover has an angry, politically engaged side that manifests itself most demonstrably in *The Public Burning*, his wild and hyperbolic rendering of the execution of Julius and Ethel Rosenberg. Gass, on the contrary, does not radically vitiate or reject narrative strategies; or rather, he relies on point of view in less destabilizing ways than do the others. Most of his work as a novelist and short-story writer utilizes the technique of interior monologue; he also leaves a consistent narrator in place. At the level of the sentence, though, is where Gass does his antirealistic damage. The rhythms and incessant alliteration he deploys in his prose; the showiness of metaphors (reminding one of Barthelme's extravagant simile, "the shoulders on her were as tempting as sex crimes" (*Sadness* 147)); the elaborately constructed quality of his sentences (which transmit a sense of completeness as much as a connection with what precedes or follows them): these are the dominant metafictive characteristics of Gass's prose. A sentence chosen more or less at random from *The Tunnel* shows quite well the stylization of the sentence that is uniquely Gass-y:

> I stood in a pool of cold and urine-yellow sunlight one early autumn afternoon, a sweater's empty arms around my neck, closing the family album on my children, one soft black page against another like the dark in which I'd mount my succeeding days; face dry, tight, smileless, smooth as an apple's skin, while I counted the overlapping shadows of their heavy steps when they went with their luggage to the car and

drove away toward college as though it were Africa (it took ten strides, ten silhouettes like played cards); for I realized that I would never sleep straight through another night again; that my belly would wake me, or my bladder, or my nose; that I would take my oblivion henceforth in pinches like snuff; and that this intermittent dah-dit-dah-dit, cutting up my consciousness in cubes, was the first signal of senescence: C for ceasing, C for shutting shop. (139)

As Kohler, *The Tunnel*'s narrator, has it, the art of the sentence minimizes the mundane quality of life. He renders this in his wife-hating tirade: "Martha hates it when I shape my sentences. She says it falsifies feeling" (154). Just in case the reader of Gass's fiction gets too complacent, thinking s/he has access to a finely balanced prose unit commensurate with the world or constructive of an alternate one, Gass will run a sentence off the end of the page as he does in *Willie Masters' Lonesome Wife* or, à la Thomas Pynchon, he will write such a long one that it is impossible to grasp in its completeness.

As vital as his link with and understanding of other writers of metafiction is Gass's contribution as a literary theorist. His importance to late twentieth- and early twenty-first-century letters, indeed, his legacy, might rest primarily on this dimension of his multifaceted work. The consensus among critics seems to be that here is a formalist, one who at every turn touts the integrity and autonomy of the work of art. This ignores the, call it postmodern, excess that is a part of everything Gass has published. (Some critics, yoking Gass's novelistic tactics to those of Coover et al., do call him a postmodern writer.) Moreover, Gass's impact on the theory and criticism of the novel has occurred from the 1960s on, a period marked by a monumental shift in literary theory. Although Gass nowhere refers to himself as a postmodernist or, especially, a deconstructor, he has, as much possibly as Jacques Derrida, Barthes, or any of their acolytes, helped to foster an intellectual climate in which the primacy of language, with all its indeterminate qualities, is valued over its referential properties; the formal limits of genre are resisted and exceeded; a critical vocabulary situated in continental notions of aesthetics (and stimulated by the interpretation of continental philosophers such as Hegel and Heidegger) has supplanted the discourse of New Criticism; the boundary between literature and criticism has been dissolved or at least miscegenated; the critic's role as handmaid to the arts has been transformed into the kind of performative role that suits Gass's (not to mention Derrida's) theatrical style.

While Gass might dismiss the diminution of the author's role that one finds in Barthes's "The Death of the Author," he in many ways—the dandified prose, the delight in maxims, the indeterminate generic forays—shares a good deal temperamentally and tactically with Barthes. Similarly, while he rejects the faddishness of contemporary critical theory—showing the same disdain for "scholar-squirrels" that Gore Vidal, another important and frequent *NYRB* reviewer, does—in many essays from the 1980s on he deploys the terminology and frame of reference that have become de rigueur in deconstructive circles. Echoing Derrida's distrust of the stability of meaning—found most notably in Derrida's pithy remark, "In the beginning was hermeneutics" (67) and in Pynchon's equally witty and doubting assessment of "the direct, epileptic word" (87), Gass writes the following in "Representation and the War for Reality," published in *Habitations of the Word*:

> Certain philosophical systems can claim to discover conditions and laws in our life because they have become so enamored of their interpretive systems, where alone such conditions and laws exist, they do not realize that they are dreaming in their dressing gowns and an unconsuming fire is lit; yet it is precisely this ancient belief that in the beginning was the Word . . . which allows them to describe the general principles of creation with such accuracy. . . . (108)

After years of positivistic literary criticism in which a work's meaning was difficult to discern, but, with techniques allied to what has been called close reading, was ultimately deciphered, the paradigm shift in reading texts has been toward a skepticism regarding fixed meanings disseminated from the Word, either theological or artistic. That skepticism, adumbrated in the above quotation, is clearly as much a part of Gass's intellectual and aesthetic armature as it is of Derrida's or, indeed, any of the relativistic critics who have proliferated in deconstruction's wake. Such skepticism also propels Gass to repeat intransigently that, as unique, rich, and sustaining as some works of art can be, their link with the "real world" is not a direct one.

Embracing the aforementioned uniqueness of the work of art does, it is true, separate Gass from the legion of recent cultural-studies critics who find in comics, pop music, television, movies, and fashion the same kind of elements and significance that literary critics have found in the classics. Nonetheless, Gass's insistence, over these many years, on the complex word-world relationship and the intractable, unstable dimensions of the former entity ally him with most of the postmodern projects. So, too, does the use of such terms as *difference* and *absence*, which have been wielded frequently by aficionados of deconstruction. In "Tropes of the Text," another essay in *Habitations of the Word*, Gass argues for the "tendency to think of the text of the novel, itself, in terms of some trope" (142) by ranging widely over the history of the novel; he concludes by asserting that the trope "sometimes begins in sameness, and then careens toward difference" (158). Such destabilization, he affirms, "brings its wretched employer nothing but confusion, nothing but Postmoderism" (159). Or, in one of those flashy metaphors that are Gass's imprimatur, he writes, in *Willie Masters' Lonesome Wife*, that his ideal reader is comfortable with such indeterminacy for

> Only a literalist at loving would expect to plug ahead like the highway people's line machine, straight over hill and dale, unwavering and ready, in a single stripe of kiss and covering, steady on
> FROM
> START
> TO
> FINISH

Wittgenstein's idea that philosophy should be written as a form of poetry finds its apotheosis in Gass's oeuvre (in which the reverse is also true). For all of the fine, cerebral fiction and theory that have been produced in the U.S. during this contemporary or postmodern period, Gass is the only one of the writers of metafiction who has married literature with a professional interest in philosophy, mixing, enriching, and contaminating (a positive word in the postmodern lexicon) both. This activity, with a noble lineage in European letters (Jean-Paul Sartre first and foremost comes to mind), has not had a similar efflorescence in North America, this despite the turn to aesthetics and thus to philosophy that Derrida and deconstruction have foisted on North American intellectual life. Coover has had and John Hawkes had extended teaching careers at Brown University and Barth similar longevity at Johns Hopkins University; these and other writers of metafiction have all written incisively on such matters of interest to aestheticians as the nature of literary language and its relation to reality. Nonetheless, only Gass has been enmeshed as much in scholarly arenas as in artistic ones.

This may be one of the significant factors in the fashioning of Gass's major opus, *The Tunnel*, which, for all the flourishes that so distinguish his fiction and essays, has a claustrophobic, academic feel to it. Regardless, for anyone who wishes to engage the preeminent figure of the seminal movement known as metafiction, the works—the performances—of William Gass stand as the most coherent, extended, extravagant, and opulent examples of the kind of writing that scrutinizes its very creation and explores experimentally and theoretically the reasons for and values of its making.

Career

Given the preceding paragraph it should come as no surprise that Gass is the only major metafictive writer-cum-theorist with a Ph. D. in philosophy; his dissertation, also unsurprisingly, had, as its subject, metaphor ("A Philosophical Investigation of Metaphor"). What is perhaps surprising is the rancor with which he writes about his upbringing. Born in Fargo, North Dakota, in 1924, Gass, in the preface to the 1977 edition of *In the Heart of the Heart of the Country*, comments on the creation of the stories therein with the following pejorative metaphor: "I was born in a place as empty of distinction as my writing desk. When I wrote most of these stories, it was a dining table, featureless as Fargo" (10). (Possibly, Gass's rich, luxuriant prose is meant as compensation for the landscape's austerity.)

Certainly no bravado is required of a writer dismissing the purportedly lackluster surroundings of his or her birthplace (though animus is probably not called for given that Gass's stay in Fargo was for fewer than two months). Some chutzpah, though, is needed by that writer in order to reject his alcoholic mother with the memorably obscene dismissal, "Even as a grown man I was still desperately boasting that I'd choose another cunt to come from" (11). Although the metaphors with which to wield contempt aren't as juicy, Gass is equally as scornful of his father for the racism and anti-Semitism to which, among other prejudices, his begetter gave voice. Directly and indirectly, Gass's outrage at his early family life filters into his writing, both fiction and nonfiction. Most notably, the lengthy scene in *The Tunnel* in which William Kohler reminisces about his youth appears to have been lifted from Gass's young life. At one point in that section Kohler describes his parents' tendencies with the following succinct summary: "a bottle-mad mother; a little Führer's been my father . . ." (236).

Lest the reader feel secure because s/he is distanced from the bile, Gass widens his target in "Even if, by All the Oxen in the World," from *Fiction and the Figures of Life*, with a diatribe against "most people": "War, work, poverty, disease, religion: these, in the past, have kept men's minds full, small and careful" (272). The effervescence of Gass's prose and the pleasure it often proffers seem at odds with the vituperation of the preceding quotations and many others besides. Nonetheless, he remains, in interviews and other forums, as consistently negative about his upbringing—and much that passes for cultural formation—as he is upbeat about the joys of literature. Indeed, as is often the case, works of art appear to be a refuge, literature an alternative world containing riches not found in the one he, by accident of birth, inhabited. Regardless, though, of the perceived familial hardships, Gass's intellectual formation and academic progress were impeded only by a stint, which he detested, in the U.S. Navy. Otherwise, an undergraduate degree from Kenyon College in Ohio was followed by a Ph. D. in 1954 from Cornell University. After completing his doctorate he began to teach at Purdue University, where he remained until 1969 when he moved to Washington University in St. Louis, the academic home of another major American fiction writer, Elkin. He taught there until he retired in 1999.

Beginning in the late 1950s, Gass has published a good deal of fiction and numerous essays, many of which have been collected and re-issued—to date in five separate volumes. The essays were written mainly for arts and culture magazines rather than academic journals. His first book, the novel *Omensetter's Luck*, a few sections of which had been published previously, came out in 1966. Since then Gass has produced a salmagundi of books—a jeu d'esprit such as the slim *Willie Masters' Lonesome Wife* commingles with a six hundred-plus-page opus, *The Tunnel*. Articles on such seemingly slight subjects as the conjunction *and* have appeared along with more momentous ones on the role of the artist in society and on the nature of narrative. Awards have been abundant; they include a Lannan Foundation Lifetime Achievement Award, the Pushcart Prize and the first PEN/Nabokov award. There have been honorary degrees granted as well as distinguished teacher citations given. Twice married, Gass has five children.

Although at the epicenter of experimentation with the form of fiction, Gass's adult life has been less the subject of scrutiny, more the stuff of routine, than, say, that of Pynchon, whose refusal to appear in public has paradoxically elicited a substantial amount of speculation; Coover, whose departure from the U.S. for a number of years had political overtones; or Hawkes, whose storied ambulance work in World War II reverberates through his fiction. As much as language is the subject of his work, both fiction and nonfiction, Gass's engagement with and fashioning of that medium seem to be the subject of his life. Although, or possibly because, his sentences have the feel of something expertly fashioned, carefully crafted, rather than something simply spewed out, the task of completing a writing project appears to be the central struggle of his life. Recalling in his preface the process of creation for the stories that were published collectively as *In the Heart of the Heart of the Country*, Gass compares his labored process to that of an anguished, protracted birthing: "we'd see the skull come out on Thursday, skin appear by week's end, liver later, jaws arrive just after eating. And no one of us, least of all the owner of the opening it inched from, would know what species the creature would eventually contrive to copy and to claim" (12). Indeed, the fiction has struggled into print, most notably *The Tunnel*, which H. L. Hix reports as having been begun in 1965 or 1966 and which was finally published in 1995.

Professor, essayist, fiction writer, reviewer: these are job descriptions that, since metafiction, among other factors, moved the novel inexorably into the university ambit (poetry's home decades before). Some other individuals have managed to fill all these roles. No others, however, have performed them with Gass's ability to be both erudite and breezy and to write the kind of prose that makes him seem to be a natural, someone who was born, as he would have it, "somewhere in the middle of my first book" (*Heart* 30).

Fiction

Although, according to Hix, "Gass considers himself primarily a fiction writer" (3), his works of fiction have been published more sporadically over the years than his essays and reviews, especially the commissioned ones. There was a creative efflorescence in the late 1960s during which *Omensetter's Luck*, *In the Heart of the Heart of the Country*, and *Willie Masters' Lonesome Wife* first appeared. Thereafter, until *The Tunnel* was finally released (after a good many collapses, in 1995), there was relative silence. *Cartesian Sonata*, which contains four novellas, including the title piece, was published in 1998.

In addition, possibly because of the scope of the nonfiction—its intellectual sweep and range of topics—the fiction reads cumulatively in a slightly more claustrophobic manner. To be sure, recurrent motifs such as typographical play, antirealistic devices such as long lists, as well as prose that is full of rhymes and rhythms, speak to a lively, expanding project. Along with the inventive wordplay that inundates his fiction, they broadcast a joy in the resources of language that outstrip the narrative needs of the work; they also interrogate the relationship of that language to the world and undermine traditional novelistic tactics. Nonetheless, they often produce literary pyrotechnics predominantly from within a narrative voice; the effect is thus occasionally more solipsistic than celebratory. Too often, the narrator's failure to be integrated into the milieus about which s/he drolly comments and around which s/he shapes stylish phrases gives the fiction a remote feel.

Punning on "remote feel," though, points contrarily toward the energy in Gass's fiction; this emanates from the constant hewing of prose's possibilities and the relentlessness of language's capabilities and limits. Drama in Gass's fictions comes from the narrators' attempts to make contact via language with the objects of their desire as well as from their desire to order the world around them and the chaotic thoughts they have. Gass's narrators may be isolated but they are also indefatigable.

The fascination Gass has with voice, with weaving a tapestry of words, precludes the radical disruption of narrative that marks the work, say, of Ronald Sukenick or Walter Abish (although *Willie Masters' Lonesome Wife* contains enough freewheeling play with the forms of fiction to provide an exception to that statement). Also, his reverence for great art causes him to forego parodying the traditional forms, the kind of absorption-rejection of literature's residue that one finds in Barth's fiction. In an interview with Arthur M. Saltzman, Gass says, "When I look at the writers who are really doing new things among American writers, who are they? Coover" ("Language and Conscience" 21). While Gass has consistently touted Coover's writing, his own temperament precludes him going in the extreme, anarchic direction Coover does. (One of Coover's characters says "There they are, man, the whole western world, all that lunacy, all that history, A to Z—shoot 'em!" (97).) While debunking the maneuvers of realistic fiction, Gass is also attracted to the creation of seamless art. He refuses the combative relationship with the reader, such as the one formulated by Barth in *Lost in the Funhouse*: "The reader! You, dogged, uninsultable, print-oriented bastard, it's you I'm addressing . . ." (127). Only the "bad" reader, whom Nabokov, too, teases, the one who reads fiction for transparent sociological or psychological truths, is chided by Gass.

While Gass's narrators aren't, for the most part, likeable, they are, like Alex in Anthony Burgess's *A Clockwork Orange*, compelling and interesting. Gass's first published novel, *Omensetter's Luck*, contains possibly the most riveting and driven of all; this is, of course, the Reverend Jethro Furber. Not that the whole novel is told in his voice, Israbestis Tott and Henry Pimber, two other citizens of Gilean (there are biblical overtones throughout the novel), a town on the banks of the Ohio River, have sections that focus on their doings; these, though, are much more limited than Furber's and are devoted to the men's perceptions of the events around which *Omensetter's Luck* is constructed. Structured thusly, the novel recalls an earlier American masterwork, William Faulkner's *The Sound and the Fury*. In the Faulkner opus three brothers tell conflicting versions of the same event while one central figure, Caddy, their sister, has no voice. In *Omensetter's Luck* three points of view are again brought into play regarding a pivotal protagonist, Brackett Omensetter, who also is given no section in which to articulate his version of the story. In addition, a preacher in the fourth and final section of *The Sound and the Fury* is offered the one still, nonlinguistic moment of communication and connection in a novel saturated with a welter of self-serving words: "And the congregation seemed to watch with its own eyes while the voice consumed him, until he was nothing and they were nothing and there was not even a voice but instead their hearts were speaking to one another in chanting measures beyond the need for words . . ." (175-76). While that blissful, nonverbal epiphany is denied Furber, the final paragraph of *Omensetter's Luck* reveals that his replacement as clergyman in Gilean, despite having "small management of words, little imagination, no gift for preaching," is heard from, leading "a boisterous choir" with a "lusty voice" (237). While evocations of the word "lusty" might trigger links in the reader's mind with the kind of verbal play that sprang from Furber's obsessive desires and thinly veiled repressions, the musical accord provides the only note of harmony and tranquility in Furber's long, highly charged monologue.

Nonetheless, it is the verbal riffs, the performances with words, orchestrated by Furber that are the crowning achievement of *Omensetter's Luck*. Brackett Omensetter might for most of the novel have had the charisma and luck of its title; however, Furber has most of its words and they—lubricious, unceasing—are what garner the reader's attention. *Omensetter's Luck* begins in a slow, stumbling, tottering way with Israbestis Tott trying to command the townsfolk's attention by being the first to relate and interpret the stories that comprise this town's history. Midst the rhythmic alliterative language—"The weeds were wilted and long in seed" (9)—that reminds one of Gertrude Stein's prose, Tott tries to tote up, for whatever audience he can find at the auctioning of the Pimber family's household goods, the events he has witnessed. An unsuccessful ancient mariner (he dreams of having been at sea and sailed around the world), he wants to make of the controversy surrounding Brackett Omensetter's stay in Gilean more than he is capable of. Thus he produces incomplete accounts that register as "the story I call the story of" (28), only to have his listener become restless and disappear. Tott is then left with the plaintive remark, "But I haven't come to the story" (28).

That story, on the face of it, seems a simple one. "Omensetter was a wide and happy man" (15), a refrain that, first uttered in Tott's soliloquy with the added sentence fragment "Fact" (15) for emphasis, is reiterated in the first line of the book's second section, "The Love and Sorrow of Henry Pimber." Omensetter continues to be the focus early on. Whenever he is spoken of, the sentences are short and unostentatious; furthermore, Omensetter is almost exclusively spoken about. He rarely speaks, and when he does, none of the intrusions of an expanded consciousness that mark the passages devoted to Tott, Pimber, or Furber is permitted. "They [the Omensetter family members] washed their wagon. . . . They brushed the dog" (31). Such are the descriptions of Omensetter that accrue, so unlike the performances of any of Gass's verbose narrators or, indeed, of Gass himself.

Pimber's melancholy is set in opposition to Omensetter's life force, his simple assertion of being; that depression culminates in Pimber committing suicide. Nonetheless, before that rash event, he dotes on Omensetter, renting him a house and being healed of lockjaw by him. Liberated by that latter act to indulge in language use that the atavistic Omensetter never feels he needs, Pimber gives in to the verbal exercises which Furber will later exceed: "He would say to his wife: here's your vulva, it's next to the nose of the beagle; or he'd say: here's your blood, dark as wet bark; or he'd say: here are the stools your bowels are shaping: on and on . . ." (46-47). Yet Pimber's curse is that he yearns to emulate Omensetter, to dispense with the welter of consciousness that weighs on him: "He had always crammed humanity in everything. Even the air felt guilty" (58). Pimber hangs himself on the branch of a tree not so much, as Hix surmises, to counterbalance his shooting of a fox in a well, but to ally himself with the "inhuman" (58) trees around him to which he utters a paean. At the end of his section, he puns on his imminent death, calling it a "leave-taking" (63).

Three-quarters of the novel remain after the close of Pimber's section. They contain the prolix maneuvers of Furber who, along with the incessant talking presence of *Willie Masters' Lonesome Wife*, is surely Gass's finest creation. Spewing a language charged with a mélange of sexual and religious nuances, full of sound and fury, Furber dominates the novel. If *Omensetter's Luck*'s major theme is the convoluted relationship between word and world, Furber demonstrates the possibilities and frustrations of bringing the latter under the complete control of the former. Making love (and hate) is still, alas for Furber, something that remains solely a linguistic foray. It was Omensetter's luck, but also his limitation, that he felt no such need; his fecundity (he has three children), never in question, is of a physical nature. Nonetheless, Furber's energy, transmitted through his skill with language (he sounds much like *Lolita*'s narrator, Humbert Humbert), overwhelms Omensetter and everyone else in the novel. It also causes all of them to mistrust him. It is this energy, though, that conveys the novel's energy; in addition, it makes this novel as different from *The Tunnel* as Furber is from William Kohler, a far more depressed and depressing monologist. Consequently, *Omensetter's Luck* is redolent of more vitality and crackles with more tension than does the larger work.

Furber, at one point in his monologue, says, "yes, words were superior; they maintained a superior control; they touched without your touching; they were at once the bait, the hook, the line, the pole, and the water in between" (113). In a novel in which water, via the Ohio River, looms large, potentially flooding the house that Omensetter rents from Pimber, the fishing metaphor above provides a microcosm for the novel's and Furber's central conflict: the attempt to regulate, dominate, and control natural forces. As Herculean as are Furber's efforts to obtain and maintain mastery with his words, his prolixity ultimately spills over the boundaries of moderation and good taste the way the Ohio River spills over its banks. Furber's early meditation accepting the fact that "Nature was the word of God as certainly as a scripture was" (67) founders when he catches sight of the Omensetter family bypassing his church to stroll along the river's edge. There, Lucy Omensetter sprawls on a rock, precipitating a torrent of speech by Furber, his words running amok with his desire. The word *nakedness* spawns wordplay that overwhelms the decorum promised in the fishing motif cited above. It becomes "nay-ked-ness" (67), a futile nay-saying that causes his patter to escalate into sound rather than sense. "Dee dum dee dum. How'd it gone? While his mother lay sleeping, Big Jack had come creeping . . . Guilty of nessss. Um . . . some, something to tipple from her mountainous nipple. Cover her nay . . ." (68). The ambiguity of the final sentence, abbreviating "nay-ked-ness" and also opening up the possibility of not covering up Lucy Omensetter, reveals the richness as well as the limitation of language, a binary that Furber wrestles with fiercely throughout the novel.

If *Willie Masters' Lonesome Wife* tests the limits of the book as body, "The Reverend Jethro Furber's Change of Heart," the final section of the novel, specifically, and *Omensetter's Luck*, generally, challenge the notion that there is a possibility in language to regulate desire. Rhymes, limericks, and bad jokes are triggered in Furber's mind; they comprise but also undermine his language skills. If Lucy Omensetter's sensuality causes Furber to unleash his desire verbally, his audacious, irreverent words also run riot over his congregation and its members' characteristics. The spinster, Samantha Tott, Israbestis's sister, gets reduced to the following bit of whimsy: "Samantha Totty . . . grew her nose . . . in her potty . . . like a rose" (78). Furber's battle with his irrepressibly effulgent word-making gets its pithy formulation in religious terms a little later in his section: "He tried to rally his thoughts and form them in unassailable squares, but not a line would hold, they broke ahead of any shooting, and the Logos wandered disloyally off, alone, rudely hiccoughing and chewing on pieces of raw potato, looking surly and dangerous" (85). Clearly, most of the time Furber tries but fails to corral Logos, preferring, in many ways, the erratic routes his language tends toward.

Again, although Gass never phrases his characters' dilemmas in postmodern or deconstructive terms, in Furber's conundrum one can find echoes of Michel Foucault's maxim that "The Bible has become a bookstore" (106)—everything is interpretable, variable, meanings spawning other meanings. As Furber articulates this at one point, "To find and utter the proper words, the *logoi spermatakoi* . . . that was Plato's game . . ." (168). Furber finally has a breakdown because the proper words elude him. Regardless, the novel's richness, indeed Gass might argue, language's richness, results from his inability to maintain propriety. Furber's imagination, as well as Gass's, is too fecund, the words at his disposal too loaded and variegated to limit him to a linear, logical exposition of anything. Furber, like Gass, is the kind of lover of language who, similar to all that author's narrators, thrives by strutting and seducing with his words; the allure of prose is as tantalizing and sexy as any buffed body. The following is Furber's way of rendering such a scenario: "The ladies egged him on; in Eve's name they dared him; so he made love with discreet verbs and light nouns, delicate conjunctions. . . . Those words of his—for her they were only the prelude to Lohengrin, but for him they were the thing, the actual opera, itself" (162).

The narrators of Gass's other fictions are to varying degrees concerned with the same dilemma but are perhaps less claustrophobically restricted to words and words alone. Indeed, in the stories collected in *In the Heart of the Heart of the Country* each of the narrators is confronted with Furber's problem: how to frame and phrase an encroaching world. Sometimes that world is malignant and threatening; at other times it is sensuous and beckoning. Perhaps because of the limitations of the short-story form, though, the narrator's formulations don't overwhelm the reader the way Furber's do. Regardless, the struggle is in many ways to dwarf and suppress the external world. There are, in *In the Heart of the Heart of the Country*, a would-be killer or killers, family life, jobs, and community that vie, via the narrators' mediations, for the reader's attention.

In "The Pedersen Kid," the adolescent age of Jorge, the narrator, lends a more direct, elementary tone to the narrative than Gass has otherwise achieved in his fiction. That Jorge still must order the events he encounters, hew meaning out of language, try to get the sequence right, is demonstrated in the following passage:

> The wagon had a great big wheel.   Papa had a paper sack.   Mama held my hand.   High horse waved his tail.   Papa had a paper sack. We both ran to hide.   Mama held my hand.   The wagon had a great big wheel.   High horse waved his tail. We both ran to hide.   Papa had a paper sack.   The wagon had a great big wheel.   Mama held my hand.   Papa had a paper sack.   High horse waved his tail.   The wagon had a great big wheel. We both ran to hide. (102)

Here, Jorge phrases the same sentences in very deliberate fashion—note the spaces that appear here and elsewhere in "The Pedersen Kid." They denote the effort required for Jorge to organize his perceptions of what is happening and has happened.

Although the piece has been read by a number of critics as a coming-of-age story, one saturated with Oedipal tensions, the above quotation (which covers only half of the paragraph that continuously reshuffles the same sentences) indicates that the way the details, even simple and realistic ones, are recorded dictates the meaning of this text, specifically, and any text, generally. The final paragraph of "The Pedersen Kid," which emphasizes the solitary state of the narrator, also appears to confer upon him the power associated with writing. Father, mother, Hans—not to mention the Pedersens in whose house Jorge has installed himself—are nowhere to be found. This allows Jorge to claim that he'd "done brave things well worth remembering" and that he was "burning up, inside and out, with joy" (105). This triumphalism is at odds with what happens in the rest of the story in which he is reluctant to go to the Pedersen farm with his father and Hans to alert the family to their son's brush with death; it also ignores the whining and carping he indulges in throughout the tale. The haltingly told story, full of bullying, threatening, and danger, reveals Gass operating within seldom imposed structures—a youth's capacity for storytelling and, concomitantly, fiction-making. It also allows for more action and more dramatic force, as well as less rumination, than are written into any of Gass's other works. Nonetheless, the demands on the narrator are consistent with Gass's aims in the rest of his oeuvre.

"Mrs. Mean" has a more familiar narrator, an adult male claustrophobe whose eye and "I" dominate the scene and the figures within it. In this case he obsesses over a woman whom he names Mrs. Mean. As with Brackett Omensetter, though to a lesser degree, Mrs. Mean gains in stature as a result of the narrator's preoccupation with her mundane doings, such as the controlling and disciplining of children as well as contending with the dandelion seeds originating on her neighbor's lawn; these become significant as the narrator monumentalizes Mrs. Mean's wrath and augments her image by means of his chronicles. This extends to a bit of doggerel "about a child called Henry" (130) who gets caught by his chin on a meat hook, an intrusion a long way from the suburban locus, domestic and bland, that the Means inhabit, however mean the wife may appear to be. Yet the narrator, who himself can be formidable, terrifying another neighbor, a Mr. Wallace, with grotesque facts and data about the malignancy of moles, promises at the end of "Mrs. Mean" that he will gain access to the Means' house. Here again is an example of authorial control, the compelling presence of voice and its ability to create and to dictate.

The next story in the collection, "Icicles," provides Gass the room for the metaphor-making, punning, and all-round exuberant language play that are his strengths. Although obsession and anxiety are frequent motifs in his fictional works, when he introduces a comic element such as one finds here as well as in *Willie Masters' Lonesome Wife* and in Furber's section of *Omensetter's Luck*, his prose has an enlivening, zesty quality found most frequently, curiously enough, in his nonfiction. Another link between *Willie Masters' Lonesome Wife* and "Icicles" involves the fascination with living in, in this case a house rather than a body; the parallel relates to a habitable space with language being the medium of caresses. Property, a frequently occurring word in this story, is the object of adoration that triggers wordplay: "Shoes, the rug—he saw the rug—and the foot of a table rising from the weave, thickening as it treed its top—was it rosily wooded?—waxed featureless and gleaming. Prop-purr-tee: a lovely sound. Was he an organ looking out? Was this how it seemed to the liver, lying . . . where?" (179). Unlike Babs, Willie Masters's lonesome wife, however, Fender, the story's main character, has a body that is aging badly; the icicles that cling vulnerably to the edges of his property and are under threat from children at the conclusion of "Icicles," remind him of an assault that jeopardizes his house and, by extension, his body.

Fender's frantic tone is offset by the calmly delivered discourse of the female narrator in "The Order of Insects." Like Fender's, though, her narrative involves an attempt to order and manage her quotidian world. Roaches in her home trigger the kind of speculation frequently encountered in Gass's narrators. How can she weave meaning out of their seemingly happenstance presence in her tidy, bourgeois house? Her involvement with them—she spins out possibilities and hypotheses about the roaches—threatens to overwhelm her the way Fender's obsession with icicles and Furber's with the erotics of the word come to dominate them. She relates that the "point of view I tremble in is the point of view of a god" (189). Ultimately, though, her controlled narrative reveals that she will reject the absorption that dooms Fender and Furber. She abandons the possibility of authorial, godlike mastery; she refuses to give in to unfettered language play.

"In the Heart of the Heart of the Country," probably Gass's best-known and most anthologized short story, also pursues the motif of narrators creating their own worlds in opposition to the mundane ones surrounding them. The story, though, offers two distinctive elements. The first is a Vonnegut-like assessment of the heartlessness that persists in Indiana (where Gass lived and taught for years), the heart, geographically speaking, of the U.S.A. In a section of the story entitled "Politics" he writes, "sports, politics, and religion are the three passions of the badly educated. They are the Midwest's open sores" (215). References to the John Birch Society and other right-wing organizations and people also appear in "In the Heart of the Heart of the Country." The scorn Gass usually reserves for "everyman," for mass culture and its unthinking adherents, gets unleashed on mid-America and its conservatism and bigotry. Education itself is not spared. Gass quotes Colin Goodykoontz, a certain "itinerant preacher with a name from a fairytale" (196), with his evaluation of nineteenth-century education in Indiana: "Ignorance and her squalid brood. A universal dearth of intellect. Total abstinence from literature is very generally practiced. . . . Need I stop to remind you of the host of loathsome reptiles such a stagnant pool is fitted to breed!" After recording this diatribe of Goodykoontz's, the narrator drolly comments, "Things have changed since then, but in none of the respects mentioned" (196-97).

The second unique feature of the story pertains to its format. Instead of being impelled by the narrator's voice, the shape of "In the Heart of the Heart of the Country" results from an accumulation of sections—for example, "Education," "Politics," "Business"—that facilitates, better than linear narration, the clinical, analytical dissection of a place. This scaffolding works contrapuntally with the emotional heart of the story. "In the Heart of the Heart of the Country" begins, "So I have sailed the seas and come . . . to B . . . a small town fastened to a field in Indiana" (191). This blatant allusion to William Butler Yeats's "Sailing to Byzantium" brings into play the recurrent motif of Gass's short-story collection, namely, the attempt to transform evanescent life into something immutable, into art, in short. The point-counterpoint—sterile, philistine, Midwestern America and the sensuous, radiant love immortalized in language—holds throughout "In the Heart of the Heart of the Country." "Birch . . . a good name. It stands for the bigot's stick" (215) is juxtaposed, for instance, to more lyrical potentialities: "The sun looks, through the mist, like a plum on the tree of heaven, or a bruise on the slope of your belly. Which? . . . We meet on this window, the world and I, inelegantly, swimmers of the glass; and swung wrong way round to one another, the world seems in" (214). Antiseptic lists of clubs, etc., found in sections such as "Vital Data," are set side by side with poetic bursts to give the story the tension, impact, and poignancy that make it a superb work.

Published in the same year as *In the Heart of the Heart of the Country, Willie Masters' Lonesome Wife* is Gass's most whimsical piece of fiction. Anthony Burgess refers to *The Eve of Saint Venus*, one of his lesser works, as "this libellum or opusculum or jeu d'esprit" (1), a small book, a playful and delightful one. His choice of diction, ostentatious, erudite and gleeful, to describe a ludic, sensuous spree of sorts suits Gass's aim as well and captures nicely the spirit of his undertaking in *Willie Masters' Lonesome Wife*. The publication of this book, first issued as a supplement to the journal *TriQuarterly*, then one of the major voices of experimental fiction in the U.S., recalls the novels put out by the Fiction Collective, a Coover-inspired venture that published some of the most avant-garde writing of the time, something Gass himself applauded.

Unpaginated, containing diverse fonts as well as photographs and footnotes, with lines of prose running up, down, and off the page, the pages themselves with different textures and feel, from coffee-table glossy to newspaper disposable: these are some of the tactics Gass has deployed to make *Willie Masters' Lonesome Wife* sui generis. The experimentation and innovation serve two major purposes. A closing introjection, circumscribed by what the author indicates is a coffee ring and superimposed on the final page of prose reads, "YOU HAVE FALLEN INTO ART—RETURN TO LIFE." This pithy remark highlights the first of Gass's two principal concerns: to draw attention to the art, the novella in this case, as artifice. Everywhere the aforementioned devices draw attention to themselves. They signal to the reader that s/he is in the realm of literature, not life. Like Nabokov before him, Gass is insistent throughout his writings and interviews that prose fiction's greatest enemy is verisimilitude, the sense that it is a window onto the world, through which a reader apprehends events and action. By doing all he can not to provide a seamless, unmediated reading experience, forcing the reader to adjust to different typographies and abrupt shifts in (minimal) story lines, to absorb fragments and digressions, and to hunt for footnotes a few pages from their asterisked indications in the main body (if there is such a thing) of the text, Gass dispels any illusion that a narrative commensurate with real-life happenings going on outside the novella is being made available.

The second emphasis in *Willie Masters' Lonesome Wife* is also encapsulated in its final paragraph: "Then let us have a language worthy of our world, a democratic style where rich and well-born nouns can roister with some sluttish verb yet find themselves content and uncomplained of." If, for Gass, the language of the novel or novella is not meant to provide easy passage to reality, it can pose more sophisticated questions about its relation to the world and forge more complex links with extralinguistic space. The focus here is frequently encountered in Gass's work: how the body of language is connected to and can express the language of the body. Desire, as Jethro Furber revealed, is manifested and unleashed as much in and through language as through direct physical expression. Babs, the eponymous heroine of the novella, is constantly vetting and coining names for the male and female sexual organs. There are also set pieces such as the invented excerpt from "Passions of a Stableboy," Gass's creation, which parodies nineteenth-century modes of rendering desire: "I shall take you in this horsey darkness, this stable quiet, this turded territory; I shall topple you to the straw ground and fill you with myself. . . ."

An extended comedic section involves a theatrical format in which a couple interacts in an Ionesco-like manner, discussing with bourgeois evasions the fact that the male, Ivan, has found a penis baked in the bun he has been given to consume. The tableau, complete with footnotes, is also reminiscent of Coover's unperformable play, "A Theological Position," in which sexual organs function as characters, discoursing on all manner of sexual and theological issues. Gass's purpose here (and Coover's as well) is to test the possibilities of language, rejuvenating it so that it crackles with sexual energy; on the contrary, the formulaic, mechanical, mundane expression of desire is seen as dampening eros. Babs seeks in her monologue, and Gass in this brief, variegated, experimental work, some fresh, exciting ways of rendering desire in print, on the page.

Decades passed between the publication of *Willie Masters' Lonesome Wife* and *The Tunnel*. Gass, of course, was actively writing and publishing, but the gestation of *The Tunnel* was a long and difficult one. Its appearance in the mid-nineties did not resolve, for critics and reviewers, the question of whether it was worth the wait. Dwarfing other works of his in terms of size, *The Tunnel* is over 650 pages long. The concentrated, epigrammatic quality of Gass's earlier prose gives way here to long, meandering passages, thinly disguised autobiographical forays into early childhood experiences, army duty, marriage, and an academic career. Limericks are peppered throughout the novel and some play with typography is evident; these strategies are implemented to deflect *The Tunnel*'s realistic feel. Nonetheless, wit and compression give way to an amplitude, a drifting even, that, for a good many readers, probably leaves the text freighted and burdened with the kind of, call it transitive and referential prose that Gass elsewhere eschews in his fiction.

The merits of *The Tunnel* have been widely debated; so, too, its, for some, offensiveness vis-à-vis the parts of the novel that engage Nazism. Critics have been divided on the book's success or lack of it. Omitted, though, from the academic debates and discussions of *The Tunnel* is the acknowledgment of the propensity of all the metafiction writers to try their hands at the great American novel, the hyperthyroid opus with encyclopedic range. Pynchon's *Gravity's Rainbow* and Coover's *The Public Burning* are just two of the novels that attempt to encompass the American character and sensibility, to come to terms with grand, extended themes, and to engage as well in experiments with the forms of fiction. Then there are Barth's expansive works, such as *LETTERS* and *Giles Goat-Boy*, which seek to recycle, update, and deconstruct the stories that underpin Western, specifically American, culture. Gass's mixture of the political (an interrogation of the guilt and complicity of Germans regarding Nazism) and the personal (detailed chronicles of William Kohler's life), though, lacks the parodic dimensions of Barth's work, the complex entanglements of Pynchon's, or the sustained fury and energy of Coover's. Also, the lengthy and occasionally jejune jibes at academic fiefdoms and squabbles, which appear to be taken more seriously than Barth, say, regards them in his novels in which university life plays a significant part, possibly limit the novel's overall impact.

Nonetheless, *The Tunnel*'s scope and heft, as well as its refusal to provide nostrums about Germany and its responsibility for the Holocaust, demand a more studied response than the comments above seem to require. Although Gass is not the only contemporary American writer to tackle such a topic, Abish's *How German Is It* offering a more compressed exploration of that monumental historical moment and its repercussions, *The Tunnel*, in its own slightly ponderous way, takes on the question: What does history do? This should come as no surprise because Gass's preoccupation in his other writings is, as has been demonstrated, what does language do? How does it reflect, (re)compose, and/or articulate the world? A professor of history, Kohler ruminates on that discipline's role in recording and shaping the events with which it contends. The section called "Mad Meg" which is devoted to Magus Tabor, a German professor who teaches Kohler and influences him enormously, contains an inquiry into this issue. The following question with which Tabor begins his lecture echoes the concerns about word and world that Gass raises with the same panache as many of his essays: "Does the word 'prick' stick us? what bumps when 'bump' is spoken? is there any blood in 'bleed'? . . . So you seek safety in your sentences?" (268). The ease with which sentences can narcotize or neutralize horrors, deflecting their effects: this—specifically German-inflicted horrors and the discussion about them—is the subject of Tabor's riveting, idiosyncratic lectures. "[H]istory usurps the past" (268): this is the danger that Tabor addresses and Gass, in *The Tunnel*, wants to redress. The academic podium in Tabor's case and the novel in Gass's are sites of resistance to the bewitchment of ordinary language.

Tunneling below the decorous surface of language the way William Kohler literally tunnels below his bourgeois home, the principal action that takes place in the present tense of *The Tunnel*, Gass tries to nurture unease about accepted versions of German history at the same time as he destroys comfortable interpretations of family life. As the creator and charter member of the "PdP," Party of Disappointed People, Kohler occasionally causes or more frequently witnesses the collapse of tidy versions of everything. At one point in the novel, he, not Tabor this time, asks, "Who clicks the shutter for the rusted gutter, the shattered windowpane or scarified loading dock, or celebrates the weedification of the parking lot? who records the trash in the alley or the garbage on the shore? who gives glass brick what it deserves—a bash—or welcomes eye sores like honored guests? who is the Arbus of the broken sash? the Cecil Beaton of the humblest door? the Ansel Adams of pigeon shit?" (360). The answer to these questions is clearly Kohler himself. His manuscript, which we read as *The Tunnel* and which he stashes as he writes it—interleaving it—in the pages of his academic treatise, *Guilt and Innocence in Hitler's Germany*, to prevent his wife from discovering it, contains his bid to be "the Ansel Adams of pigeon shit." By memorializing the vistas named in the first question, he aspires to emulate Claude Lanzmann in his film *Shoah*.

The contrapuntal elements of *The Tunnel*—pettiness (PdP, university politics, episodic bits of philandering) and monumentalism (his witnessing of and minor role in Kristallnacht, his attempt to understand Germans' predisposition to Nazism as well as fundamental human qualities)—are meant to provide the novel's drama and to sustain its interest. Whether lengthy sections on fathering a child and on having a small penis, to name two personal concerns explored, are juxtaposed successfully with Kohler's forays into ethical and moral spheres is for readers to decide. Certainly, the novel contains gist for the scholarly mill. There are abundant allusions in it, from the tossed-off title of a section, "Blood on the Living Room Rug," which alludes to Gertrude Stein's parodic detective novel, *Blood on the Dining Room Floor*, to references to Anna Livia Plurabelle of James Joyce's *Finnegans Wake*. There are also the aforementioned concerns with the theory of the novel. "I am an intransitive man" Kohler enigmatically states one of the many times he is pondering his situation (468). *The Tunnel*'s last trace, on its final page, is a graphic of the PdP. If the novel registers intransitively, seems like Kohler's tunnel to be built for no purpose, then, by the end of the novel the reader would certainly have gravitated to the Party of Disappointed People. Gass, though, is too erudite a writer, too interesting a thinker for the PdP to gain a majority. When Kohler makes love with language to his paramour, Lou, merging literal rivers with rivers of prose, to give one example of Gass's continuing legerdemain in the novel, *The Tunnel* tunnels under the detritus of language and experience to give the kinds of frissons one expects from Gass.

Cartesian Sonata, the latest work of fiction that Gass has published to date, contains four novellas. Each features a beleaguered figure akin to Gass's earlier creations, whose ordering and coping mechanisms also remind one of the ways Gass's corpus of characters shapes and comes to terms with the world. Despite that common motif, the stories are a variegated lot; they are sophisticated pieces that have woven into them literary allusions as palpable as the Byzantium reference that launches "In the Heart of the Heart of the Country." The least successful, but ironically most metafictional novella, is the first one, "Cartesian Sonata." Written in three parts, it is, as the narrator succinctly states in the opening sentence, "the story of Ella Bend Hess, of how she became clairvoyant and what she was able to see" (3). Yet things do not unfold in a straight-forward manner; indeed, the first section of "Cartesian Sonata" is something of a throwback to the early days of metafiction in which the writer foregrounds the construction/description of Ella Bend Hess by an authorial "I": "I decided she looked too much like a witch, and since she really was a witch, it wouldn't do to have her look precisely like one" (4).

Moreover, teasing references to *Willie Masters' Lonesome Wife* and *The Tunnel* appear early in "Cartesian Sonata." Direct addresses to the reader are another metafictional element here; so, too, is the way Gass draws attention to specific letters and words. Ella's clairvoyant streak is the focus of her section, the second part of the novella. Here, too, Gass's predilection for words' palpable nature is manifested. One of Ella's early contacts, a Professor Logos no less, relies on the dictionary, not globes, palms, or tea leaves as his con-duit to a supernal, yet textual truth. "This, he said lifting *Webster's New Collegiate*, is the book of the world, the one true honest holy book; it's all in here, the order of everything. Do you know what the world is, Mrs. Hess? It's *word* with an *l* in it!" (40). Mr. Hess's section, the final one, is, despite his more mundane, earthbound desires, full of lyrical flights, giving all three narrators their shot at fixing the appropriate words to their various takes on Ella's—and their—worlds.

"Bed and Breakfast" might surprise the reader searching for literary high jinks. The name of its main character, Walter Riff, short for Riffaterre, could possibly refer to Michael Riffaterre, an academic and author of *Fictional Truth*, to name one of his books. Also, the abundant descriptions, first of a hotel room and then of a bed and breakfast, along with the myriad books on their respective shelves, could be construed as a kind of Alain Robbe-Grillet-like realism that by overwhelming the reader with data and detail jeop-ardizes the very photographic enterprise being undertaken. None-theless, the novella can be read as a tender look at an understated and attractive place with its reports on the nooks and crannies of the Ambrose couple's bed and breakfast. "Bed and Breakfast" has all the attention to detail that a more orthodox writer, bent on verisimilitude, might devote to evoking the scene. Although the discovery of a discretely deposited G-string threatens to disrupt the domestic order that saturates the tale and provides the narrator his equilibrium, this too gets subsumed into comforting prose that is far cozier than the acerbic and caustic style usually found in Gass's fiction: "the heart's been here and cared for even this little lost place; nothing has been neglected; nothing has been overlooked, nothing rejected. Even this, Walter said in amazement, his face in the satin. Ummm . . . this. This too" (143).

Books, specifically one listing bed-and-breakfast establishments, are what propelled Walter Riff toward his Illyria, and books or literariness saturate "Emma Enters a Sentence of Elizabeth Bishop's." Emma Bishop, so named, has a moniker that is charged with literary heft: "one half of her a fiction, she felt, the other half a poet" (145). Her life, though, is an impoverished one. A gender-bending anorexic, at the mercy of a voyeuristic father, she lives through literature and language, generally, as most of Gass's characters do, commenting ". . . I am the ex of ist . . ." (150). Rejecting other sustenance, she buys books with her meager income, but only those written by women. In the novella's one strongly metafictive touch, she recites a lengthy list of flowers and weeds: ". . . Emma collected and admired and smelled their names and looked at their pictures in books" (180). (The list, one of Joyce's favorite techniques, is used by many of the writers of metafiction, most notably Barthelme, to outstrip, even obliterate the text's narrative needs.) The toughness of Elizabeth's Bishop's verse, its resistance to cliché and comfortable language, draws in and unnerves Emma Bishop whose life is as remote from ease as is most of Elizabeth Bishop's poetry.

"The Master of Secret Revenges" introduces a comic touch, something that, when it is present, enlivens Gass's fiction. This final work in *Cartesian Sonata* has a mock-heroic tone, reminding one perhaps of that idiosyncratic novel by Steven Millhauser, *Edwin Mullhouse: The Life and Death of an American Writer, 1943-54, by Jeffrey Cartwright, A Novel*. The Millhauser novel features a narrator who drolly recounts and appropriates the adolescent ramblings of a "writer," who can be labeled such only by his inventive biographer. Ditto Luther Penner whose childish diary entries (e.g., "April 1. Got a wagon for my birthday. No red wheels" (194)) and feckless revenges are faithfully recorded by the doting narrator of 'The Master of Secret Revenges." As he grows older, Penner becomes, if not more sophisticated in his revenges, certainly more erudite in his justifications of them, citing, among others, Proust, Gide, and Shakespeare as authorities. His "An Immodest Proposal" gains him, again according to the narrator, cult status as the author, in a couple of senses of that word, of revenges for all manner of slights. The consistent tongue-in-cheek quality of the story makes this one of Gass's zestier and lighter works of fiction. The discrepancy between Penner's doings and musings and his faithful amanuensis's elevation of those "achievements" is sustained throughout "The Maser of Secret Revenges."

Nonfiction

Paradoxically, despite the limitations of the review format for one and the specificity and possible ephemeral quality of the essay topic for another, William Gass's nonfiction writings are among the best and most inventive of his era's literary output, regardless of the genre. Gass might celebrate the preeminence of Ralph Waldo Emerson's essays, their pertinence and intelligence, as he does in "Emerson and the Essay" (found in *Habitations of the Word*), but his own combination of breeziness and erudition produces essays on a wide range of topics—mass culture, the nature of prose in fiction, directions of the contemporary novel, to name a few—that will probably stand as seminal statements for and about late twentieth- and early twenty-first-century culture, specifically the culture of the novel. It is, in fact, Gass's learning and intellect, focused on a concrete, delimited subject, that allow him to concentrate on flamboyant formulations of the problem or conundrum at hand, something that the fiction, with its lack of necessity, does not permit him. The circumscribed topic contributes to the compression and tension that, in part, give his essays their optimal impact. The danger, of course, is that an occasioned review can be rushed and can be localized; Gass, however, by concentrating for the most part on the broad ramifications of his subject and on the implications of the tomes or authors under review, circumvents this problem. Moreover, the wit and metaphor-making he turns on sometimes abstruse topics give his essays a liveliness rarely seen in the usually ponderous realms of intellectual discussion.

A recent review essay that Gass penned for *Harper's* (January 2004) shows the methodology he has developed over fifty years. The occasion is Susan Neiman's book, *Evil in Modern Thought: An Alternative History of Philosophy*; nonetheless, it is roughly a third of the way into the article before the work in question is even mentioned. Before that, Gass takes on the monumental topic of evil with the verve and panache he, more than any writer, lavishes on complex philosophical issues: "Perhaps the cigarette is. Evil. Because it has within it, like Old Nick in 'nicotine,' habituating elements that mimic the resolutions of intention. Because it encourages cancer to attack the lips that lip it, the lungs that suck its smoke, the eyes its blown smoke stings" (77). Like the cigarette smoke here that is concretized if not rhapsodized, this prose exhaled by Gass is the kind that makes the concept of evil palpable. (He then can turn to Neiman's take on its toxicity.) Not incidentally, the essay even offers a way to explain Kohler's behavior in *The Tunnel* as well as the thesis of his magnum opus on German guilt: "Evil . . . is a mosaic made of petty little pieces placed in malignant positions mostly by circumstance" (83). Containing a yoking of Popeye the Sailor's perspective on power with Michel Foucault's, Gass's essay eschews Neiman's argument as its framework in favor of his own pithy disquisition on a large topic.

Fiction and the Figures of Life, which came out in 1970, contains previously published material, a substantial portion of which first appeared in the *New York Review of Books.* It stands as the vade mecum for many of the writers, critics, and aficionados of metafiction, codifying its principles, outlining its manifesto, acknowledging its shapers, precursors, and seminal practitioners. Indeed, it announces the importance of metafiction as a movement. *Fiction and the Figures of Life* contains memorable apothegms such as the following: "The soul, we must remember, is the philosopher's invention, as thrilling a creation as, for instance, Madame Bovary" (5); "the novelist can learn more from the philosopher, who has been lying longer . . ." (5). Not only witticisms, these maxims point to a skeptical, relativistic philosophy that is suspicious of metaphyics, not to mention theology.

Trenchantly, too, Gass demands a different take on what fiction is and how it should be read both by those who consume it and by those who study it professionally. The following diatribe from "The Medium of Fiction" appropriately marks the shift away from realism that Gass demands:

> For most people, fiction is history; fiction is history without tables, graphs, dates, imports, edicts, evidence, laws; history without hiatus— intelligible, simple, smooth. Fiction is sociology freed of statistics, politics with no real party in the opposition; it's a world where play money buys you cardboard squares of colored country; a world where everyone is obediently psychological, economic, ethnic, geographical—framed in a keyhole and always nude, each figure fashioned from the latest thing in cello-see-through, so we may observe our hero's guts, too, if we choose: ah, they're blue, and squirming like a tickled river. For truth without effort, thought without rigor, feeling without form, existence without commitment: what will you give? for a wind-up world, a toy life? . . . six bits? for a book with a thicker skin? . . . six bucks? I am a man, myself, intemperately mild, and though it seems to me as much deserved as it's desired, I have no wish to steeple quires of paper passion up so many sad unelevating rears. (30)

Lest the academic critic somehow feel s/he has avoided the brunt of the above attack, Gass in the next essay, "The Concept of Character in Fiction," excoriates him or her with some more stirring and fulminating remarks, this time with a taunt that has a traditional critic reading a painting by Picasso in a too literal, realistic way. He concludes this assault by pithily writing, "Here you have half the history of our criticism in the novel. Entire books have been written about the characters in Dickens, Trollope, Tolstoi, Faulkner. But why not? Entire books have been written about God, his cohorts, and the fallen angels" (39).

Other essays in this collection such as "The Artist and Society" and "Even if, by All the Oxen in the World" set out, in equally combative fashion, to contest the virtues of popular culture and to champion the uniqueness and importance of meritorious art. These pieces are, perhaps, less successful on the level of argument because they have been made frequently; nonetheless, Gass's dexterity with prose and his bold images make these articles seem fresh.

Importantly, too, in *Fiction and the Figures of Life* Gass scrutinizes the work of those who have influenced and those who have produced metafiction. (He also clobbers more plot-oriented writers such as John Updike.) "Gertrude Stein: Her Escape from Protective Language" anticipates the current fascination with Stein by deconstructive as well as queer theorists. For Gass, Stein's genius lies in the fact that she created works that resist, most fiercely, interpretation and transparency. *Finnegans Wake*, might, Gass writes à la Stein, demand intense concentration on the part of its readers; however, it is interpretable, readable, the way *Things as They Are* is not. Her work seeks "contexts that will limit the functions of its words to that of naming" (90). That is, Stein's project involves stripping the English language of the associations its words have accumulated throughout years of usage, as well as through the history of its literature. This antireferential undertaking, an intellectual enema of sorts in which each word acquires the quality of an object, is what Gass reveres about Stein.

Although he finds the literary games that Nabokov and Borges play a bit too cerebral, too clever, Gass exalts them, too, for the techniques they use to deflect any possible realistic interpretations of their works. "Mirror, Mirror," Gass's homage to Nabokov, begins with an image related to the title of his review that configures in language "mise-en-abyme," the situation of a reflection that reflects a reflection ad infinitum, something that has become a catchphrase in a postmodern milieu for the destabilization of language, as well as the lack of a solid base upon which literature supposedly depends. In the next essay, "Imaginary Borges and His Books," Gass links that author with Wittgenstein and his "battle against the bewitchment of our intelligence by means of language" (128). Borges's unwillingness to regard metaphysics as anything except the reified equivalent of an artistic construct is captured in the following passage:

> Thus the effect of Borges' work is suspicion and skepticism. Clarity, scholarship, and reason: they are all here, yet each is employed to enlarge upon a muddle without disturbing it, to canonize a confusion. Ideas become plots (how beautifully ambiguous, for Borges, that word is), whereupon the notty tangles the philosopher has been so patiently picking at can be happily reseen as triumphs of esthetic design. (129-30)

Gass understands that for Borges "beliefs . . . are merely materials" (130).

That philosophy and religion have a nominalist status for Coover (as well as other writers of metafiction) is one of the reasons Gass champions his work in a review of *Pricksongs and Descants*, Coover's radical, experimental collection of short stories. Of avant-garde writers, Gass asseverates, "each wishes to instruct us in the art of narration, the myth-making imagination. The regions they have begun to develop are . . . regions of the mind . . ." (107), rather than specific, well chronicled, geographical sites. Pithily, again, Gass acknowledges that the result of Coover's meddling with the form of fiction is "the scrambling of everything, the dissolution of that simple legendary world we'd like to live in, in order that new values may be voiced" (109).

Gass's prescience regarding Coover's revolutionary literary agenda applies to Barthelme's oeuvre as well. Gass begins his review of *Unspeakable Practices, Unnatural Acts*, a collection of stories he aptly assesses as Barthelme's best to that point, with a droll introduction that mimics Barthelme's methodology, his process of democratizing meaning whereby mundane descriptions are juxtaposed to intellectual musings as well as surreal occurrences. Snow White, the eponymous heroine of one of Barthelme's novels, exclaims, "Oh I wish there were some words in the world that were not the words I always hear!" (6). This example speaks to Gass's rejection also of clichés, of mechanical sterile language. In his review "The Leading Edge of the Trash Phenomenon," Gass hones in on Barthelme's parody of what passes for communication among people: "The words we hear are travelogues of gossip; they are slogans, social come-ons, ads, and local world announcements; phatic, filling our inner silence, they produce an appearance of communion, the illusion of knowledge. Counterfeit, they purchase jail" (98). Gass wants no part of such incarceration, inside or outside of the novel.

It is important not to underestimate the impact and incisive nature of *Fiction and the Figures of Life*. Part theory, part polemic, part evaluation: the essays define a movement, speaking to a major shift in the writing of fiction and literary criticism in North America. Although less influential perhaps, *On Being Blue*, published in the mid-seventies, shows Gass at his erudite, irreverent best. Here the extended interplay between the carnal and the philosophical is scintillating. The beginning of *On Being Blue* replicates Gass's preferred opening tactic. Instead of outlining his thesis, he treats the reader to an impressionistic riff on the word *blue* that demonstrates his key concept, to wit, "a random set of meanings has softly gathered around the word the way lint collects" (7).

The word in question here, *blue*, triggers diverse associations, among them, erotic ones. Gass affirms, "As we shall see, and be ashamed because we aren't ashamed to say it, like that unpocketed peppermint which has, from fingering, become unwrapped, we always plate our sexual subjects first. It is the original reason why we read . . . the only reason why we write" (10). So Gass teases out sexual blues before other hues in ways that remind one of *Willie Masters' Lonesome Wife*. *On Being Blue*, though, contains a good deal more than Babs- or Furber-like, logophilial, sexual self-indulgence. Not surprisingly, what is done with a unit of language, *blue* in this case, preoccupies the author: "not the language of love, but the love of language, not matter, but meaning, not what the tongue touches, but what it forms, not lips and nipples, but nouns and verbs" (11). Whereupon Gass ransacks literary sources—Cocteau and Colette, Henry Miller and Henry James; painting—from Giotto to Jackson Pollock; and philosophy—Plato, most notably: all this to dredge up the many intellectual and cultural shades of blue that have seeped into our world as insistently as blue skies.

Without abandoning the techniques—metaphor-making, rhyming, and other sorts of wordplay—that turn *On Being Blue* into a literary triumph, Gass persists throughout this short but dense book in asking how the word relates to the world, signifier to signified. Sensuality and its relation to as well as evocation by language is Gass's topic, one that has been treated ad nauseam by didactic writers seeking to reign in the danger or exalt the potential of alluring or taboo words; pornography, its limits and/or liberation, gets unconventional treatment in *On Being Blue*. Yet Gass's strong sense of what the language of sexuality does comes through here not as bombast or homily but rather as illumination, argument itself crafted as tantalizing art: "Books whose blueness penetrates the pages between their covers are books which, without depriving us of the comfort of our own commode or the sight of our liberal selves, place us beside a manufactured privacy" (84-85). A little later, Gass yields the maxim, "For the voyeur, fiction is what's called *going all the way*" (85).

How flesh is made word is the weighty subject Gass breezily engages. His legerdemain, including lists and lyricism, permits him to go all the way, turning readers into voyeurs if they weren't already. The genre, though *On Being Blue* is, on the face of it, an exposition of a word's properties, philosophical and otherwise, is not necessarily classifiable as essay or literary criticism. Sentences are microcosms of this encyclopedic work that cites all shades of blue; e.g.,

> For our blues we have those named for nations, cities, regions: French blue, which is an artificial ultramarine, Italian, Prussian, Swiss and Brunswick blues, Chinese blue, a pigment which has a peculiar reddish-bronze cast when in lump-form and dry, in contrast to China blue which is a simple soluble dye; we have Indian blue, an indigo, Hungarian, a cobalt, the blues of Parma and Saxony, Paris, Berlin, and Dresden, those of Bremen and Antwerp, the ancient blues of Armenia and Alexandria, the latter made of copper and lime and sometimes called Egyptian, the blue of the Nile, the blue of the blue sand potters use. (59)

Three collections of essays, spanning the last thirty or so years, have followed the publication of *On Being Blue*. That their impact has not been as great as that of *Fiction and the Figures of Life* is probably due to Gass's voice being recognized, his hobbyhorses being ridden once (or twice . . .) again. Nonetheless, *The World within the Word*, *Habitations of the Word*, and *Tests of Time: Essays* continue to feature the perspective of an intellectual, a scholar, and a creative writer, someone who can treat arcane philosophical subjects as well as more timely issues, in a lively, unpedantic, but insightful manner. The essays in the three collections also reveal Gass's scope and varied audiences. While some of them were first published in newspapers, others were read at academic conferences or were first printed in scholarly journals. "The Doomed in Their Sinking," "Malcolm Lowry," and "Three Photos of Colette" are themselves tours de force, as much creative as critical. The familiar litany of effects is enacted; in addition, though, these are poignant pieces with as much feeling as flamboyance. "The Doomed in Their Sinking" contains a bravura performance by Gass on the subject of suicide. Ostensibly a review of A. Alvarez's *The Savage God* and Jacques Choron's *Suicide*, the essay becomes a meditation on Gass's own mother as much as on literary figures who have killed themselves and who people Alvarez's book:

> Though Hart [Crane] shed his bathrobe frugally before he jumped, my mother, also saving, would have worn hers like the medal on a hussar

straight through living room and loony bin, every nursing home and needle house we put her in, if those points hadn't had to come out (they confiscate your pins, belts, buckles, jewelry, teeth, and they'd take the air, too, if it had an edge, because the crazy can garrote themselves with a length of breath, their thoughts are open razors, their eyes go off like guns). . . . (*World* 3-4)

Much like the exhibitionistic Sylvia Plath, who fascinates Alvarez, Gass's mother has the decorum stripped away from her. Gass reveals his early family life as a frank way into understanding suicide, providing autobiographical explanations more than disinterested criticism.

The Lowry essay also leaves criticism a long way behind in its introductory remarks. Five or six pages elapse before the subject of the essay, Douglas Day's *Malcolm Lowry: A Biography*, is even mentioned. Before that Gass re-creates the situation and ambiance of *Under the Volcano*, the alcoholic Consul's love affair with the cantina. It is as much a short story along the lines of and in homage to Lowry's novel as it is the lead-in to a review. Later, Gass turns to registering the impact Lowry's prose makes (he does this with his other favorite writers as well): "The paragraph encloses us like the fuselage of the plane. We progress down narrow overlapping phrases toward the bottom of the page, pushing our way through adjectives which gather like onlookers at an accident" (30). Not only does Gass impressionistically inhabit the degenerate realms occupied by Lowry's legendary Consul with his here claustrophobic prose, but he also concisely summarizes Lowry's modus operandi: "Lowry could not invent at the level of language, only at the level of life, so that having lied life into a condition suitable for fiction, he would then faithfully and truthfully record it" (36).

Just as the Day biography gets dwarfed by Gass's own Lowry-like reconstructions in "Malcolm Lowry," so too does Yvonne Mitchell's *Colette: A Taste for Life* act only as the stimulus for his rich emendations in "Three Photos of Colette." Reminding one of Gertrude Stein, Gass constructs in language three photos of Colette, three vignettes from her full life, adapted from images published in Mitchell's book. Again here, Gass's article develops a portrait of Colette that can be read without the prop the book under review provides. Revealed in his snapshots are the complex dynamic of her relationship with husband, Willy, her feminist stirrings, Willy's exploitive use of her writing, and Colette's will to write as well as her physical decline.

The longest chapter in *The World within the Word* is "Gertrude Stein and the Geography of the Sentence." Already lionized by Gass in *Fiction and the Figures of Life*, Stein here is subjected to the kind of close reading Gass rarely undertakes. His purpose is to unearth what he calls a polytype text, a text that is *scriptible*, writerly, open to the play of meanings. Again producing a vocabulary that links him to deconstructive criticism, Gass calls *Tender Buttons*, in many ways Stein's most experimental work, a "metatextual metaphor" (92). The passage that Gass singles out for treatment "does not describe some object which the title designates as much as the title describes the passage" (92). At one point in his interpretive maneuvers Gass quotes the Stein sentence that could stand as a testament to his as well as her literary effects: "Certainly glittering is handsome and convincing" (84).

Not everything glitters in *The World within the Word*, though. Gass's vituperative side comes through in a couple of the essays. Joseph Blotner's biography of William Faulkner is savaged as a pedantic, deadening exercise. In "Sartre on Theatre" Gass has sharp words for the doctrinaire writer that, according to him, Sartre sometimes was. Yet Gass himself tries to avoid being doctrinaire in his piece on Henry Miller. Antipathetic as he says he is to Miller's obsession with himself (and his penis), Gass nonetheless celebrates those moments in Miller's work that come alive: "in spectacular bursts, in similar fits and starts throughout his *oeuvre*, there is an eager vitality and exuberance to the writing which is exhilarating . . . and the language we watchfully hear skip, whoop and wheel across Miller's pages makes an important esthetic point, especially to those of us who are more at home with Joyce or Woolf or James or Proust . . ." (257).

In the final three essays Gass, freed from even a nominal review focus, returns to his favorite subject, the convoluted relationship between language and reality that is adumbrated in the collection's title. Literature's role in this dynamic draws special attention. One aperçu of his worth noting is the one in which he ranks the novel, not poetry, as the genre that most fertilely ransacks its resources. There, too, he cites the works of "Nabokov, Borges, Beckett, Barth . . . Gaddis . . . Calvino" (305) as valuing aesthetic concerns over realism.

Habitations of the Word has a title that also contains intimations about language's place in the world. It opens with the essay on Emerson in praise of his production of that genre and its possibilities in a contemporary arena. The concluding paragraph of "Emerson and the Essay" reveals one contradictory aspect of Gass's work. Seemingly of the Party of Disappointed People when he fashions his fictions, chronicling a depressed, solipsistic lot, Gass, when he turns to the essay, a public forum, is often upbeat. Emerson's "only recourse," Gass wrote, "was to write, to fade when he had to—die—and then to rise once more inside us when we say, 'In this refulgent summer, it has been a luxury to draw the breath of life . . .'" (49). In this celebratory vein Gass pens his paean to the word *and*, which, he informs readers at the beginning of his article, occurs 3,381 times in *A Portrait of the Artist as a Young Man* and 7,170 times in *Ulysses*. The remainder of "And" serves to monumentalize and concretize that word. Like Stein again, Gass gives it heft and range rather than consigning it to the transparency of an invisible plus sign. "[E]ssential for excess" (170), a postmodern overwhelming of the reader, "ands" are given more than their due in an essay that first and foremost transmits a love of language's possibilities and ramifications. Stein and Hemingway especially come in for praise. "And" concludes, " 'And'   then some" (184), a tribute to Gass's desire to keep adding to the treasure trove of creative word usage.

"Tropes of the Text," first presented in 1982 at an international conference on postmodern fiction, advances Gass's now familiar argument regarding the interpenetration of discourse and action. Elsewhere in *Habitations of the Word*, most notably in "The Death of the Author," Gass revisits a postmodern debate initiated by Foucault and Barthes regarding the revaluation and diminution of the author's role creatively and culturally. Gass's firm support for what he perceives as the author's heroic task, the resistance to and transformation of mundane reality, doesn't allow him to accede to the submission of author to text, a tenet insisted upon by Barthes and Foucault.

Although impassioned, the selections that comprise *Tests of Time: Essays*, Gass's most recent collection, are possibly the weakest of his nonfiction works. There is, of course, still the remarkable dexterity with language. For instance, in "The Writer and Politics: A Litany" Gass writes unsympathetically about the Marquis de Sade, "For de Sade, every sexual act was political, and buggery was simply a way of marking your ballot" (131). Such witticisms, though, yield to more clichéd observations on writing and politics in contemporary society. Also, in "The Test of Time," Gass renews his tirade against mass culture: "the evidence is that whenever people have a choice . . . they will select schlock with a greed and certainty of conviction which leaves no doubt where their preferences lie; . . . they crowd into movies which glorify stupidity; their idols are personalities, their dreams sentimental, their realities dubious gossip" (109). Gass refuses to have anything to do with the au courant cultural studies perspectives that find more sophisticated responses to and interaction with mass culture by its consumers. In "Anywhere but Kansas" he resolutely touts experimental fiction ("innovation that comes to something is nearly always formal" (32)) as the most important resource with which to resist mainstream entertainment and its, for Gass, pernicious, deadening effects. Indeed, he creates a portmanteau word, "innoversive"

(36), to try to express the multifaceted qualities of works that eschew or alter conventional forms. Yet he also acknowledges, as a professor of philosophy who happens to be one of the leading commentators on and theorists of contemporary fiction, that, because of this vocational placement, he is free of the internecine squabbles over literary and critical territory that mark university departments of English literature.

Some more nourishing comments about literature as well as a tribute, in "Quotations from Chairman Flaubert," to Flaubert's all-encompassing love of aesthetics, of style over content, conclude the tome. Only "How German Are We?" introduces sparkling new material, in this case the chronicle of a trip to Cologne, Germany, that is transformed into a meditation on prejudice, specifically, anti-Semitism; this still later migrates into a commentary on the writing and reception of the *The Tunnel*. "For twenty-five years," Gass asserts, "I have been writing about resentment . . ." (212). The point he develops is that rejection of *The Tunnel* on the grounds that Kohler is so aberrant that he cannot be identified with, especially by American readers, is misguided. Gass quotes Sinclair Lewis whose response to the sentiment that fascism couldn't flower in the U.S. is as follows: "The hell it can't! Why there's no country in the world that can get more hysterical—yes, or more obsequious!—than America" (213). Gass's own notion of his novel is that it asks how German—in the malignant Second World War sense of that term—can "we" be. "Its answer has pleased few. Its answer is—very" (215).

The Critics

Like many writers of metafiction, Gass has received a good deal of critical attention, this because metafiction lends itself to intellectual discourse. Also, as with the rest of that highly articulate coterie (except for the reclusive Pynchon), Gass has been interviewed frequently by academic journals. Moreover, those interviews contain incisive, extended questions. In, for instance, "A Conversation with Stanley Elkin and William H. Gass," Jeffrey L. Duncan begins his query with the following: "In your essay 'In Terms of the Toenail,' you talk about the weakness of much recent fiction as a fear of feeling, and you cite Beckett, Borges, and Barth. And you say they've been led too far towards fancy, as Coleridge called it, neglecting somewhat in the forming of their figures the full responsive reach of their readers. They are too much a passive term in this relation" (56). Dense aesthetic and metaphysical issues get an airing in interviews such as these; a recent count from the *MLA Bibliography* turned up thirteen interviews out of sixty-eight citations on Gass.

Gass's cautionary comments, presented in "The Artist and Society" in *Fiction and the Figures of Life*, with respect to the ease with which "critics, poets, novelists, professors . . . those used to shooting off their mouths—they shoot . . ." (278), are seemingly overlooked. The parenthesis that follows the above quotation regarding the effect of such commentary—"(no danger, it's only their own mouth's wash they've wallowed their words in)" (278)—also is apparently ignored.

In addition to the *Review of Contemporary Fiction*'s 1991 and 2004 special issues on Gass, the *Iowa Review* and *Critique: Studies in Modern Fiction* have published numbers devoted to Gass's work. He is also the subject of two books from two series devoted to contemporary American literature, one published by Twayne in 1990 (*William Gass* by Watson L. Holloway) and the other in 2002 by the University of South Carolina in its Understanding Contemporary American Literature series (H. L. Hix's *Understanding William Gass*). The more recent of the two, Hix's book provides a solid reading of all of Gass's fiction to date, with ample citations from those critics who have commented on the work. Its best chapter is "Twenty Questions on *The Tunnel*" in which Hix, the editor of a casebook on that novel, seeks to articulate the elements of autobiography appearing in the novel and their purpose, the mixed reception of the novel, the significance of the metaphor of the tunnel, the function of the long section devoted to Kohler's academic colleagues, etc. Perhaps because of the limitations of the series, Hix does not try to provide a framework within which to understand Gass or to assess his place in the panoply of contemporary literature and theory. Also, occasionally Hix overemphasizes religious and biblical interpretations and references that sometimes clash with Gass's irreligious sensibility.

Larry McCaffery, in *The Metafictional Muse: The Works of Robert Coover, Donald Barthelme and William H. Gass*, a 1982 work, presciently contextualizes Gass's achievements vis-à-vis the development of metafiction. Philip Stevick, in "William Gass and the Real World," reaffirms this placement, finding in Gass's statements about fiction the most succinct and compelling formulations about those writers "we have come to think of as the prominent postmodernists or postrealists or metafictionists" (71). Others, such as Ned French in "Against the Grain: Theory and Practice in the Work of William H. Gass," stress that "the construction of his novels is realist" (99), even if the theoretical essays, more than any of Gass's other works, are adamantly antirealist.

In the Heart of the Heart of the Country has garnered a good deal of approbative and insightful critical response. " 'yung and easily freudened': William Gass's 'The Pedersen Kid,' " by Kevin J.

H. Dettmar, offers a reading of that selection as an initiation story, one "with a particularly overt Freudian bent—a *Bildungsroman* or *Kunstlerroman*, written by a man who knows his Freud" (88). Moreover, Dettmar sees in "The Pedersen Kid" a postmodern as opposed to modern handling of the "Freudian symbols—flagrant, loud, *audacious*" (93). (Hix too finds this to be the style with which Gass embeds literary allusions in his other fictional works.) The link with writing is also stressed by Dettmar who emphasizes that Jorge's "first important act on taking possession of the [Pedersen] house is to write it, for it is only through writing that it becomes fully his" (98).

Melanie Eckford–Prossor in her article on "The Pedersen Kid"—"Layered Apparitions: Philosophy and 'The Pedersen Kid'"—divulges a different emphasis, stressing a philosophical rather than a psychological reading: "To the extent that Jorge grapples with expression and order in language, he works through certain philosophical problems that Wittgenstein, prompted by Moore's 'defence of common sense,' probed in *On Certainty*" (105). This argument connects with Gass's central focus: (un)reliability of language, how stories can, or cannot, explain events that have taken place. Epistemology, it is Eckford-Prossor's contention, is Gass's concern in "The Pedersen Kid."

In "Where Words Dwell Adored: An Introduction to William Gass," Arthur M. Saltzman fetes Gass with the following opening remarks:

> William Gass builds sentences, sentences that are their own best excuse for being, sentences that seduce, like a bold, new Annunciation, through the ear. They can be as delicately suspended as a bridge of web spun by the spider that serves as metaphor for the artist in *Omensetter's Luck*; or they can be arches of triumph, solid and lasting and right as pillars set in concrete; or they can lie quietly, feeding and fattening on our attention before we notice that we are noticing their tug at the imagination. (7)

Saltzman overlooks one other characteristic of Gass's sentences: their showy, excessive, erudite quality.

Critics, Gass states in one of his interviews, render safely and comprehensibly the meanings they discover in texts; the artist, for him, must be bolder. Despite some inevitable repetition of ideas, Gass, even when he opts for criticism, strives for boldness and innovation. He is a writer who can turn philosophy into art and art into philosophy. Above all, he is mindful of his medium. His caring admonition to the writer at the conclusion of *On Being Blue* is a fitting way to conclude this overview of Gass because he, himself, lives up to this credo:

there's one body only whose request for your caresses is not vulgar, is not unchaste, untoward or impolite; the body of your work itself; for you must remember that your attentions will not merely celebrate a beauty but create one; that yours is love that brings its own birth with it, just as Plato has declared, and that you should therefore give up the blue things of this world in favor of the words which say them. . . . (89-90)

Thanks to Carolyn Dirks, Librarian, St. Jerome's University, for her invaluable bibliographical assistance.

Works Cited

Barth, John. *Lost in the Funhouse.* 1968. New York: Anchor Press, 1988.

Barthelme, Donald. *Sadness.* New York: Pocket Books, 1972.

—. *Snow White.* New York: Atheneum, 1967.

Burgess, Anthony. *The Eve of Saint Venus.* New York: Norton, 1970.

Coover, Robert. *A Theological Position.* New York: Dutton, 1972.

Derrida, Jacques. *Writing and Difference.* Trans. Alan Bass. Chicago: U of Chicago P, 1978.

Dettmar, Kevin J. H. " 'yung and easily freudened': William Gass's 'The Pedersen Kid.' " *Review of Contemporary Fiction* 11.3 (1991): 88-101.

Duncan, Jeffrey L. "A Conversation with Stanly Elkin and William H. Gass." *Iowa Review* 7.1 (1976): 48-77.

Eckford-Prossor, Melanie. "Layered Apparitions: Philosophy and 'The Pedersen Kid.' " *Review of Contemporary Fiction* 11.3 (1991): 102-14.

Faulkner, William. *The Sound and the Fury.* 1929. New York: Norton, 1987.

French, Ned. "Against the Grain: Theory and Practice in the Work of William H. Gass." *Iowa Review* 7.1 (1976): 96-107.

Foucault, Michel. *Language, Counter-Memory, Practice: Selected Essays and Interviews.* Trans. Donald F. Bouchard and Sherry Simon. Ithaca: Cornell UP, 1977.

Gass, William H. *Cartesian Sonata.* New York: Knopf, 1998.

—. *Fiction and the Figures of Life.* 1970. Boston: Godine, 1978.

—. *Habitations of the Word.* 1985. Ithaca: Cornell UP, 1997.

—. *In the Heart of the Heart of the Country.* 1968. Boston: Godine, 1981.

—. *Omensetter's Luck.* 1966. New York: Penguin, 1997.

—. *On Being Blue.* Boston: Godine, 1976.

—. "On Evil: The Ragged Core of a Sweet Apple." Rev. of *Evil in Modern Thought*, by Susan Neiman. *Harper's* Jan. 2004: 77-84.

—. *Tests of Time: Essays*. Chicago: U of Chicago P, 2003.

—. *The Tunnel*. 1995. Normal, IL: Dalkey Archive Press, 1999.

—. *Willie Masters' Lonesome Wife*. 1968. Elmwood Park, IL: Dalkey Archive Press, 1989.

—. *The World within the Word*. 1978. Boston: Godine, 1979.

Hix, H. L. *Understanding William H. Gass*. Columbia: U of South Carolina P, 2002.

Pynchon, Thomas. *The Crying of Lot 49*. 1966. New York: Bantam, 1978.

Saltzman, Arthur M. "Language and Conscience: An Interview with William Gass." *Review of Contemporary Fiction* 11.3 (1991): 15-30.

—. "Where Words Dwell Adored: An Introduction to William Gass." *Review of Contemporary Fiction* 11.3 (1991): 7-14.

Stevick, Philip. "William Gass and the Real World." *Review of Contemporary Fiction* 11.3 (1991): 71-77.

Wetzsteon, Ross. "Nabokov as Teacher." *TriQuarterly* 17 (1970): 240-46.

William H. Gass
(Photograph by Michael Eastman)

A William H. Gass Checklist

Fiction

Omensetter's Luck. New York: New American Library, 1966; New York: Penguin, 1997.

In the Heart of the Heart of the Country. New York: Harper & Row, 1968; Boston: Godine, 1981.

Willie Masters' Lonesome Wife. New York: Knopf, 1971; Elmwood Park, IL: Dalkey Archive Press, 1989.

The Tunnel. New York: Knopf, 1995; Normal, IL: Dalkey Archive Press, 1999.

Cartesian Sonata. New York: Knopf, 1998; New York: Basic Books, 2000.

Nonfiction

Fiction and the Figures of Life. New York: Knopf, 1970; Boston: Godine, 1978.

On Being Blue. Boston: Godine, 1976; Boston: Godine, 1991.

The World within the World. New York: Knopf, 1978; New York: Basic Books, 2000.

The Habitations of the Word. New York: Simon & Schuster, 1985; Ithaca: Cornell UP, 1997.

Finding a Form. New York: Knopf, 1996; Ithaca: Cornell UP, 1997.

Reading Rilke: Reflections on the Problems of Translation. New York: Random House, 1999; New York: Basic Books, 2000.

Tests of Time. New York: Knopf, 2002; Chicago: U of Chicago P, 2003.

Robert Lowry

James Reidel

What did you say with Robert Lowry about love? Do you know anything about what it means for a humanish human being? Does he know better?
—Simone de Beauvoir to Nelson Algren, 5 March 1951

As Lionel Trilling and others debated the death of the novel in the mid-1950s, Robert Lowry experienced his career suicide as a novelist. The way that tragedy played out has prevented an overdue reconsideration of his life and a body of work that was praised in the years after the Second World War. He had all the trophies of what a professional author did after 1945, writing at least one of each of the period's "war novels, veteran's-return novels, race novels, or New York novels" (Aldridge 197). Reviewers labeled him "a virile, pungent" stylist, a writer of "peculiar virtues," a "conscientious craftsman," "never without impact and immediacy." Academic critics saw him initially as making modest, workmanlike advances on the overwhelming influence of 1920s modernism. They had yet to be charmed by the cunning indirections of postmodern texts; Lowry's were expected to be simply "moving and significant—a sort of direct humanness" (Hartman 314). This was not to last.

Lowry by 1951 was one of the neo-Hemingways in John Aldridge's *After the Lost Generation*, dispraised for their thick-laid negation and lack of technical innovation (88). And as he rose from behind the shadow of a previous generation, he was eclipsed by a postmodern one. He does not qualify as a producer of literature under most yardsticks, a producer of those necessarily difficult books, like a Gaddis or Barthleme, writers esteemed by Frederick Karl in *American Fictions, 1940–1980*, where Lowry is "modified Hemingway" that "allows for few modulations" (113). From this point Lowry disappears from any consideration save for a few blips that come from Europe. These are intriguing mentions, like Lowry being called, by Emilio Sanz De Soto, a "fasciste dément" (26), but they make taking him on more like the task of the *advocatus diaboli*.

The other limitation found in Lowry's development is not getting beyond the state-guide-like regionalism of the 1930s—in his case it is a micro-, even hyperregionalism. Lowry's transparent eyeball looked out from the dead end of Hutton Street in Cincinnati, where his career began, and ended by way of his promising debut in the hipster-era, in the Village where he was one of Anaïs Nin's "transparent children" (95). His Emersonian lens rolled brutally, romantically, and narcissistically from one end of Hutton, closed off by the technology and logic of the Pennsylvania Railroad (for which his father worked), to the other—an Edenic floodplain where he would hunt rabbits, walk among the stones of the pioneer graves, or be trapped again by the rising waters of the Ohio. Its ultimate value for Lowry is a becalming nihilism, which he actualized in his careerless metatext, that surrounding life in his later years no longer set into words: "What he wanted was to read, to walk around, to look at things. Not to be anything more than exactly and precisely nothing. Uninvolved. He was through with the world, he had buried himself. He'd come back here to the womb, to Doanville, because he was through, because he wanted no more travel, no more excitement, no more nothing" (Lowry, *Find Me in Fire* 48–49).

As close to "home" as this reads, Lowry's world has much in common with the inescapable hells of European existentialists; and his is far worse than Vonnegut's Midwestern-placed "asshole of the universe." Self-taught, he parallels the intellectual Sartre and Camus more than he knows. But Lowry did read their forebears, de Maupassant and Dostoyevsky, and could say that he conversed with the latter during his long mental illness, recording the Russian's praise during an imaginary analysis that also included the psychiatrist who had given up on him. Other European strains exist, too. Kafka did not sit in, but he could have. Only Lowry's Cincinnati–New York–Rome axis and the messy whorl of his American grain obscure how much of the tall, thin, and meticulously written Prague insurance company clerk rubbed off. (His presence and demeanor obscure this too; as diarized by Nin, he was an "inflated child" (144), more Goth than Gothic modernist, in keeping with the alter egos of his fiction, "brutal . . . ugly, sinister. Bitter" (165).) Yet much of Lowry's best writing is about those confined, inescapable, and usually dark spaces of existence. Even his most spatially American novel, *The Big Cage*, is a concatenation of cubicles and withdrawals and not just the on-the-road book that Kerouac knew before he wrote his.[1] Lowry also has his metamorphoses. It is writing from the perception of a woman, not as the surreal cockroach or Philip Roth's breast—though he does see through cat's eyes in two stories without violating the naturalism of his usual method.

Despite these hidden European lines that other, younger writers would exploit with more discipline, Lowry offers something else to bring him back into view, to even find him a place in the canon. It is itself a postmodern conceit, for he is an *outsider artist*. He is not unlike the untrained and reclusive folk painter—even more so he is the psychiatric-case artist whose works sell in the gallery world for what he sees and we cannot. Nevertheless, here he will not be so ennobled with R. D. Laing's day-pass that the mad are really the saner. Indeed, had the psychoanalyst-turned-poet treated Lowry, he would have discarded this idea.

"I have had the most interesting literary career in Twentieth Century America," Robert Lowry wrote as though for a prize-acceptance speech, a career "completely satisfying to me for its great variety and grand scope of publication." His audience, however, were the recipients of his curious 1975 résumé, where, among his many publications and an old photograph of him in uniform, he could also capitalize on his experience in telephone sales for aboveground swimming pools and handing out towels at the Y.

The irony of such a lapsed man of letters began early in Cincinnati, Ohio, where Lowry was born on 28 March 1919 to Beirne Clem Lowry, a Pennsylvania Railroad conductor, and his wife Alma Collas Lowry, a former telephone company operator. Robert was the younger of their two children, his sister Ruth being two years older. Though the Lowrys lived in lower Linwood, one of the poorer, river-bottom neighborhoods subject to flooding by the nearby Ohio and its tributary, Duck Creek, they were considered one of the better-off families on Hutton Street. Beirne would soon be promoted to yardmaster of the Pennsylvania's Undercliff yards, which ran perpendicular to Hutton Street and which could be crossed by an Escher-like footbridge to Eastern Avenue, where the trolley line ran. It appears in Lowry's fiction and even has its own story, "The Bridge," from which this cadence of second-person sentences is taken, a cadence that reappears in Lowry's work, usually as an argument in the narrator's head:

> You cannot crawl under it. It is all fenced in.
> You cannot go another way.
> You have to go up the steps and over it.
> You have to do it in silence, because any wasted breath and you may not make it. (Lowry, *New York Call Girl* 113)

Lowry's childhood here where Cincinnati ended in bottomland fields was both urban and pastoral, dissonant and idyllic. The events in his life reflect this, from being stuffed with food by his doting mother to being forced to witness a neighbor shoot a sick dog. He never saw his probable sexual abuse by a teenage girl as victimhood, but rather as a pleasantly warm, wet experience—like the assignations he had already had with a little neighbor girl. He had the experience to come halfway with the babysitter, and this, more than reading Henry Miller, contributed to the casualness and candor about sex in his work.

The other precociousness in Lowry's life is that he began to write and see himself as a boy-wonder writer, an image he would never let go. To him (and certainly to his contemporaries who developed "normally" after their debuts in the 1940s) and the general public, the American novelists of the Jazz Era were as much celebrities as the era's cinema stars and aviators. To want to be like Hemingway was as natural for Lowry as the other boys wanting to be the next Lindbergh. During the late 1920s, he began to type his own stories on a toy Simplex wheel typewriter and make his own books and magazines filled with his detective and prizefighter stories, jungle adventures, and the like, inspired by comic strips, penny dreadfuls and boys' adventures, radio and movie serials, and sports broadcasts. Lowry also read and collected the Little Blue Books printed by E. Haldeman-Julius, which stimulated his many interests and led to his own little book-printing ventures, from the highly collectible prewar Little Man productions to his manic and fetishistic mimeographings of the late 1950s, which resemble cargo cult objects invoking his lost high-flying career of the previous decade.

Writing, seeing his name and words in type, and the tactile pleasure of the printed objects associated with his name became the way Lowry played. It gave him an early start, but he was never the perfectly divided self of adult–child that we find in other writers. The adult gap between the outward, civilized person and the inner, organic anarchy of fantasies and fears is at its thinnest in Lowry. His creativity is so transparently play—especially during his mentally uninhibited years—that he would have made a revealing subject for Gregory Bateson's human and animal play research during the 1950s, when the renowned anthropologist observed only children and zoo animals. And the secrets that Lowry might have revealed would force a disturbing reassessment of even the most serious thinkers and creators, those "players," in the way he failed at being a player. What he might prove could be one reason for the *omerta* that fell around him to the point that even those still living who knew him remain guarded—including Gore Vidal, who rated Lowry's *The Wolf that Fed Us* as having a "virtue of being felt"; compared to Norman Mailer's *The Naked and the Dead,* it was "not created out of stern ambition and dogged competence" (33).[2]

When Lowry was nine, the *Cincinnati Times-Star* printed one of his mystery stories in its "Sunshine Page" for young readers. This experience left him exhilarated, and he still talked about it to the end of his life. However, in his novel *The Big Cage* he seems to recall his mother's reaction to her gifted son's first success: "She just looked at me sadly then. She wanted me to be little and innocent; to resemble other kids; to coast along and just grow. And here I was going at it furiously at the age of eleven, hell-bent for glory or the booby hatch . . ." (91–92).

At Withrow High School Lowry was a reporter for the student newspaper and a voracious reader of Hemingway, Faulkner, Fitzgerald, de Maupassant, and all the new names that appeared in James Laughlin's New Directions anthologies. He came to the attention of Delphine "Duffy" Westheimer, who reviewed books for the *Times-Star* and whose family is still well known for their cultural philanthropy. She introduced Lowry to her "salon," in the mansion district of Avondale, as an exotic specimen who came literally from across the tracks of working-class Linwood. She plied him with books, let him help her write reviews, and pulled strings to get him a scholarship at the University of Cincinnati. Lowry depicted her as the character Sary Farber in *The Big Cage*; he also drew on his other mentor, Mildred Cook O'Nan, a librarian, whose letters to William Saroyan resulted in Lowry's connection to the novelist who then personified the kind of success that Lowry's supporters wanted from him.

In the fall of 1937 Lowry enrolled as a premed student rather than an English major. Being a psychiatrist, he thought, might be "a possible alternative" if he could not make it as a writer—a practical solution that was not only driven by his parents but also by his first exposure to analysis. *The Big Cage*, which is relentlessly autobiographical, gives evidence that Duffy Westheimer had succeeded in getting a resentful and resistant Lowry psychoanalyzed that summer. His manic writing and antisocial and oppositional behavior alarmed her. He already had a confrontational edge that would manifest itself later in hit-piece or revenge-themed fiction, written with little disguise of the intended victim, and in sudden and precipitous fallings out with even close friends. (That Lowry was never successfully treated for a deleterious cocktail of such indicators, including his lifelong bizarre and inappropriate advances on young women, suggests that he suffered from Asperger's Syndrome, a form of high-functioning autism that can be correlated with creative genius. This relationship is explored in Michael Fitzgerald's *The Genesis of Artistic Creativity*.)

His first months at the university, however, were taken up with founding the publishing enterprise that would become the Little Man. Stirred by European surrealist magazines, Laughlin's New Directions, and independent small presses that printed handsome, limited editions of modern poetry and fiction, Lowry mixed serialization, radical typography, graphic art, social commentary, and avant-gardism with his editing and, as a self-reward, samples of his own writing. (The foil stars that he pasted on one of his last Little Man productions, *The State of the Nation,* are the kind used by teachers for their students' best work.) The Little Man's name originated from an incident when Lowry was five years old and sitting at the kitchen table with his grandfather and namesake, Robert Collas, who had pasted a cartoon of a funny little man from a newspaper comic strip on the kitchen wall: "we both laughed like hell," he wrote in an unpublished fragment, "Of course there was Henrik Ibsen's magazine THE MAN. . . . I was a great admirer of Ibsen. . . . And then too 'the little man' was in the headlines in those days, the days and years of the Great Depression when 'the little man' was glamorized and eulogized and given a job on the Works Progress Administration. . . ."[3]

Lowry had won university funding for the *Little Man* magazine on the understanding that it would be a student-run journal with contributions mainly by students. This arrangement, the uneven quality of the submissions, and a revolt led by his fellow editors for his "dictatorial ways" made him abandon the magazine and drop out of college in March 1938. He had also been showing too much favoritism to a married graduate student, Shirley Wheeler, with whom he was also having an affair. (Her poem in the *Little Man* faced his love poem to her.) She had solved any outstanding inexperience he had, not only with sex but with driving—she also provided him with the idea of hopping a freight to "Tibet." The couple got as far as Little Rock, where Wheeler's mother retrieved her troubled daughter. Alone and still in love, Lowry continued on to Texas and then hitchhiked east, back to Scranton, Pennsylvania, where he reunited briefly with Wheeler, who had promised her family to return to her husband. Lowry then went on to New York City.

From April to June 1938, Lowry lived in Greenwich Village, where he tried to support himself by selling his short stories to magazines. Finding no takers, he returned to Cincinnati and, backed by the Westheimer family, reformed the Little Man. He also took a partner, James Flora, an Art Academy student who would later be celebrated as an innovative illustrator of record covers and children's books. Much of his style, based on marionette-like figurations, was developed in the books that he and Lowry produced. The first new Little Man production was a reproduction of a Thomas Mann letter to Lowry and Flora, written during his lecture tour on neohumanism and endorsing the Little Man as a center for the aspirations of young and progressive artists in America. It was followed by small ingeniously printed and illustrated chapbooks, including the work of Saroyan, William March, Weldon Kees, Gilbert Neiman, and a number of cult figures such as the proto-Beat sonneteer Charles Snider, whose discovery Kerouac credited to Lowry.

Lowry charged very little for the colorful letterpress chapbooks that he, Flora, and Hugo Valerio, another illustrator, designed. Even by the populist standards of the Depression, Little Man prices were always just a few pennies more than trolley fare. Lowry advertised his press in small literary magazines and New Directions anthologies in exchange for advertising space in Little Man issues. These were sold through subscription and in a handful of bookstores. An early supporter, Frances Steloff, featured stacks of Lowry's Little Man wares in her Gotham Book Mart, including a literary magazine that he printed for two student editors at the University of Wisconsin, *Diogenes.*

From 1939 until 1942, the Little Man operated out of Lowry's home on Hutton Street—the printing press was in the basement—and from the apartment living room of his first wife, Bella Cohen, whom he married in 1941. Bella was seven years older than her husband and worked for the Division of Public Relief in Cincinnati. The marriage took place as much to elude the draft as it did for love, for the Selective Service was not yet calling up married men.

Lowry lost any exempt status in early 1942 and left for boot camp in Alabama in June. From that point he began writing the hundreds of letters and V-Mail he sent to Bella (or "Mookie," which rhymes with his comic-strip character-sounding pet name, "Bookie"). These reveal a passionate relationship—with little held back about their sex life—and the energy that Lowry put into his writing and literary interests despite the vicissitudes of army life and relocating first to a base near Spokane, Washington, and then in October to Ft. Huachuca Military Reservation near Douglas, Arizona. There Lowry, now a corporal in the army air forces and attached to an aerial photo-reconnaissance unit, the 953rd Topographic Engineers Company, learned mapmaking and edited and produced the 953rd's magazine, *Phisterus.* He also continued to fold up the Little Man. Bella during this time acted as her husband's agent for this and for sending out his manuscripts. She also followed him from camp to camp on rare weekends that were carefully timed by the "rhythm" method.

The army provided Lowry with the experiences that would inform much of his fiction, the work for which he should even now be well known. Initially, he was horrified by the war—before 1941 he could have been considered a pacifist. After his first bayonet drill, he came to see his situation as a punishment, that he "deserved it" for not resisting the war and the encroachments of an American-style crypto-fascism—a punishment for inaction that would be the irony and rough justice that the characters of his fiction would suffer. To Bella, he came close to expressing the worldview that informs everything that he wrote:

> don't laugh darling Mookie—I'm in a position of terror and fear; confused but sort of serious too darling. You see—somehow this killing's got to stop. This regimentation—all conditions in which one man holds

the power of life or death over another man. Mookie sweet, this isn't the little C.P. urge that every college freshman feels to reform the world—every day I go through I know better and better that in this one way I was living a little-boy life not knowing what terror could be, not knowing what horrible things *Are* in the world. (Lowry to Bella Lowry, 8 June 1942)

Douglas, however, was like that prewar army base in Carson McCullers's *Reflections in a Golden Eye*: settled, boring, and sexually tense. In such a setting Lowry could find and instigate his own material among the other soldiers, the Mexican bar whores, and a teenager he picked off the porch of her parents' home when he saw her watching him. Mary Beth Nelson became Lowry's third muse and a female mirror of himself, even a protégé. Before he embarked for the invasion of North Africa, while still in New York, he compelled Bella to pay for a parcel of *Little Man* remainders from Gotham Book Mart that Lowry wanted sent to the high-school girl whom he had already tried to seduce, along with a book of Klee reproductions and Hemingway's *The Torrents of Spring*. "[I]t's a wonderful thing to find someone like this," Lowry wrote Bella, "a really honest person who, working all by herself without any encouragement from anyone, comes on the good things alone, develops an extraordinary taste without any prompting" (Lowry to Bella Lowry, 16 Aug. 1943). Throughout his long tour of duty, Mary Beth reciprocated, sending him her short stories, poems, and small paintings, nudes of Mexican girls who posed for her or whom she imagined. Lowry already knew that these were outward expressions of her real sexual preference, and this made him identify with her all the more. He even sent her feminist literature.

In Bari, on the boot heel of Italy in Apulia, Lowry drafted *The Big Cage* and published in mimeograph an illustrated version of his novella *Casualty* under its original title, *War*, which he tried to distribute among the soldiers like the semi-official newsletters he produced for the engineers. His officers, however, deemed its content defeatist and antiwar, and Lowry was court-martialed and demoted to private for the misuse of army equipment and stationery. Disturbed over the shame this brought his parents, Lowry nevertheless continued his self-publishing between sojourns to the brothels of Rome, taking over an Italian print shop in Bari to produce two "Piccolo Uomo" story collections in 1945.

That same year he had to choose between Bella and Mary Beth, Cincinnati and New York. For her part, Bella had refused in her last letters to leave her job and clients and come live with him and the vagaries of the New York writer's life that he proposed. Mary Beth, however, even though involved in a lesbian relationship at college, agreed to join him in the autumn in a cold-water flat on Downing Street in Greenwich Village, her interest sustained, perhaps, by Lowry's plastic physical appearance—he could modulate it from the feminine softness of his mother, whom he resembled closely, to that of a thick-bodied tough—and by the good news that he had been hired by James Laughlin as a project manager and book designer for New Directions.

While Lowry designed the covers and text for books by Dylan Thomas, Federico García Lorca, Thomas Merton, and Pablo Neruda, he did the same for his first hardcover, the revised and expanded *War* that New Directions published as *Casualty* in 1946. The novella, about the last days of a disgraced young soldier in the Italian theater, brought him to the attention of book reviewers and Doubleday's fiction editor, Ken McCormick. But by this time Lowry had already been discovered by the fiction editor of *Mademoiselle*, the legendary George Davis. Davis had become intrigued with Lowry after reading his story "The Ticket, the Train, the Journey Out"; he found it in one of the small, unusually designed books that Lowry had printed in Italy which had subsequently made its way into a secondhand bookstore on Fourth Avenue that the editor frequented. The story—in which Lowry had channeled much of what he knew about Mary Beth—about a creative, sexually ambiguous adolescent girl, appealed to Davis, who had made his own contribution to gay fiction with the novel *The Opening of a Door* (1931). The next day, he gave his editorial assistants the task of finding Lowry so that the story could be bought and reprinted in *Mademoiselle*. It did not take long, for a telephone call to New Directions revealed the author to be on the staff.

Confronted by the intriguing combination of an ostensibly straight man living with the very girl in the short story—made stranger by the couple sometimes dressing alike in corduroy coats—Davis brought Lowry into the circle of Truman Capote, Carson McCullers, and others, including the African American painter-playwright Charles Sebree and the poet Owen Dodson. When Mary Beth left after her relationship with Lowry became abusive, Davis gave the rising young novelist a room in his Yorkville brownstone on 86th Street in New York's German district.[4] There Lowry drafted his next novel, *Find Me in Fire,* which Davis practically midwifed, and was introduced to the next two women in his life, first McCullers's sister Margarita Smith (Davis's assistant at *Mademoiselle*) and Frances "Frankie" Adelman Abbe, who became Lowry's second wife. The latter matchmaking may have been both an act of kindness and way out of a disappointing arrangement for Davis, even an act of revenge. Lowry, as perceived by Davis's co-workers, was a sexual tease and grifter with whom the editor was infatuated, taking advantage of him for the free room and constant loans of money that he offered.

Despite Lowry's lifelong chronic need for income, with his Double-day advance for *Find Me in Fire* and forthcoming work, he had a modicum of income and independence in 1948. He started living with Frankie and her son (by her first husband, the photographer James Abbe II) and married her in that same year, just before leaving for an extended stay in Italy and France to coincide with translations of *Casualty* in both countries. There he finished his collection of war stories in *The Wolf that Fed Us* and the novel *The Big Cage* (both published the following year by Doubleday). He also enjoyed the celebrity that came with publication of the Italian edition of *Casualty,* the translator of which, Giorgio Monicelli, praised Lowry for transforming "realism into a redemptive poetry . . . and his apparent defeatism into a love of humanity" (Monicelli 18–19).[5] Monicelli, responsible for introducing much American postwar fiction to an Italian audience, was also in a position to know of the praise Hemingway had given Lowry in response to an Italian publisher who asked him what he thought of Lowry: "Best writer in America today—il migliore scrittore che oggi abbia l'America" (qtd. in Monicelli 16).

So anointed, Lowry returned from Europe in 1949 because the now pregnant Frankie wanted to give birth in an American hospital. She may have had another reason to return: her husband had been unfaithful in both Rome and Paris—perhaps even flagrantly in their suite at the Hotel Saint-Cloud. He had also become obsessed with a Doubleday assistant editor he knew as Judy Bailey (now the editor emeritus Judith Jones at Knopf), whom he continued to practically stalk, even when she took a new job at the Ober agency, where Lowry himself went after many years of being represented by Macintosh & McKee. However, with the birth of his first son, David Beirne, Lowry agreed with Frankie to move to the Connecticut suburb of West Redding in 1950. There, with money from his advances, paperback and translation rights, and a new job as a book reviewer for *Time,* he was able to afford a comfortable 1840s farmhouse and a new Hudson Hornet.

In contrast to his upper-middle-class milieu—the inventor of the corn-chip snack Fritos lived across the road—Lowry began sketching his next Doubleday novel, *The Violent Wedding,* which explored the taboo of an interracial relationship between a boxer modeled on the real-life Sugar Ray Robinson and a troubled young woman artist. Set in the boxing camps of rural New Jersey and the hipster bohemia of Greenwich Village, this manuscript, Lowry hoped, would make him the most important and controversial author in the country. His research for the book took him to Robinson's training camp and to the climactic bout with Jake LaMotta in February 1951 (nearly missing it after an afternoon of drinks and writers' shoptalk with Nelson Algren), which Lowry used as a chapter and a stand-alone short story, "Blood Wedding in Chicago," published in the *American Mercury*. This passage is a mimesis of the swaggering reportage of the *"Time* man" of Marshall McLuhan's famous *Partisan Review* essay, "The Psychopathology of *Time* and *Life*," and painterly, too, in the way it riskily celebrates diversity (long before *that* became trite) and seemingly resonating in prose what the abstract expressionists were doing with their Black & White shows of that same year:

> All the people you always see at fights were here, except that tonight there were more of them. Instead of two or three platinum and peroxide blondes in seven-and-a-half-inch heels, I counted eighteen—all with chins held high and lashes lowered to half-mast. Gorgeous Negro women all around me offset the blondes with a beauty that most white people have no idea exists, since in their isolation they deal only with the Negro girls not pretty enough to do something better than vacuum rugs and scrub pots in a white woman's house. This sweep of faces in the great bowl of the Stadium made a black-and-white checkerboard pattern, a pattern that added a colorful border of latent violence to the square patch of brilliantly lit canvas which surrounded it. (*New York Call Girl* 184)

As Lowry took on the themes of an increasingly restive and liberated society, he deracinated himself from Hutton Street and wrote in registers that made both his Harlem boxer and the passing black chanteuse in his 1951 story "Passing Star" believable. He showed that social justice had taken on a life of its own. Yet in his personal life he turned away from being Doubleday's agent provocateur. As his father's health declined and it became clear he would lose that connection, he increasingly romanticized his roots. He decorated the room in which he wrote with railroad memorabilia and even started to wear a railroader's denim shirt as he worked. He had hoped that his literary success would impress the elder Lowry and even make up for his father's refusal to take a promotion with the Pennsylvania Railroad, which wounded the son's self-esteem. But the East Coast career was a brittle accomplishment, for Beirne Lowry, a freight-train conductor and a farmer's son from West Virginia, did not see it as a real man's work. This insecurity and a "professional" one of not betraying that self-made boy genius—the Little Man incarnate, that "big, affable kid" in Ken McCormick's glimpse at the real nature of his author—also made it hard for Lowry to conform to the *politesse* and rigors of that unforgiving cultural cityscape that was New York after the war. He may have been more put out with the role of the intellectual than those who suffered from his dismissive—and often acute—book reviews in *Time* and the *Saturday Review of Literature*. (Gore Vidal took umbrage at what he had written about his friend Anaïs Nin.) Another source of professional insecurity may have come from his pursuit of Judith Bailey, which was the stuff of high and hushed gossip about his sanity.

That Lowry's womanizing contributed to the events of early summer 1952 is uncertain. But his uninhibited libido was a source of mental discipline in the way he understood it—as he told Truman Capote while pointing to his own head and then his crotch, "I'm not all *here*. But I'm all *there*." This means there was a practical dimension to the bizarre personality change he underwent and the breakdown that followed: Lowry may have "wanted" to frighten his second wife into a divorce to feed his writing again with his favorite subject, himself alone, in love, and disappointed with both, even as he moved away from autobiographical fiction in *The Violent Wedding*. And if there was no "other woman," the crisis would open up some unexplored self-territory from married life in West Redding.

If there were elements of theater as well as real pathologies that faced Frankie when she returned from Los Angeles with the infant David after a three-month absence, during which she visited her family following the suicide of her father, her reaction backfired horribly on Lowry. Frankie was devoted to making their relationship work and his books achieve monetary success as well as the critical kind. (She was Lowry's typist and editor, a role she had played for George Davis's boarders when she lived next door to 7 Middagh Street during the war years.) When he reacted violently after his two-year-old son repeated what one of his relatives had told him, that he was Jewish because his mother was, Frankie had her husband committed to Connecticut's Fairfield State Hospital and signed a permission form for a series of twenty-two shock treatments. Lowry was later transferred to the Bronx V.A. Hospital, where he finished *The Violent Wedding* and managed to recover enough to be discharged.

He returned to his family in West Redding and resumed writing and working as a part-time editor for the Popular Library, a publisher of paperback editions (including Lowry's, which attracted readers with lurid and often sexually explicit covers). However, once again he began to act bizarrely. He even kidnapped Frankie's son, James Abbe III, for a day. Finally, he could no longer socialize with friends and neighbors without getting into some accusatory argument with his wife. Alcohol, which had once made him the bad boy of George Davis's cocktail parties, now left him an open psychological wound in mixed company. The couple agreed to separate in early 1953.

In the summer Lowry moved into a hotel in Danbury and sold the West Redding farmhouse, furniture, and even the letterpress he had used to print his Little Man books, using his share of the money to buy a "Toro red" 1953 Hudson Jet, which he used for making forays to the Village to pick up women or drink at the White Horse Tavern, where his bar mates would have included Delmore Schwartz and James Baldwin. The publication of *The Violent Wedding* put him on an upswing for a time, but there was no wide readership for a book with an interracial relationship (and by the time there was, in the 1960s, authenticity would clearly limit what a white writer could do). Nevertheless, a confident Lowry, freed at last from his wife and son, found the sign he had been looking for: a redheaded ticket-taker and actress at the Cherry Lane Theatre named Katherine Kelleher—who went by the more slatternly "Kit." In a performance of *The Plough and the Stars* she pointed to Lowry in a half-deserted row and cried out, "I see a star," and he was smitten.

A few days later, in early July, Lowry, intent on meeting Kit, started hearing the voice of God as he drove down toward New York on the Hutchinson River Parkway. "Bob, I am giving up. You are the last man. I am giving this world to you. . . . You are the new Christ." Lowry, who had recently signed a contract for a new collection of short stories, *Happy New Year, Kamerades!*, was in no condition to disbelieve and started "taking charge of the world" by ramming and sideswiping cars on the busy highway with his new Hudson. He was arrested after he crossed the state line.

Lowry spent the rest of 1953 and part of 1954 in different mental institutions. His treatment at New York's Harlem Valley State Hospital included insulin shock therapy, in which epileptic-like seizures and coma were induced to relieve the psychotic patient's symptoms. (The Nobel Prize-winning mathematician John Nash, whose story is told in the book and film *A Beautiful Mind*, was also treated in this way.) Lowry's constitution and stamina and his manic need to edit proofs forced his doctors to use a more rigorous regimen in implementing what is now a dangerous procedure. It left him increasingly, and inexplicably, anti-Semitic. Given his two Jewish wives, his Jewish benefactors in Cincinnati, his many Jewish friends and associates in the army and in his "good years" after the war, and his taking on bigotry in his fiction, no one expected this from Lowry. Nevertheless, his way of shocking his second wife and doctors did not come out of thin air. Lowry had absorbed the folk prejudices of his upbringing and had repressed them to the point of being little more than class envy or being true to the aesthetics of realism and Cincinnati's upstairs, downstairs—this despite Duffy Westheimer[6]: "Because Lillian Sunday did not go to the tuberculosis hospital that time, like all the times before. Instead she got on as a housegirl in Avondale, and she got more nervous and thinner all the time . . ." (Lowry, *Hutton Street* 13)

Lowry actually felt a bond to Jews who were not so much assimilated as taking the step of repressing their identity and reinventing themselves, much the way he had reinvented himself as a writer from the railroad people who lived around the Undercliff Yards. And for his Jewish wives and some Jewish friends, this made Lowry a member of an attractive outgroup that had room for others taking an existential risk (which he preserved in those character dyads of his fiction). His first wife, so wounded by waiting through the war years to find him in love with another woman, ironically kept his "gentile" name to make herself employable in Cincinnati, where Pound's "suburban prejudice" still exists.

The shocking symptoms of his illness (and the disturbing possibility of it all being an act over which he lost control) hardly made Lowry the celebrated cause that Ezra Pound was. And he had none of the entertainment value of a Robert Lowell, as famous for his psychotic outbursts as his poems. Instead, Lowry lost one friend after another who might have interceded for him. Chandler Brossard felt endangered by Lowry, and George Davis, who had let Lowry spend a night at his house, woke up to the fear of being murdered. He eventually decided he could do no more for his friend after Lowry wrote him the day after his first insulin shock treatment at Harlem Valley State Insane Asylum and begged Davis to form a committee of influential men, preferably writers such as W. H. Auden, Carson McCullers ("well, of course, she's not a man, but she might be willing to help"), Charles Henri Ford, Richard Wright, Janet Flanner, Jean Cocteau, Truman Capote, Maxwell Anderson, the ethnographer Colin McPhee, cartoonists Bill Maudlin and Virgil Parth, to sign a petition to free him or write letters to protest his being committed against his will.

Ken McCormick and the Popular Library's Charles Heckelmann stuck by Lowry. For much of 1954 and 1955, he had work and income from a new novel for Doubleday, *What's Left of April*, and a new short-story collection, *The Last Party*. Lowry, promising her that he would be rich and famous again, successfully romanced Kit Kelleher through the mail and moved in with her upon his release from the Bronx V.A. He even took lessons with her at Stella Adler's and Herbert Berghof and Uta Hagen's acting schools (although this seems to have been to keep an eye on her). Kit refused to marry Lowry, even after she divorced her husband and made him pay for an expensive abortion so that she could continue her career. Eventually, this impasse led to his moving in with a sailor with whom Lowry had his only admitted homosexual relationship. Then, following his arrest for attempting to break down the door to Kit's apartment, Lowry was persuaded to commit himself. Upon his release, he recuperated at his parents' home in Cincinnati through much of 1956 and 1957.

While Lowry was still with Kit, he had met a younger woman, Anne LoBianco. After a long courtship on visiting days at King's

Park State Hospital, she flew into Cincinnati's Lunken Field, less than a mile from Hutton Street, and the two were married in 1958. As Lowry's third wife, Anne tried to support him as he restarted his career in their new apartment on Bleecker Street overlooking the San Remo Café in the Village. Lowry's mental condition, however, had degraded so much that he was content to run off homemade mimeographed magazines, doggerel verses, and short stories that were more a reprise of his childhood publishing than a revival of the Little Man. He had little contact with his old milieu and with the Beats save for a few contacts with Jack Kerouac (for whom Lowry printed a section of *Some of the Dharma*). The Ober agency dropped him—as did Doubleday. Ken McCormick even told Lowry, who had once been his most promising writer, that Doubleday had lost money on every one of his books. A collection of previously unpublished short stories, *New York Call Girl*, relieved Lowry of his contractual obligations. And James Laughlin's secretary endured years of telephone calls from an increasingly rancorous Lowry in need of money.

Lowry's reputation was not helped by the film adaptation of his short story "Layover in El Paso," *That Kind of Woman* (1959) with Sophia Loren and Tab Hunter. His writings in his magazines and his increasingly eccentric behavior marginalized him. The islands of lucidity and false sanity became fewer, but he managed to novelize the screenplay of *That Kind of Woman,* write a few more striking short stories—collected in his last hardcover, *Party of Dreamers*—and hold a clerk's job at Doubleday's Fifth Avenue bookstore so that he could support his growing family.

His son Beirne was born in 1959 and Giacomo ("Jack") in 1962. The birth of the second son, however, put a strain on the Lowrys' marriage and caused yet another breakdown. This time, however, because she had promised not to commit him, Anne compelled her mother-in-law to take Lowry back to Cincinnati for the last time. From that point, his career effectively ended. His involvement with American Nazi George Lincoln Rockwell further tainted him, and it required some mercy on the part of those few friends and editors who remained in touch. But in the end Chandler Brossard, James Laughlin, and Ken McCormick could no longer endure his letters with even their envelopes festooned with swastikas.

From his mother's home and, after her death, from different residency hotels and group homes, Lowry continued to produce odd bits of poetry and prose. Laughlin published a short piece based on Lowry's father, and the *Carleton Miscellany* and other magazines occasionally published his last unremarkable writings. Even with all the manic energy that went into this—Lowry was diagnosed as a manic-depressive in the 1970s—there was nothing of his old craft and the professionalism his old editors once enforced. His twilight years were self-parodies of a younger Lowry, check-ins at the V.A. psych ward, a fourth wife and one more live-in girlfriend. Even the cocktail hours and fine drunks of his New York years were burlesques—more often a peach schnapps shared, if at all, with his mother and the side effects of lithium, which gave him the shambling walk seen so often in downtown Cincinnati during the 1980s and 1990s. Nevertheless, Lowry had some sense that he was his generation's *Crack-Up* and that he had not performed this role or much of his career very well. For this, Lowry apologized in a 1964 unpublished memoir that honored Laughlin:

> I was ready to go in 1953, when I was at the top of my career . . . and with all the force of my great literary voice fully expressed, fully written, finally put down and forever. . . . But the decadence, the rottenness, of my work since . . . is quite evident, in spite of refinements of style and a new imaginative flair, as well as a willingness and daring to deal with *any* kind of subject matter. In short, I regard *all* of my work since THE VIOLENT WEDDING as corrupt and senile and rotten, whatever interesting literary and stylistic and imaginative qualities may be discovered about it.

When a third chance at a comeback arrived in 1994, it came too late. A German journalist, looking for a new American cultural import to fill in for the late barfly and writer Charles Bukowski, took an interest in Lowry and wrote a major piece about him in *Der Spiegel*. This rediscovery attracted a German publisher and a book deal to have several of his old Doubleday novels translated. But Lowry did not live to see them in print or even cash the check he received for signing. He died of heart failure on 5 December 1994.

Lowry's texts would seem to have a place more in a cultural microhistory than a study of neglected books. On first reading, too, they seem to lack the complexity that would require much discussion, a body of critical writing. Yet his road novel, war fiction, boxing novel, and myriad short stories, which cover the Age of Anxiety that was the 1940s, form a bridge to Kerouac, Heller, Pynchon, even Raymond Carver—but his work is not influential. It is more interesting for the way it deals with influence. Lowry is a dead-ender for the "schools" of Hemingway and, to a lesser degree, Thomas Wolfe. He also belongs among the women writers of his time—especially for his studies of young women and girls—with Carson McCullers, Jean Stafford, Mary McCarthy, those who are not included in *After the Lost Generation*. Lowry is and comes close to getting his own chapter in that book. Aldridge found him interesting enough to include among the Neo-Hemingways: he, along with Vidal and "their terse little books," *Williwaw* and *Casualty*, had "helped to carry the tradition of Hemingway into our own decade" (133). But, Aldridge concluded, Lowry and others of his generation showed "little evidence of new developments" and did "little to flavor the material present" (88).

This survey of Lowry's published fiction begins with a selection of his prewar, self-published Little Man imprints that brought him notice and show his early promise. Lowry's postwar, hardcover debut for New Directions and Doubleday continue this discussion and reveal aspects of his maturity that were not apprehended during his professional career. The work that followed Lowry's mental collapses in the 1950s is also examined book by book until his illness forces any critic or reader disposed with goodwill to draw a line that he drew himself albeit jaggedly.

Defense in University City (1939) and Hutton Street (1940)

Lowry took secret pride in being the mysterious James Caldwell praised by Ezra Pound in a "Rome literary-artistic newspaper."[7] *Defense in University City* was Lowry's first book, printed as a stapled folderol in the Little Man series in 1939. It is more a theater piece than a long short story, for Lowry, after some research and mental preparation, had recited a dramatic monologue that his Little Man collaborator, James Flora, transcribed. This took place over the course of an evening in Lowry's Cincinnati apartment, from which he was evicted the next day for all the shouting and pacing that had gone into re-creating James Caldwell's account of his experiences in the Spanish civil war. The method was not untested by Lowry—it was an extension of his writing without looking back, without revision, and publishing the results (a métier that proved untenable as his mental illness progressed). Part of the nineteen-year-old Lowry's preparation was the influence and appropriation of that war experience of the moderns. Lowry skipped the "youthful disillusion" of Dos Passos (Aldridge 64). From the vantage point of that strange *Sitzkrieg* of an isolationist United States redoubled in the heartland of Cincinnati, he could jettison the pretense of the Hemingway hero, too—in fact, he replaces him with an antihero who anticipates Billy Pilgrim and Yossarian. Lowry also replaces those "damn good times" for his new model, *lumpen*-Jake Barnes with the daily grind of the Depression.

Caldwell's story begins with his recruitment into a foreign brigade charged with the defense of Loyalist Madrid in 1936. His motivation is not to "consolidate the Communist front" or his reading "a lot of books by Marx and Engels" (1). It is from being "God damn sick of breadlines and looking for jobs every morning" (2) and misanthropic, for despite the brotherhood of the common man he hears about, Caldwell is "sick of turdish friends" (2). There is, though, something higher than the listless negation of Caldwell's joblessness and fecalhood: a vague sense that "we had to do it before they got over here and beat the hell out of us" (3). Brute survival is the only ideal for Caldwell as well as his lost innocence (and infantilism). Lowry depicts this in Caldwell's seeing himself and his fellow brigadiers as a drunken children's crusade with too few "steel hats," tanks, and good leaders. His pacifism is a foxhole conversion, not from a moral or religious conviction: "in a war nothing is right" because the elites who *do* wars cannot get them right and you are at the mercy of competencies (17). Lowry is harshest, though, on his own kind: "Nobody said anything in the truck. The man next to me was wounded in the arm. He was crying. He was sitting all bent over, crying like some small child. There was nothing you could say to a man like that. That's what happens to your fat little American boys when there's no artillery to break em up on front" (12–13).

Caldwell is finally wounded himself and sent back to recover in a New York City charity ward. Lowry delays the nature of the wound so as to set Caldwell's revelation on the stage as he and other veterans are feted at a rally in Madison Square Garden that is part of celebrating the twentieth anniversary of the Russian Revolution. There, he observes "the dark thin girls you always see" (18), code for the women and camp followers of the Cause (the kind Lowry would marry). He also finds in the crowd his competition for them, the winners, "the fat greasy men in glasses you always see," the *Partisan Review*-reading intellectual, those "pretty bright people," next to whom, earlier in the story, Caldwell "couldn't hold a candle" (2). Such an erection and the performance with a literal one are not possible for him. Yet Lowry, the envious, generational beta-male writer to Papa Hemingway, takes on the coup of Jake Barnes's testicles in the shocking, closing revelation of what the fascist machine guns took from Caldwell, which hang from the Statue of Liberty: "They were my nuts" (19) is both a riposte and a respect-bite that Lowry would repeat in other work.

According to Stanley Weintraub, *Defense in University City* was "the most intriguing first-person account of the war in Spain by an American volunteer, one that registered the profound disillusionment of those who had poured themselves into the Cause only to discover that Spain had become a pawn of the great European powers" (226). The problem, as Weintraub researched his cultural history, *The Last Great Cause*, was that Caldwell was really Lowry and his story a fiction. The need for this authenticity, where fiction and New Journalism began to blur in the 1960s, is still an unfortunate development for the purist storyteller that Lowry was. But *Defense in University City* is no less invented than *The Red Badge of Courage*, as Lowry pointed out. He had, like Crane, researched his "story," using what he could find in Cincinnati: newsreels, *The Spanish Earth*, picture stories in the popular press. He even appropriated Robert Capa's *Life* magazine image of the dying soldier in a cloth hat, and his battle scenes seem to come from *Homage to Catalonia*. However, the resemblance to Orwell is coincidental, for Lowry would have had a hard time finding the first edition published in England.

The Little Man Lowry writings are stylistically his most heterogeneous. Lowry can sound like Joyce or the funny papers in the same work, as is the case in yet another one-story 1939 chapbook, "I'll Never Be the Same." It begins as a penitential prayerlike mea culpa before it segues into stream-of-consciousness writing that may have been typed directly out of Lowry's font box. Nevertheless, he moved quickly in making these disparate voices and styles into his own with the stories that he printed in *Hutton Street* under his own name in 1940. James Flora's whimsical wood engravings decorate this book, beginning with a cabala-tree-like map of Hutton Street on the wrappers. The stories are a fusion of Grimms' fairy tales (the naïveté of "Star-Money" comes to mind), Dick-and-Jane-simple sentence cadences, and the social naturalism of the period, like that of William Carlos Williams in his fiction of the 1930s, and of the common-man novels of Hans Fallada (which were available in English translation during the Depression years). There is that American style of regionalism, too, but it is reduced from a *Winesburg, Ohio* scale to that original center in Lowry's fictive cosmography: "It was getting dark on Hutton Street, a blue mist was settling over all the houses; and in the evening everything became smaller. Under the moon Hutton Street in winter time was like a toy world down which a child could walk like a giant" (6).

United by interpolations that celebrate a false spring on Hutton Street in winter, the stories use Lowry's neighbors as starting points or are barely altered transcripts of their real lives. They reveal a young married couple's lovemaking ("This Is Our House"), a tubercular young woman's short life and epiphanous death ("The Beautiful White Hospital"), and family violence ("The Paper Seller's House"). The plight of the neglected elderly and the disposable children who do not live long enough to imprint Hutton Street with a memory are also themes. Lowry may have planned a larger collection of Cincinnati stories, perhaps with a four-seasons structure. Bella sent *Hutton Street* to several trade publishers as a teaser. After Pearl Harbor, however, the market for books set in a prewar world disappeared, and Lowry, in the army, redirected his energies. But while keeping up with news from the home front—one of his Little

Man contributors had shot his wife—he asked a revelatory question that is applicable to the "found object" method used in *Hutton Street* and in work to come. "Do you sometimes feel," Lowry wrote Bella, "that certain people hover about your life, some of whom you hardly get to know—people who seem to be working out a little pattern with their lives that you can see . . . a pattern which has meaning all in itself, the ends gathered up as in a well-written story" (27 Sept. 1942).

The Piccolo Uomo Books (1945)

Lowry's hand-printed and graphically interesting Piccolo Uomo collections, sixteen booklets with three stories each, are like maquettes for the hardcovers that Lowry was denied as he waited out the war in Italy. They have until now been considered more as bibliophilic objects than steps in the development of Lowry's talent.

The Blaze beyond the Town (1945) collects three of Lowry's army-life stories. The title story is set in the Nighttown of Douglas, Arizona, where the fear of death in war fuels, under the copper-smelting sky, the drinking and screwing, even the soldier farting in the booth of a seedy cantina. There, a group of young soldiers confront "It," a drunken Mexican "with a dark feminine hand," who after standing and smiling and staring at them, suddenly punches one of them. The ensuing fight would seem gratuitous violence among stock characters—the Mexican, of course, is beaten to a pulp—as flat and tensionless as cardboard. But Lowry uses every surface of text to show nihilism as the new cardinal sin and what its punishment should be—he would be consistent here until the end of his writing. "He was the best man," says the character Joe, perhaps the Joe Hammond of *Casualty* and *The Wolf that Fed Us*. "He brought everything and we brought exactly nothing." For this, Joe reasons, "all of us ought to be killed in the war . . ." (21).

The stories in *The Journey Out* (1945), the second Piccolo Uomo book, are portraits of two teenage girls and a young woman. Though Lowry's investment in soldier stories, like so many of his contemporaries, is considerable, he is as comfortable and androgynous in writing about women and their experiences as Henry James—and his debut as a professional writer owes to it, for the title story, in full "The Ticket, the Train, the Journey Out," caught George Davis's eye for *Mademoiselle*. Here Lowry, though restricted by his own gender and endomorphism, could cross over, cross dress really with and without the clothes—"In the shower room at school—all of us girls so ashamed of ourselves" (34). He understudied his teenage protégé, Mary Beth Nelson, in person and in her wartime letters, her nude paintings, her still ductile sexuality—"And when a boy would look at me I wanted to be dead. How much I didn't want to be a girl. I didn't want to be a boy either" (34). (Lowry was aware that she had lost her virginity to another woman at the University of Chicago.) The resulting short story is a pocket *Portrait of the Artist as a Young Man*. Lowry riffs on Stephen Daedalus's self- and body-conscious-ness and makes Joycean word sounds that seem to toy with his first wife's name,[8] which may be as much Lowry's subconscious infidelity as it is the story's weather: "Bloom-a-loom! mused Nancy Ann. A-loom, a-loom. That kind of thunder is purple and orange. But you couldn't write it on paper. . . . it's like an aged giant very hoarse and very far away, maybe in a cave, bellowing his last breath. Bellowing! Now there's a word. It's worth three hundred dollars, that word. It seems like almost a *bad* word. Maybe because it's like belly. 'The bellowing belly'" (29).

The girl, Nancy Ann, escapes Douglas, Arizona, her widowed mother's dependence on her, a boy who has proposed to her, and the normal life she detests, to attend college in Chicago and be an artist. She falls asleep on the train and instead of seeing herself painting and writing in an urban–academic bohemia, she is trapped in a nightmare where everyone she left is already well established: her despised boyfriend is her professor and the others from her past have been nightmarishly recast. Here is Lowry's gesture of surreal-ism that found its way into prewar American avant-garde writing and reappeared to express postmodern anomie in such settings as Joseph Heller's B-25.

Casualty (1946)

Lowry's novella about the disciplining and death of Pfc. Joe Ham-mond is an expanded version of a short story written and printed in 1944, when Lowry was nearly cashiered for using an army mimeo-graph machine and stationery. For that offense, he was court-mar-tialed under the auspices of his commanding officer, the president's son, Colonel Elliot Roosevelt, and demoted from sergeant to private. Lowry's friend Gene Newstrom, a mission model sculptor, was also tried for illustrating the pamphlet. He believed the verdict had more to do with Lowry's perceived antiwar content and defeatism than the misuse of army printing supplies. The real protest, however, was not against the war with the Germans but rather against the army and, by extension, the structured America that produced it—this microcosm provides Lowry's dramatic structure. (Had there been no war, he could have found that structure working in a car dealer-ship.) The Purple Heartlessness of a "meaningless routine" and the disconnect "with the war or with his former life" (38,39) provided him with a miniaturist's set piece, the kind in which he excelled, to present a single, sociologically defined character, yet another version of himself, and its limited consciousness, only aware of its subtraction and negation: "worming your way up a hill would have its advantages. Even getting killed, he thought with a laugh, would have its advantages. The truth of the matter is that each of us feels his own death more acutely than any real death around him. This sedentary life that's been going on for two years over here is the realest kind of death because we don't have any decisions about our personal lives, our future or our present" (77).

Hammond does not have a Catherine Barkley to think about in Italy, but rather his girlfriend back in Virginia, to whom he piously masturbates, which is at once an expression of the impossibility of a grand Hemingway romance in this war, of its unreality, and an ironic homage to the same and to the master because his student sees himself and his era as debased. His vicissitudes are not the retreat from Caporetto in *A Farewell to Arms* but the vaguely homosexual Lieutenant Pinkman who catches him performing a drunken friend's guard detail. The punishment is really a reprimand, and the lack of any real drama or tragedy is, by Lowry, added to the American style of oppression, which is muted and unviolent. Hammond is even free to go to Rome where he drinks away the annotativelike thoughts Lowry gives him about being wronged by the "rotten political army" and has real sex only once, rendered closer to the nausea of the European existentialists than to any kind of American writing: "He felt like vomiting, but he got himself drunkenly out of the chair somehow. He felt no passion, no interest in the girl or in sex or in life" (151). This is writing that holds a finger up to *Catch-22* but only mystified the first wave of postwar critics. Aldridge granted that Lowry at least showed "signs of developing a distinctly personal idiom" (111). However, he was ultimately disappointed: "The distance between [the Neo-Hemingways'] war world and Hemingway's is the distance between the tenderness Frederick Henry felt for Catherine and the fleeting pity of Lowry's Joe Hammond as he set about his systematic rape of Rome" (116). There is no rape—but it is true of the dysympathy that Lowry forces on the reader with its shock reckoning in that crushing of Hammond's head under a two-ton truck that leaves him in the street "not even kicking" (153).

Find Me in Fire (1948)

Unlike the now neglected Neo-Hemingways of *After the Lost Generation*, whose attempts to improve on the master's technique annoyed the handful of critics who considered them, Lowry's appropriations are less mannered, less academic. It is very much central to that inkling of a "personal idiom"—that is, Lowry is like the painter who copies out of picture magazines instead of off museum walls. There is no homage, no deference—just the rude economy of compulsion and sampling that allows for what is original in Lowry to surface. There is no overstudy because Lowry is probably incapable. Jake Barnes's testicles can be appropriated the same way that Duchamp repurposes a urinal albeit without the theory.

Art brut was the norm for Lowry—yet during the professional phase of his career he did work with an editor and mentor, George Davis, who must have seen that his discovery needed intercession to force from him more than the rough cut. *Find Me in Fire* is their book, Lowry's second published novel and first Doubleday hardcover. While Davis's hand can only be surmised, the way the novel is structured shows that Lowry had been "guided" into seeing the disparate characters of his shorter fiction as relatable and capable of being interwoven into a single narrative. The evidence—which must have struck at least some casual readers of the 1940s—is Lowry's cannibalization of a section from "The Ticket, the Train, the Journey Out," his first *Mademoiselle* story. What is known is that Davis provided Lowry with a fresh scene so that he could write in character again, without the entanglements of now being one of New York's literati, and with just enough difference from Hutton Street to make it new—the editor's own hometown of Ludington, Michigan, where Lowry spent part of the summer of 1947 as a guest of Davis's parents and friends:[9] "I wrote the fire-and-sex chapter this week—I think it's the best thing I've ever done. A great relief to be writing the book in Ludington—with not another writer around and everyone bright-eyed curious to know what I'm saying about them (they stop me on the street)" (Lowry to George Davis, 29 Aug. 1947).

Lowry's best and most deeply felt characters exist in *Find Me in Fire*. Jim Miller is an amputee coming home from the war. The bobby-soxer and love object Petey Jordan is another version of Nancy Ann, the tomboy–artist. Her friend and mentor, Genevieve Aronson, a librarian, is the town's only Jew and an agent of social justice based on Lowry's first wife. Len Sharpe is her other project, an African American teenager as troubled as the boy in *The Quiet One*, Helen Levitt and James Agee's film that appeared in the same year as Lowry's novel. Len's troubles, however, are not so innocent; and here Lowry seems controlled in imagining disturbingly real and speculative adolescent power fantasies—not unconsciously revealing his own strange and damaged semitophilism and where it was taking him:

> "Anyhow there he was, all alone in there, and struttin up and down in front of the mirror. Just struttin up and down with his hands on

his hips. Then all a sudden he raised up his hand, like this, straight
out."

"Like Hitler!"

"Sure, like Hitler. An struttin up and down. He think he gonna be
dictator, tell all the white people where to get off."

"An marry that Jew lady in the liberry." (59)

Though not a masterpiece, even with so many provocative scenes,
such as the masturbatory washing of Jim's stump and his sex acts
with their afterglow of despair, *Find Me in Fire* drew much praise if
not sales. A private memo from the director of Doubleday's publicity
department to George Davis termed the book a "perfectly stunning
job" and Lowry himself as a "top, new literary talent," with the only
regret being that the author was abroad and could not promote the
book in his own country (Louise Thomas to George Davis, 22 July
1948). Indeed, the novel, with its Midwestern noir years ahead of
its time, would receive more of an audience in Europe, where it was
translated into Italian and into Dutch as recently as 1965. In a
1990 monograph about the fiction of the cold war, *Find Me in Fire*
was even praised by a professor of American literature in Sweden:
"Lowry's theme is the violence of the postwar world and the need to
tackle the new situation and leave the old world behind—fittingly,
some of the most poignant scenes occur in the Doanville cemetery,
the representation of the old world that has died" (Axelson 46).

The Wolf that Fed Us (1949)

Lowry's first trade collection of short stories included stories that
went back to his first Piccolo Uomo book and his subsequent appearances in *Mademoiselle*, *Western Review*, and new writing anthologies. This book commanded praise—from Hemingway, Vidal, and
other writers and from academic critics in the early 1950s, such
as Aldridge and Ray B. West, Jr., who first printed "Layover in El
Paso," one of Lowry's most celebrated short stories gathered in *The
Wolf that Fed Us*: "From Capote and Bowles as a . . . center, a few
other writers of the forties seem to range in two directions: in the
direction of the symbol for its own sake, as in the case of Shirley
Jackson . . . or toward the pure, Anderson-like sentimentality. . . .
Better than these . . . is Robert Lowry, whose volume of short stories
The Wolf that Fed Us combines the sentimentality of Anderson with
the toughness of Hemingway or of Anderson at his best" (115).

As in the fiction collections that followed, Lowry here is an
experimenter and a neorealist who can modulate risk-taking, especially in sexual content, with the polished commercial writing that
got him into the better paying venues without too much artistic

compromise on his part. He is, in fact, virtually devoid of the disciplined ambition that would become a character trait of many of his contemporaries. He could still rely on placing stories that were two-finger typed without revision (and in this Lowry had a point when he imparted to Kerouac that he had reinvented automatic writing before the Beats). The way *The Wolf that Fed Us* is packaged, too, shows Lowry's nonconformance with the commercial imperative of trade-house publishing. The collection strays with what were to editors filler stories that did not fit the package—the one that Ken McCormick must have intended: episodes about the American occupation in Italy, GIs and Italian girls, the values and mores of nylons, cigarettes, and sex for food. But there is another kind of homogeneity in this looser anthology—one that Aldridge made to show that for the Neo-Hemingways the "frame of Italy" and the war were their only viable dramatic structure. To him, Lowry had only transferred "the war emotion intact to another setting. His women act the same whether they are Italian or American, in Italy or America, and his ex-soldiers in New York are identical with his infantrymen on leave in Rome" (110). Lowry, however, had actually written stories from a "frame" of Douglas, Arizona, one barely removed from the *ur-* of Hutton Street.

The opening story, "The Toy Balloon," flows from the anxiety of Lowry's boot-camp letters to Bella, in which he protested the way the war had separated them physically and emotionally. It documents one of their assignations as he moved about the country—this one in a San Francisco hotel. The fireworks and balloons of sex that fail in *The Sun Also Rises* go up for Lowry in what is an incredible subversion of Hemingway, of subtle influence and differentiation that went unnoticed. Here one of Lowry's dyads, with this karmic urgency, exists in a "room [that] took off like a balloon." The narrative is prose-poem-like, resembling or anticipating *Howl*—"The prophet masturbating and sinking himself, leaving dung floating on the waves" (14).[10]

Yet suggesting a certain phallocentrism on Lowry's part, his real subject is the fear of and power of women—the title directly evokes the she-wolf of Rome. Bella's character is but one wolf ("If you really are an animal you should have a mouth to bite me with, he said, and she bit him" (13)). Lupe in "The Church" is yet another who might be led into a back room to have sex with a "squarefaced soldier," but she can "swallow him, put him inside her" (32). In the title story the newly minted businesswoman and bar owner Nina Bonte seems practically lifted from Pavese's *Among Women Only*. For her, and the other women in this collection, Lowry's "rape" of Rome is a consensual one, even Oedipal. Joe Hammond, for his making her see herself as a by-product of fascism—because "Maybe he's Jewish, she thought" (115)—can be dismissed through her empowerment. She simply washes her face of what he wants her to see in cold sexless water and coolly returns to selling her liquor—the mother's milk of the she-wolf—with the evaporative decision not to "think of the soldier again" (120). He is as much consigned as the dead soldiers are in the dungeon of "Visitors to the Castle," Lowry's dark comedy of a town's revenge on the *Americani* for failing to bring Fiorello La Guardia.

The Wolf that Fed Us is Lowry's most myth-larded work, and yet this is virtually unseen with the requisite war-flavor notes. Red, in "Layover in El Paso," with the pun so in the face that it is missed, is the sex slave and prisoner of Kay, his Calypso and Circe, "somebody like Katharine Hepburn" (37), who belongs to that lost wartime demimonde of the American passenger train. However, it is she who does the abandonment—making Red a kind of Ariadne in uniform. This story would eventually become a film vehicle for Sophia Loren and Tab Hunter. "The Terror in the Streets," the slickest of Lowry's newer Village stories, would be adapted for the *Schlitz Playhouse of Stars*. With its trick ending for a young woman painter frightened by one of the postwar Bleecker Street Goths described by Milton Klonsky, this story, like the others in the collection, is of such contrast that it could be said that Lowry lacks a style let alone a personal one. He seems to mimic or echolaliate outside influences (the *New Yorker*, *Story*) and other writers (Shirley Jackson) for what to sound like next. But the fetishistic attention he gives to his women characters frustrates getting the stories' skillful arrangements just right, presumably frustrating his editors and agents, even though it is the essence of his one marketable quality: the sexual content that was now advancing through the culture. It is such a personal investment, too. The frightened girl is a pastiche of all of Lowry's women to date and her roommate simply wears his mother's name, a "wash" that reveals with its thinness that such women are the only kept-wet colors in his paint box.

The Big Cage (1949)

No matter what way Doubleday and Popular Library commodified and sexed up the undressing and sleeping around of Lowry's characters, he was not consciously pushing or holding back the envelope of light pornography. He was not a sexual adventurer like Henry Miller and Anïas Nin. (He panned one of her books.) There is, after "Toy Balloon," more interest in depicting joylessness in his sex. He simply added that to zeroing out any affirmative message, which made him a tough sell in a land of bulging automobiles and postwar hubris, even with the mushroom cloud puffing what unease there was and resonating with the mission-creep nihilism that affected Lowry as he moved from George Davis's orbit. (Davis, on reading the first draft of *Find Me in Fire*, was appalled at how Lowry had ended it with Jim Miller's suicide, as though unnaturally eager to echo the self-murderous ending of *Casualty*.)

The Big Cage, however, is anodyne, affirmative. It is Lowry's other portrait of an artist—the Nancy Ann–Mary Beth one being its divertimento. It is also the first novel that Lowry wrote, dating from 1944 and revised and expanded in Italy again in 1948 and 1949. He invented almost nothing in his story of becoming a writing tyro; the only gesture made to fiction seems to be renaming Hutton Street, his sister, others, and himself as the outsider Dick Black, whom—and *which*—he personifies in the hardcover's publicity photo. There Lowry is the *noir* hipster, Mailer's White Negro par excellence.

Lowry's early awareness of himself as someone different and dispossessed, his tactile joy at typing short stories, his discovery of sex and being discovered by the adults, and his founding the *Little Man* magazine at college—*The Big Cage* of the title—are retold with the emotional and personal investment of Thomas Wolfe's Eugene Gant. Dick Black, however, expresses a postmodern black humor that writers after Lowry would use more fully in depicting the absurdity of the self-romance. This is not to say that Lowry is not fascinated by himself and his demiurgic powers to make it in New York, that he can wax with a sentimentalism that is more true to the 1930s: "Though I'd sensed from the beginning the irony of human existence—this cage of flesh and circumstances that binds the spirit and denies the visions that the imagination conjures up—I'd made the mistake of believing that only I yearned for escape, never realizing that the cage that held me was as big as all humanity" (342). Because of this book, Hemingway, who loathed Wolfesque, took back in private what praise he gave Lowry. He must have seen an advance copy of *The Big Cage* and, rather than produce a blurb for Lowry's new book, it facilitated an omnibus displeasure in a letter to Malcolm Cowley: "You could put Lionel Trilling, Saul Bellow, Truman Capote, Jean Stafford and . . . Robert Lowry into one cage and jack them up good and you would find that you have nothing" (681).[11]

As expected, Lowry's self-hero caught the eye of most book reviewers, and his strange new, yet underdeveloped conceit of a prefailed writer only further soured some qualified praise that he had at least been faithful to imitating a modern. Also going unnoticed is "the strangest Iseult in modern fiction"—a serendipitous description supplied by the anonymous writer of Lowry's jacket copy. This is Nancy Williams, whom Lowry created from his Last Flapper, Shirley Wheeler. She imprinted him with what has to be

the teleology, the purpose of him writing at all: to re-behold his
molls and models as Hutton Street's Pygmalion, as postmortems,
as messages in bookstore windows and the newspaper book page
that he had *won*.[12] After *The Big Cage*, this would increasingly look
like revenge, too.

The Violent Wedding (1953)

"To prove himself," Aldridge wrote in 1951, thinking of Mailer, Irwin
Shaw, and the other war novelists, "he must . . . write a second novel
outside the frame of the war and take up characters and situations
that will demand some imaginative support from him" (97). Lowry's
fourth novel met this criterion for a "dramatic situation" with the
pairing of Paris "Baby" James, a boxer modeled after Sugar Ray
Robinson, and Laine Brendan, a composite of the many young
women who lived in postwar Greenwich Village and studied with
the Art Students League and the like. It is, therefore, more social
commentary than a boxing novel, mixing into that genre another
theme along with a hard-boiled account of left jabs and footwork:
the motivations behind that first wave of interracial couples who
appeared in the more tolerant quarters of northern cities in the
years leading up to *Brown v. Board of Education*. Nevertheless, *The
Violent Wedding* is Lowry's contribution to that shelf that includes
George Bernard Shaw's *Cashel Byron's Profession* (1882), Jack London's *The Game* (1905) as well as his prizefighting reportage (which
Lowry certainly read as a boy), and Orio Vergani's *Poor Nigger*
(1930). It was also part of a literary fad, riding on the coattails of
Budd Schulberg's *The Harder They Fall* (1947) and Nelson Algren's
The Man with the Golden Arm (1949).

What is surprising, even to readers now, is the way Lowry handles
such controversial material, going beyond Len Sharpe or the cameos
of black MPs in *Casualty*. The dominance of the African American
prizefighter, the racial guardedness of the lovers, even the dialogue is
unaffected. The stereotyping is an expression of realism; it never gets
beyond what would be natural for the characters themselves. Lowry
narrates convincingly as a black man—tapping his Hutton Street
otherness and an intimacy with postwar Harlem—through Paris.
The resulting cleaner, even minimalist innovations disappointed one
early reviewer who expected a more florid relationship between the
author and his personae: "You get a curious impression of a nerveless
narrator standing off to one side and describing the action of his
puppets in neat clinical documentary prose" (Hine 29–30).

To readers more attuned to Gordon Lish's writers, Lowry does get
well inside Laine. She is Nancy Ann grown up with, perhaps, her
appearance and background informed a little by Lowry's obsession

with Judith Bailey, who, like Laine, attended Bennington College. Lowry views the couple not only alone and together but also through Dick Willis, a white sports reporter torn by whether he is experiencing prejudice, jealousy, or both as he waits to pick up Laine after Paris tires of her. Willis is a representation of Lowry's own conflicted views at the time, a sublimation of the book-researcher's role that took him to the training camps of New Jersey, where he shadowed Sugar Ray and became steeped in the black boxing culture. Through Willis, Lowry portrays the anxieties of his own type, the liberal, progressive white male—a self-representation that is hard to square against the mental patient who five years later wrote in one of his crackpot, hand-cranked magazines that his novel was a send-up, that he had given "the Negro . . . his day in American literature" as well as a "beautiful blonde mistress."

The treatment of Laine's death is a more troubling sign. She is the suicide that George Davis denied Lowry. Her taking sleeping pills to end her life and pregnancy is also her well-crafted non-event, a personal, technical knockout to what follows: Lowry's colorful reenactment of the "St. Valentine's Day Massacre" of 1951, the Robinson–LaMotta fight in Chicago. Her rationale has little to do with carrying a mixed-race child; rather, she is incapable of being a trophy woman—of being another of Lowry's Eurydices. He sends her, this fresh new composite of women, back to hell. She is a receptacle of the author's punishment with her piled-on years of low self-esteem vis-à-vis unsatisfactory white lovers. The last of them is Dick Willis—who is just another Dick Black, a Bob Lowry. He ruthlessly lays her despite her troubled state. He *gets his turn in* in a near-necrophiliac act as she looks on, already out of her body, a ghost of herself, with "dead eyes" (198). This quasi-rape makes *The Violent Wedding* the first in a line of misogynistic works that come with the decay of Lowry's talent.

The "Later" Fiction

The two novels and four short-story collections that Lowry published between 1954 and 1962 form an uneven coda, one that is stylistically unsettled in ways that are good—as though he were succeeding in going back to his prewar, pre-Doubleday freedom, before the novel-writing pushed against the ceiling of his talents and, perhaps, sidetracked the kind of storytelling in which he excelled. It is also disappointing because what is really unsettled is Lowry's mind. Nevertheless, he kept producing publishable work alongside much republished fiction, some of it indicative of what could have been a second wind for his career and an earlier rediscovery in his native country and elsewhere.

Happy New Year, Kamerades! gathers *Defense in University City, Casualty*, and other stories published or written before Lowry's mental illness. "Little Baseball World" is one of several standouts, a 1947 *Mademoiselle* story based on Lowry's sister Ruth and her obsession with the Cincinnati Reds and their radio announcer, Red Barber, during one of their near-glory seasons during the 1930s. It is still anthologized as a classic baseball story and was used to form a chapter in *The Big Cage*. Ruth's partially paralyzed and spastically emotive right arm is depicted as though it were a character in its own right—and Lowry does this without exploiting her condition, ennobling this shy, physically challenged woman without sentimentality.

The title story is a leftover Roman episode from *The Wolf that Fed Us*, in which a carload of drunken soldiers hurry to the Eternal City for New Year's Eve 1944 and find it cold and deserted. The characters are stock Lowry army buddies that show how Lowry's success had influenced him to make his stories screen-ready. The dialogue and scenes are perfect for the period's method acting along with character parts for Jack Ward and William Bendix—but the gratuitous violence is too far ahead of its time. Another example of this is the story that Lowry agonized with George Davis over publishing, "The Victim," in which a former soldier, Eddie, forces himself into a Yorkville apartment furnished like Davis's at 305 East 86th Street, with its Austrian manservant, a cat like the one Lowry had left behind when he moved out, and its owner, Arnold, a gay television studio executive. There, Eddie, obviously Arnold's former partner in a rough trade relationship, punches his former lover and benefactor—and then, in the deserted house, slits the cat's throat with a Swiss army knife to hurt him further, dumping the carcass on Arnold's bed. Davis had refused to read it despite Lowry's urging. "I could only think," he wrote Frankie Lowry, "that the story was filled with hate, that so many people had reacted to it in a way that made me certain that I had better not read it . . ." (22 April 1953).

"Be Nice to Mr. Campbell," which earned Lowry his only O. Henry award, is an Oedipal comedy that was adapted for the *Starlight Theatre* in 1951 and even anthologized in the textbook *Parent and Child in Fiction* (1977) as instructional in understanding the fears and anxieties of children in single-parent homes. The title character is recognizably Lowry during his courtship and seduction of Frankie Lowry, made difficult by the presence of her jealous little boy. Less of a chestnut is "For Girlhood and for Love," which originally appeared in 1947 as "The Consolation Prize" in the first number of *Epoch*, an influential journal of postwar new writing. This story, with its typography indicating what a young woman hears and thinks as the anesthesia takes effect, again shows Lowry's ability to write a woman's self-doubt and sufferings like an *intime*, like someone who would be comfortable playing with dolls to show us these stories—and again it is Mary Beth Nelson.

Another collection, *The Last Party*, also needed Lowry's pre-crack-up fiction to fill it out due to a paucity of good new stories, one of which is a disturbing echo of "The Consolation Prize." "Child Bride" tells the events that lead up to its dreamlike abortion; and Lowry's ear seems so true to what actually took place that he even incorporates what could be remembered dialogues between himself and Mary Beth, right down to his character being rebuked for finding a butch-coded young woman to be a more "authentic" lesbian.

An obvious reprisal piece, like "The Victim," is the title story. "The Last Party" is autobiographically linked to Lowry's separation from Frankie Lowry. His character invites their neighbors to a grotesquely uncomfortable party in a soon-to-be-sold house. Then he sleeps with one of them, not caring, as the story ends, that he will be discovered in bed with another woman by the Frankie character as she unexpectedly returns. A permutation of this victimology, with a thinly disguised Robert Lowry as the cheated-on hero-as-injured-party, forms the basis for his final two novels.

Lowry's fiction always required for its structure his personal memories and mythology. He could sublimate his autobiographical representations to the point where only he, his family, and his women might see themselves mirrored in his work—and even those renderings are, though uncomfortably too real for their life models, never undisguised by him in anything else he said or wrote. The narcissism in his later work became more of an obvious and distorted mirror, but it differs only in that it becomes a form of self-justification and the dangerous practice of analysis on himself. A few years earlier he had achieved the objectivity and capacity for the complex experiences of *The Violent Wedding*, but his new novels retell the story of his breakdown, even as he tries to represent it in the old manner so that there is a semblance of craftsmanship rather than raw, brute life.

The civilizing effect of the 1950s—that "mixture of imitation, counterfeit, economic advances, [and] personal aggrandizement" (Karl 49)—a houseful of antiques, and suburban cocktail hours left Lowry a gentrified hipster in West Redding. His breakdown was, in part, his reaction, maybe his protest; but he still needed to behave as a novelist and an increasingly suburban, middle-class readership wanted to see the world he wanted to leave behind. *What's Left of April* (1956) is Lowry's mimicry of the Cheeveresque. His heroine, however, is totally his creature. She is an unbelievable pastiche of women—part housewife–divorcée based on Frankie Lowry and part fashion model–actress after Kit Kelleher, the woman nearest Lowry during the osmotic writing of the new novel. She is also part Lowry himself, a vehicle for examining the wrong moves that placed him in his suburban disaster, reimagined as the rise and fall and comeback of an ingenue from Cincinnati. His pathologizing, together with his attempts to make it fiction, comes close to being psychopathology as it makes for some harrowing writing in an otherwise banal book. There is even an element of criminality in the way Lowry frees and punishes Carol Parks from motherhood with an accident in the road involving a little boy not unlike his son. But the only bloodletting is menstrual: the bobby-soxer's "first period" chapter in the promising first part of *What's Left of April*. The second half of the book is almost tacked on like bad architecture and more the story of Carol's husband's degradation, indeed, her victim—Frankie's—Jim Ramsey, the hero of Lowry's sequel.

Nothing was left to chance during the writing of *What's Left of April*. Ken McCormick made Lowry submit one chapter at time to prevent him from straying from his narrative or introducing defects to the plot that were now attributable to his uneven mental state and psychiatric care. (This did not, however, limit Lowry's contact with McCormick's staff, for he had become infamously difficult to work with and could be constantly on the phone asking for help.) Despite the precautions, the novel was panned and its piecework construction and other flaws exposed. Carl Hartman, in the *Western Review*, in which the Carol Parks girlhood chapters had been published as a short story titled "A Cruel Day," felt Lowry should have left an otherwise successful story alone rather than vitiating it and rendering it "almost meaningless" by the "slicked up and uninteresting surface plot" written around it (314). Here Lowry's method of using a short story for the seed of a longer work or incorporating it into one failed.

Lowry had originally killed off both Jim Ramsey and his son. But McCormick ordered him to write the father back in, which resulted in the novel that ended Lowry's contract with Doubleday. It would be a disservice to him to go much further in treating his next and last novel as part of his fraying talent or find it a place among *The Bell Jar* and other novels about mental illness. Readers who do find a copy of *The Prince of Pride Starring* (1959) will find passages that treat some of the same disparities faced by McMurphy and Chief Bromden against Big Nurse and the Combine. But they will also see things in it that make its writing seem as far as one can get from a cult novel. It is a *reprisal document* by a mental patient directed at his former wife and, perhaps, even at Anne Frank for diluting Lowry's monist victimhood with the six million of the Holocaust. (The confessional poets would soon overcome this moral impasse by the conceit of adding themselves to that number—Sylvia

Plath with the least discretion.) Jim Ramsey never rises to being Lowry's Winston Smith, as a believable victim of the state. Even his anti-Semitism is received knowledge and, as the critic Frank Schäfer observes in his review of the German translation, Lowry more "performs it—unlike the example of a Céline or an Eliot—as role-player's prose (a madman's)" (35).

Despite having self-published a book that made him a pariah (unsold copies of *The Prince of Pride Starring* were remaindered through the American Nazi Party's bookstore), Lowry's last two hardcover short-story collections provide an almost bittersweet ending to his career. *New York Call Girl* (1958) includes many of the stories that Lowry published in the revived *American Mercury*, including "Passing Star" and "Blood Wedding in Chicago." His introduction, the afterword, the thanking of his editor, agent, and parents are virtually a plaintive admission that his career was over, which to him it was in 1957, hors de combat from the Village writer's life and recuperating at his starting point on Hutton Street in Cincinnati. Despite the promise of sex in the title story, Lowry's call girl is the author of a fragmentary memoir. She is more disembodied by her vocation, amorally observing herself at a distance. She is not the stock prostitute with the heart of gold but rather in Lowry's telling a sex worker, one of the first to be depicted this way. There is also much filler from Lowry's first decade—a telling sign of how debilitated he had become.

Lowry was not ready for this swansong of his, though some of his writing had become even more bizarrely prejudiced and pathologically misogynistic as in the case of *The Knife* (1959), a mimeographed novella similar to Patricia Highsmith's mysteries but devoid of craftsmanship. Instead, he tried for a comeback in *Party of Dreamers* (1962), his last hardcover trade book and one filled with too many possible directions rather than a redirection of focus or style. The stories, written in the temporary stability made possible by his third wife, are for the most part new work, with several stories having already appeared in new writing venues such as the *Carleton Miscellany* and *Fresco*. He even tried to spoof himself, responding to the kidnapping, trial, and execution of Adolf Eichmann in "The Nazi Midgets," in which he accomplishes a miniature *Tin Drum*-like satire; the English translation of Günter Grass's novel had appeared in 1959, in time for Lowry to make his outsider art from it. However, unlike Oscar, Lowry's midget sees his scaffold in Israel and leaves his story without its implicit justice. Other stories in the collection are experimental, elusive, encrypted. "A Roar in the Village" is the best of these, in which the Kafkaesque meets Hemingway kitsch. It owes to an obsession with lions that Lowry had[13]—and an earlier story in *The Last Party*, "Cat about Town," where the animal's point of view is first used to observe human relationships in New York. The new story reads like a fractured fairy tale and a North American analogy rather than precursor to magic realism, with its performing cat that "can make up sentences" (132) with wooden blocks and that grows to be "a towering creature of jungle proportions" (134). It is also an allegory of Lowry's career and the way it ended in New York right down to being left alone in an apartment in the Village, which Lowry lines with cork, in a nod to the reclusive Proust's bedroom, so that no one hears the cat roaring occasionally and asking, "But who can hear me?" (137).

Notes

[1] In a dispute with Lowry over his claim to the origins of Beat literature, Kerouac did concede that, "you wrote very well about cincinnata [*sic*]."

[2] Vidal was probably familiar with *Casualty* as well. However, according to Lowry in *XXIII Celebrities*, a chapbook memoir printed by the bookseller Nicky Drumbolis, Vidal insulted him by referring to it as "Catastrophe" during a *Mademoiselle* photo shoot at Gotham Book Mart in 1946. And Lowry was aware of his feelings and war fiction vis-à-vis Norman Mailer. The two had met in Paris in 1948 for drinks, a meeting that Mailer still recalls as a "guarded" occasion, given that both novelists "were like young contestants vying for the same prize so neither of us was particularly ready to compliment the other nor to look for friendship." At the time, however, Mailer was agonizing over the success *The Naked and the Dead*, which had just been published and "was doing very well in sales." Mailer complained to Lowry that now the people who "take books seriously won't read it." This self-pity, he felt, must have offended Lowry, who had not been "recognized enough for his genuine talents" (Norman Mailer to Robert Nedelkoff, 24 March 2005). Lowry's recollection of the meeting is in his *American Mercury* critique of hipster intellectuals, "Don Quixotes without Windmills." In that essay he invents the "Underground Man Model 1950," who is actually himself:

> A couple of summers ago, in Paris, I ran into an ex-GI who was hiding out from the truth: his war novel, which he had written for people who used to read *Story* and *The New Anvil*, had turned out to be a big fat bestseller, a book-club selection and all the rage among the overstuffed reviewers he had always thought he hated. While the royalties and acclaim were pouring in, he huddled in shame in a dark Paris flat, harboring Spanish Republicans and ideas that there had been some terrible mistake. "I think it was my publisher," he told me lamely. "He took it in his head to make it a bestseller and he spent enough money on advertising to put it over." His only mistake was his assumption that his opinions could not possibly be popular opinions: that his book (comfortably liberal and no more explosive than the thoughts of ten thousand other ex-GIs) could not possibly appeal to anyone except an

underground, diehard, radical few. The last I heard of him he had reached Hollywood, where he was still working hard at preserving his illusions. (655-56)

I thank Robert Nedelkoff and Heinz Wohlers for this information.

[3] The primary sources for this essay include many unpublished documents (Lowry's letters to pen pals, his voluminous ephemera, and the like) that are only in my personal archive. For the sake of readability, citation is provided for sources that can be easily located at this writing.

[4] The Yorkville house was, for the postwar culture set, as interesting and significant as Davis's other celebrated residence at 7 Middagh Street in Brooklyn, his boarding house that counted among its guests W. H. Auden, Paul and Jane Bowles, Benjamin Britten, Carson McCullers, and other mostly gay artists.

[5] My translation. The full English text can be found at www.robert-lowry.de.

[6] Duffy Westheimer interceded again on Lowry's behalf, helping pay for psychiatric treatment in the mid-1950s at the request of his mother.

[7] My translation of Ezra Pound's Italian:

"Little Man," a new, nearly underground publisher, presents a new writer who, having left his testicles (nuts) in Spain, declares himself disillusioned with Bolshevik ideology: *Defense in University City* by James Caldwell deserves an Italian translation and is short enough to be publishable in Meridiano.

(James Caldwell, not to be confused with the novelist Erskine Caldwell, is in that line of Hemingway and McAlmon.) (Pound 16)

[8] Bella's maiden name, Cohen, the same as the Nighttown madam in *Ulysses*, is a literary allusion that, for Lowry, was left silent.

[9] Lowry did check in with Davis via airmail to be jealous at the rising star of Truman Capote: "That fairy Hucksters [i.e., "Shut a Final Door"] that Capootle managed to slip into the Atlantic this month! You can only compare it with the Haidless Hawk, which it is worse than. Did this one burst the bubble at last?" (Lowry to George Davis, 29 Aug. 1947).

[10] The Beats were cognizant of Lowry. He may even have been one of the "best minds" whom Ginsberg evokes at the beginning of his signature poem.

[11] The catalog of Hemingway's personal library reveals that he owned five of Lowry's novels and short-story collections and, ironically, that Lowry is better represented in the collection than all of these contemporaries.

[12] Shirley Wheeler's family, at the time of her death, found a copy of *The Big Cage* in her library. So Wheeler had followed his career. She also enjoyed some literary success with her biography of her mother, *Dr. Nina and the Panther* (1976).

[13] Lowry had painted a lion mural on a wall in his Bleecker Street apartment and owned an enormous plush toy lion in his later years that occupied a chair in his room. These and the cat-turned-lion may be just some of Lowry's strange nods to Hemingway, who factors at the top of a "canon" in Lowry's last glossy magazine appearance:

". . . I need hardly add that he invented the lion," Marietta said, "the elephant gun and the deep-sea fishing boat."

"Why did he invent the deep-sea fishing boat?" Paul asked.

"I don't know why he invented the deep-sea fishing boat or anything else. I only know that he did and that's all."

"Clever of him," Paul said.

"Yes, wasn't it?" . . .

"All of us forgot to mention Gore Vidal," the girl with the short, straight hair said as they walked down the street five-abreast. "We mentioned Truman Capote, didn't we? All right, what about Bob Lowry, Walter B. Lowery and Malcolm Lowry? What about Alfred Hayes and John Horne Burns? Maya Deren? Croswell Bowen? Kenneth Fearing? Kenneth Patchen? Kenneth Rexroth?" . . .

"No, you can't mention anybody any more unless you say what they invented," Marietta said. "And anyway, Ernest Hemingway invented all of those people. Or most of them. I don't know. I'm beginning to forget what he did invent, now."

"He invented Ernest Hemingway," Paul said. ("An American Writer" 90)

Works Cited

Aldridge, John W. *After the Lost Generation: A Critical Study of the Writers of Two Wars.* New York: McGraw-Hill, 1951.

Axelson, Arne. *Restrained Response: American Novels of the Cold War and Korea, 1945–1962.* Westport: Greenwood, 1990.

Fitzgerald, Michael. *The Genesis of Artistic Creativity: Asperger's Syndrome and the Arts.* New York: Jessica Kingsly, 2005.

Hartman, Carl. "Mr. Morris and Some Others." Rev. of *What's Left of April*, by Robert Lowry. *Western Review* 11.3 (1957): 311–16.

Hemingway, Ernest. *Ernest Hemingway: Selected Letters 1917–1961.* Ed. Carlos Baker. New York: Scribner, 1981.

Hine Al. "Do Men Read?" Rev. of *The Violent Wedding*, by Robert Lowry. *Saturday Review of Literature* 27 June 1953: 28–29.

Karl, Frederick R. *American Fictions, 1940–1980: A Comprehensive History and Critical Evaluation.* New York: Harper & Row, 1983.

Lowry, Robert. "An American Writer." *Esquire* May 1959: 90.

—. *The Big Cage.* New York: Doubleday, 1949.

—. *The Blaze beyond the Town.* Bari, Italy: Piccolo Uomo, 1945.

—. *Casualty.* Norfolk: New Directions, 1946.

—. *Defense in University City.* Cincinnati: Little Man, 1939.

—. "Don Quixotes without Windmills." *American Mercury* 71 (1950): 653-58; rtp. as "Is This the Beat Generation?" *American Mercury* 76 (1953): 16-20.

—. *Find Me in Fire.* New York: Doubleday, 1948.

—. *Happy New Year, Kamerades!* New York: Doubleday, 1954.

—. *Hutton Street.* Cincinnati: Little Man, 1940.

—. *The Journey Out*. Bari, Italy: Piccolo Uomo, 1945.

—. *The Last Party*. New York: Popular Library, 1956.

—. *New York Call Girl*. New York: Doubleday, 1958.

—. *Party of Dreamers*. New York: Fleet, 1962.

—. *The Prince of Pride Starring*. Cincinnati: National Genius Press, 1959.

—. *XXIII Celebrities*. Toronto: Letters, 1990.

—. *The Violent Wedding*. New York: Doubleday, 1953.

—. *What's Left of April*. New York: Doubleday, 1956.

—. *The Wolf that Fed Us*. New York: Doubleday, 1949.

Monicelli, Giorgio. Introduction. *Naja* [*Casualty*]. By Robert Lowry. Trans. Giorgio Monicelli. Milan: Elmo, 1948. 7–20.

Nin, Anaïs. *Diary, Volume 4: 1944–47*. Ed. Gunther Stuhlman. New York: Harcourt Brace Jovanovich, 1971.

Pound, Ezra. *Idee fondamentali: "Meridiano di Roma" 1939–1943*. Ed. Caterina Ricciardi. Rome: Lucarini, 1991.

Sanz De Soto, Emilio. "Des Créateurs Contre la Barbarie: Les écrivains et la guerre d'Espagne" [Creators against Barbarism: Writers and the War in Spain]. *Le Monde Diplomatique* April 1997: 26–27.

Schäfer, Frank. "Antisemitisches Gift? Über den vergessenen amerikanischen Schriftsteller Robert Lowry" [Anti-Semitic Poison? About the Forgotten American Writer Robert Lowry]. *Kommune* Sept. 1998: 35–36.

Vidal, Gore. *United States: Essays 1952–1992*. New York: Random House, 1993.

Weintraub, Stanley. *The Last Great Cause*. New York: Weybright and Talley, 1968.

West, Ray B., Jr. *The Short Story in America 1900–1950*. New York: Regnery, 1952.

A Robert Lowry Checklist

Novels and Stories

Defense in University City. Cincinnati: Little Man, 1939; rpt. in *Robert Lowry Journal* 3a. Harrlach, Germany: Heinz Wohlers Verlag, 2004.

Hutton Street. Cincinnati: Little Man, 1940.

The Blaze beyond the Town. Bari, Italy: Piccolo Uomo, 1945.

The Journey Out. Bari, Italy: Piccolo Uomo, 1945.

Casualty. Norfolk: New Directions, 1946.

Find Me in Fire. New York: Doubleday, 1948.

The Wolf that Fed Us. New York: Doubleday, 1949.

The Big Cage. New York: Doubleday, 1949.

The Violent Wedding. New York: Doubleday, 1953; rpt. Westport: Greenwood, 1970.

Happy New Year, Kamerades! New York: Doubleday, 1954; rpt. as *This Is My Night*. New York: Popular Library, 1955.

The Last Party. New York: Popular Library, 1956.

What's Left of April. New York: Doubleday, 1956.

New York Call Girl. New York: Doubleday, 1958.

That Kind of Woman. New York: Pyramid, 1959.

The Prince of Pride Starring. Cincinnati: National Genius Press, 1959.

Party of Dreamers. New York: Fleet, 1962.

The Mary Beth Stories in *Robert Lowry Journal 4*. Harrlach, Germany: Heinz Wohlers Verlag, 2005.

The Knife in *Edition Depression no. 3*. Ed. and intro. James Reidel. Harrlach, Germany: Heinz Wohlers Verlag, 2005. [Artist's book in limited edition.]

Robert Lowry
(Photograph by Sam Rosenberg)

Ross Feld

M. G. Stephens

> He met her in the Library
> Where all things have their history
> But nothing living may endure—
> Among the dogs of literature.
> —Henry Weinfield,
> "Beauty and the Beast" (*Sorrows* 62)

1

Ross Feld (1947-2001) was the author of four novels, *Years Out* (1973); *Only Shorter* (1982), which recounted his first bout with cancer when he was in his twenties; *Shapes Mistaken* (1989); and *Zwilling's Dream* (1999). His first book was *Plum Poems* (1972), though, and his last, *Guston in Time* (2003), was about his friendship with the older and by then famous painter Philip Guston, an artist whom Feld assayed twenty years earlier in a catalog to the painter's work. Feld was born in Brooklyn, and attended the City College of New York. From 1978 to 1994, he reviewed fiction at *Kirkus Reviews*, and was a regular contributor of essays on art, fiction, and poetry to *Parnassus* magazine. Early in his career, he had worked at Time-Life, and then for Grove Press as an associate editor to Gilbert Sorrentino (Feld, "Oz Is Home"). He struggled with lymphatic cancer in the early 1970s, survived this illness, married, and eventually moved, when his wife Ellen became a doctor, to Cincinnati, Ohio, where he remained for the last twenty years of his life.[1]

I knew Feld early in my own writing career when he was nineteen and I was twenty years old, living on the Lower East Side. We attended the workshops offered by the Poetry Project at Saint Mark's in the Bowery and often drank together in such artists' and writers' bars as Max's Kansas City, the Lion's Head, and later Saint Adrian and Company. As a student at the City College of New York, Feld edited the university magazine *Promethean*, publishing older writers like Gilbert Sorrentino and Paul Blackburn, and younger writers like Bradford Stark, Henry Weinfield, and Feld himself. Some of my own earliest published poems appeared in *Promethean* when Feld was its editor. Soon enough he had left the university and began to work for Time-Life, and then Grove Press as an associate editor aligned with Gilbert Sorrentino, the press's literary editor. Of course, the job was not all Beckett, Genet, and Burroughs, though. In one of the few autobiographical sketches that Feld wrote in his lifetime, he reminisced about other work that he and Sorrentino did.

> A lot of Grove's list at the time consisted of milled-by-the-yard porn novels. As sop thrown for seeing them through the list, the editors were allowed to write over-the-top jacket copy for these. Sorrentino and I particularly enjoyed making up blurb quotes—as well as inventing the "experts" providing them. The one of Gil's I cherished most was a French foot-fetish authority named A. M. LeDeluge; I myself concocted an Indian "erotologist" named Unduli Seerijius. ("Oz Is Home")

A lifetime later, I am reminded of those early days when I knew Feld. I especially recall those times when I come across a poem like William Carlos Williams's "To a Poor Old Woman," in which the poet writes that the poor old woman is

> munching a plum on
> the street a paper bag
> of them in her hand (67)

Or coming upon the more iconic "This Is Just to Say" in which the poet admits:

> I have eaten
> the plums
> that were in
> the icebox (55)

Whenever Feld came to Joel Oppenheimer's workshops, which was irregularly and sporadically attended by Feld, though he often hung out with Joel in the Lion's Head bar or with other writers from the Poetry Project, myself included, at Max's Kansas City on Park Avenue South, just north of Union Square, invariably he had a new poem, usually about plums.[2] It was no surprise to us then that several years later Ross Feld's first book would be *Plums Poems* (1972), yet even before the book was published Feld had drifted away from the Poetry Project and away from poetry toward the "Land of Prose," to borrow a phrase from a poem by Feld's friend, Henry Weinfield (*Sorrows* 22). He had gone off to the MacDowell Colony, an artists' and writers' retreat in New Hampshire, to finish his first novel, which would be titled *Years Out* when published in 1973. It was during this period, too, that Feld left Grove Press, suffered his first bouts with lymphatic cancer—an experience that would be chronicled in the next decade with his second novel, *Only Shorter* (1982)—moved to Ithaca, New York, met his wife Ellen, and got married.

The 1980s would prove the most fertile for this writer as his third novel would come out seven years later: *Shapes Mistaken* (1989),

Feld's magnum opus of subtlety, comedy, and economy of expression. He also wrote a monograph on his friend, the painter Philip Guston (1980) in that decade. Then he would lapse into a ten-year fictional silence. During this time he would write countless essays—some of his best writing, in fact—and most of this critical and literary work appeared in *Parnassus* magazine. His last novel was *Zwilling's Dream* (1999), like *Shapes Mistaken*, a light-hearted comedy with dark and tragic undertones, leaving an aftereffect not unlike Shakespeare's *Midsummer Night's Dream* (1600) in which the delight of the lovers' language finally settles into the pit of one's stomach in a darker, more tragic way as witness how the great Shakespearian critic Jan Kott interpreted this brooding play in his seminal work, *Shakespeare Our Contemporary* (1964). Like all dark humor from Mark Twain onward, we laugh, then we feel uncomfortable. Then we cry. Such is the similar way with all of Ross Feld's novels.

2

In his introduction to *Guston in Time*, the poet and translator Richard Howard calls it "the last of Feld's novels as well as his best criticism" (5). In fact, it is neither fiction nor criticism as Feld wrote in these forms, but his one unapologetic autobiographical book, unusual only because he was a writer who spent his life keeping himself out of his writing. Yet he admired writers such as Adam Phillips and Stanley Cavell, thinkers who combine philosophy and psychology in their writings, but also have personal themes in their books. He noted that Phillips, in his book *On Kissing, Tickling, and Being Bored* (1993), shows how psychoanalysis makes possible recovery of the past, and is "prelude to autobiography." In that sense, Feld's poetry and novels were prelude to the second of his Guston books. Elsewhere in the Cavell/Phillips essay, Feld suggests that "the future is something we already understand as a sanctioned contingency—the job is to make the present one also" ("Relievers"). But, of course, fiction-writing is about the past; Feld seems to suggest that voice is where the past resides, creating all its various pitches, timbres, and tonalities. What Feld admires about Stanley Cavell are his stances on "acknowledgment, love, poetry, autobiography, voice—states of being that nudge us out of our heads and into the phenomenal world, where we can be seen as well as see." He quotes Cavell as saying: "Certain questions of ear that run through my life—questions of the realities and fantasies of perfect pitch, of telling pointed stories, and of the consequences of a scarred tympanum—become . . . *questions of the detection of voice.*" (The italics are mine.) Cavell goes on to say that his conception of philosophy is "the achievement of the unpolemical, of the refusal to take sides in metaphysical positions, of my quest to show that these are not useful sides but needless constructions."

If I were to replace the word "philosophy" with the word "fiction," Ross Feld's ideas about the novel begin to come into focus. Certain questions of the ear did run through Ross Feld's life. His pitch was about prose, though; he told pointed stories, and his scars had to do with his body structure—a misshapen back at birth—and the cancer he experienced in his early twenties, a kind of cancer that up until that time was deemed fatal. The detection of a voice—put in more lay terms—the finding of one's voice was Ross Feld's lifetime mission as a writer. That his voice was subtle, elusive, bristly with intelligence and opinion, allusive, commanding, slyly comic, quietly tragic, confidently dramatic—all of this was evident in his life and work. That he was a product of Brooklyn, a New York writer even after all those years in the Midwest, I think is evidenced in his books, their themes and characters, almost always about bright, sensitive, Jewish New Yorkers.

3

The voice in all its permutations, and naming, these are important milestones of poetry which Feld brought to his fiction. Voice, naming. Fiction as the achievement of the unpolemical, of the refusal to take sides in metaphysical positions . . . needless constructions. His characters may feud and bicker. But Ross Feld remains outside the fray, not the omniscient author so much as the anti-poet writing prose, a writer who remained throughout his life deeply skeptical of the personal utterance in writing. In that sense, the second Guston book is not even close to being his best novel or critical work; it is an aberration, an oddity in his literary opus. Other than their initial appearances in magazines like *Parnassus*, the best of Ross Feld's critical writings have yet to be collected in book form. And, really, his last novel is *Zwilling's Dream*. All Feld's novels are good, but *Only Shorter* and *Shapes Mistaken* are exemplary. One was a melodrama verging on tragedy, the other a tragicomedy verging on melodrama. *Zwilling's Dream*, a solid bit of prose, was a comedy of errors. *Years Out* was a coming-of-age novel by a poet who considered himself an anti-poet.

His good friend and classmate from the City College of New York days, the poet and translator Henry Weinfield has said that Ross loved the poet Jack Spicer because he attacked "the big lie of the personal," but that Ross was an anti-poet, like Spicer, because it had to do with "his own vulnerability, which he didn't want to admit, and which poetry brought out." Then Henry said something which I think is the crux of the matter regarding Ross Feld, and could be considered the thesis underlying all his work. He said: "The truth is that Ross was essentially a poet, not a novelist" (E-mail 15 Sept. 2004). Yet who is this anti-poet, this fiction writer and critic who forever remained a poet in all his prose?

Of his last book, *Guston in Time*, published posthumously, the writer and critic Susan Sontag says: "Unlike my friend Richard Howard, I never had the good fortune to meet Ross Feld—just admired him, intensely, from afar. What a describer, what an intelligence! Here is a writer who, whatever the subject, is incapable of commonplace responses and diction. (Randall Jarrell is another.) His last, singular book is essential Feld: a thrilling, giddy rush of subtle, mature judgments. But never was Feld's acuity so partnered as here; Guston, of course, is no mean subject. These two high-octane minds in dialogue, in deep, respectful friendship, resound in their letters like a piano sonata for four hands that's part Schubert, part Busoni. And then there's the enclosing arch of Feld's visionary evocation of Guston's quest and Guston's vulnerability."[3]

The anti-poet eschewing all personal revelations in print came to the end of his own mortal coil with a personal essay, one of the few I know of his writing. His publisher, Counterpoint, posted it on its website in connection with his last novel, *Zwilling's Dream*. Entitled "Oz Is Home," it is a literary reminiscence about coming of age in New York City, and especially how the downtown art and poetry scenes influenced him. Some of it is nearly word-for-word repeated in his last book on Philip Guston. In the other parts, he writes of getting his education in the Brooklyn Public Library. Unlike the present day student of a creative writing program who learns to write from classroom models, Feld received part of his literary education by hanging out in bars and jazz clubs downtown (Max's, St. Adrian Company, the Lion's Head, the Five Spot Café) and by attending events at the Poetry Project at Saint Mark's Church. Keep in mind that Feld was a teenager, precocious and daring.

"After hooking up with some people involved in a little magazine while still in high school," he writes, "I found myself involved in an astoundingly generous correspondence with the poet Denise Levertov. Levertov, as the poetry editor of *The Nation* at that time, would encourage and chastise me, clucking over God awful poems but also publishing better ones. Somehow she treated me not as a precocious phenom but as an unseasoned apprentice whom she considered perhaps capable of taking over a corner of the fresco should the studio's master be called away" ("Oz Is Home"). He goes on to say that

> this was how all the writers I eventually came to spend time with—Gilbert Sorrentino, Fielding Dawson, Joel Oppenheimer, Frank O'Hara,

Paul Blackburn, LeRoi Jones—treated me. . . . The older writers weren't in search of acolytes. If anything, they wanted you to write not as they did but as their heroes did. That I began to write novels in the first place had a lot to do with my understanding of what a certain kind of American poet attempted upon the model of William Carlos Williams: writing prose defied the lyrical in you, allowed the world in to a greater and messier degree than the pressures of pure language permitted. And though poets like William Bronk, Levertov, Robert Creeley, and Gil Sorrentino were more my first readers than other novelists were—and despite the fact that it took me some years and more books to finally break away from too tight a registration of language—I've never felt sorry to have early learned a poet's economy. ("Oz Is Home")

A prose writer with a poet's economy: I think that sums up the Ross Feld whom I knew back in 1966 when I was twenty years old, and he was a very worldly nineteen-year-old. Feld was forever understated and modest about his accomplishments, and nothing illustrates this point more than a letter Feld once wrote me in which he responded to a review I had written of *Only Shorter*. I had compared him with Flaubert, especially how medicine and doctors come into the narrative. Though not a doctor, Feld had been a patient in his early twenties when he was treated for cancer. But his wife Ellen was a doctor, and one imagines him asking her endless questions on medical issues. Regarding my review, he said that "it's far from being the truth, but so are most pleasures" (Letter 12 Aug. 1983). The author's note on his first book, *Plum Poems*, simply says that "Ross Feld does not want much said about himself except that he was born in Brooklyn in 1947 and recently went to the Mac-Dowell Colony to finish a novel." His publisher added: "Mr. Feld is yet another American isolato. He is not peddling his personality or striving for the Literary Light."

Fiction was his passion, but nonfiction might be his greatest gift. This is important to establish immediately because Ross Feld was a writer of great sensibility, a literary artist with a sublime critical faculty. Poetry was the craft he seemed to abandon for writing novels, and yet poetry was what he returned to, time and time again, in his literary and critical essays. (In that sense, he is very much like his earliest mentor, Gilbert Sorrentino, a prose writer whose energy and concision owe so much to a literary foundation in poetry.) In a speech Feld delivered at Notre Dame University in 1992 on the Objectivists, he called himself "a recovering poet." But I suspect that Feld was being disingenuous about his total abandoning of poetry. In a letter he wrote to me in the early 1980s, he still mentions writing poems. "Even the poems I write aren't ship-shape or well honed" (Letter 25 June 1982). Perhaps, like Brecht, it will come about that Ross Feld wrote poems throughout his prose-writing career, and a fat volume of them will appear posthumously. I'd like to think that that is the case.

Be that as it may, his was an exemplary literary life in the late twentieth century. Novelist, essayist, poet, critic, and editor, Ross Feld wore many different hats. But I believe all his prose was influenced by his love and knowledge of poetry, first, and that, in turn, his novels, though appearing to fit into a more traditional niche with urban, Jewish writers like Saul Bellow and Philip Roth, really are more language-driven constructs—more oddly articulated narratives than their seeming surface realism might suggest. More than any other writer whom I knew from my early twenties, Ross Feld exemplified the Isaac Babel tenet that "you must know everything." He reviewed books prodigiously for *Kirkus* from 1977 to 1994.[4] He also wrote long, involved literary essays for *Parnassus* magazine, including ones on Charles Baudelaire, Primo Levi, Cormac McCarthy, William H. Gass, Charles Bernstein, Eugenio Montale, Guillaume Apollinaire, Stan Rice, John Updike, and John Ashbery. His essays on Jack Spicer, though, are the most revealing of Feld's roots in poetry.[5]

4

Feld was born in Brooklyn on 18 November 1947, and as he noted in the author's note in his first novel *Years Out*, "attended public schools and the City College of New York." He grew up on Argyle Road in Brooklyn, and went to Erasmus Hall High School, graduating in 1965. Although the *New York Times* obituary said he graduated from City College of New York, he did not. Like his Saint Mark's Poetry Project mentors Joel Oppenheimer and Seymour Krim, and his Grove Press mentor, Gilbert Sorrentino, Ross Feld attended university but then became a dropout, which was a kind of badge of honor that everyone wore in those halcyon days. Unlike so many of his peers, he did not seek out dissolution once he dropped out of college. Instead he went to work as an editor—for Time-Life and Grove Press from 1968 to 1970. From 1970 onward, he worked as a freelance editor for the next thirty years. Back in the late 1960s, though, he attended workshops at the Poetry Project, and was a protégé of Gilbert Sorrentino, working as his associate editor at Grove Press.[6]

Although Feld was certainly a part of the Poetry Project, he aligned himself more with Sorrentino (at work) and made other allegiances and friendships at that adjunct of the Poetry Project, Max's Kansas City, the artists' and writers' bar par excellence. Max's was named by Joel Oppenheimer for the poet Max Finstein who, among other things, ran off to New Mexico with Oppenheimer's first wife (Gilmore 142).

> Fast flashes—the women
> who love him, Rena, Joyce,
> Max, the *mensch*, makes
>
> poverty almost fun,
> hangs on edge, keeps traveling. (Creeley 292)

Max's Kansas City's owner was Mickey Ruskin, an odd but important figure in the early days of the Lower East Side poetry scene in the run-up to the Poetry Project at Saint Mark's (Kane 38-39). Feld liked to hang out at the bar with his fellow Brooklynite, Archie Rand, the painter, or with older writers such as Fielding "Fee" Dawson, a Black Mountain writer and painter, or even a fellow Time-Life worker and poet, Joe Early, or the essayist and editor of *For Now* magazine, Donald Phelps.

Archie was a tough, young guy from Brooklyn, a prodigious talent and as equally precocious as Ross. (Both of them were still in their teens when Max's first opened, and they began to hang out there.) Joe wrote short, cryptic poems, influenced by Robert Creeley and Gilbert Sorrentino, among others. Fee held court at the bar, regaling people with his stories of the Cedar Bar, now defunct, but once several blocks south of Max's. He knew Franz Kline. Well, Fee knew everyone from the Cedars, as they called it. His book about Franz Kline, *An Emotional Memoir of Franz Kline*, was just about to be published. Donald Phelps, gargantuan, stuttering, looking like the cartoon character Humphrey Pennyworth in *Lil' Abner*, also held court at the bar.

"You can learn as much about poetry and life at this bar," Ross once told me, "as you can learn in Joel's poetry workshop."

Gilbert Sorrentino's novel *Imaginative Qualities of Actual Things* (1971) would not appear for a few more years. But Max's was filled with people who bore uncanny *correspondences* with characters in his novel. In fact, one could patch in parts of Sorrentino's novel, and the collage might easily resemble any night at Max's Kansas City on Park Avenue South.

> *Some Things Sheila Henry Grew to Care for: 1966-1967.*
> Larry Poons' work: Bart Kahane pointed out his excellence.
> Larry Rivers: She met him at a party.
> Pantyhose: SMOOTH UNBROKEN LEG LINE.
> *Madame Bovary*: She understood her anguish.
> Guy Lewis: Who even drunk yet hath his mind entire.[7]
> Bunny Lewis: Her gentle guidance of Guy's life and writing.

> Samuel Greenberg: Probably the most underrated poet of his time.
> Emanuel Carnevali: Probably the most underrated prose-writer of his time.
> *Barbary Shore*: It has Mailer's most brilliant flashes of pure prose.
> Harry Langdon: Really the best of the Great Clowns.
> Ricard: More subtle and somehow more—*exact*—than Pernod.
> Murray Mednick: Had claim to the top rung of the American theater.[8]
> Frank O'Hara: He died.
> Jack Spicer: He died.
> Leo Kaufman: He was a sweet guy.[9]
> Che Guevara: He was a *man*.
> Ho Chi Minh: He was a *great* old *man*.
> Anal intercourse: She almost fainted with the pleasure.
> Algernon Blackwood: As good as Poe in his way.
> Lou: He loved her. (10-11)

This list of real and imaginary characters suggests the surreal atmosphere of a place like Max's, an artists' and writers' bar that more resembled a fictional setting than a real-life hangout. Lou Reed and the Velvet Underground played music in the upstairs room. Minimalist and pop art paintings hung on the wall (Donald Judd, Dan Flavin, and Andy Warhol), chrome sculpture stood in the front (John Chamberlain's car fender sculpture), and artists and writers everywhere.[10] In his last book, Feld describes how the older painter Philip Guston looked and dressed, and I'll be damned if it isn't an apt description of the young Ross Feld, too. "He dressed pretty much according to Brooks Brothers: oxford shirts, khaki pants, brown Weejuns, a roll-collared over-sweater" (*Guston in Time* 53). Feld goes on to describe a slightly messy older artist, his breast pocket filled with his Camel cigarettes. Instead of mess and sprawl, Ross Feld was as neat as a pin, topping this outfit off with a corduroy jacket, the same one he wears in the jacket photo of his first novel, *Years Out*.

His voice was loud with bourbon and cigarettes, and his head was stuffed with quotations from William Carlos Williams and Robert Creeley. But he most liked to quote to us from Jack Spicer:

> Let us fake out a frontier—a poem somebody could hide in with a sheriff's posse after him—a thousand miles of it if it is necessary for him to go a thousand miles—a poem with no hard corners, no houses to get lost in, no underwebbing of customary magic. . . . (*Controversy* 436)

Ross Feld was not the first person to quote Jack Spicer's "Billy the Kid," but he probably understood the poem—and the poet—better than any of my peers. A poet from the Poetry Project by the name of

Jerrold Greenberg also liked to quote from Spicer, this same poem but a different section of it. Jerry was almost the antithesis of Ross. Where the latter was stiff-backed and formal,[11] preppy and businesslike, Greenberg affected the sleazy countenance of the street hustler, including a pencil mustache, white suits with black shirts and a colorful tie, and even white loafers with those gauzy black socks preferred by wiseguys the world over. Jerry had dragons tattooed on his arms, and used pomade to slick back his hair, making him look more like a pimp than a poet. What these two young poets had in common was a nexus at the newly started Poetry Project at Saint Mark's in the Bowery and a love of writers like Jack Spicer.

> So the heart breaks
> Into small shadows
> Almost so random
> They are meaningless
> Like a diamond
> Has at the center of it a diamond
> Or a rock
> Rock. (*Controversy* 439)

The Poetry Project may not seem like the place to associate a writer like Ross Feld. His novels were written ostensibly in a realistic mode. After his first book of poetry, he seemed to abandon poems forever. The Poetry Project became a place associated with New York School and, later, Language poets, not second- and third-generation Black Mountain writers. Feld's influences were writers like William Carlos Williams, Robert Creeley, Gilbert Sorrentino, and, as I have noted, Jack Spicer. He was not a formal experimenter but rather a young writer with a long memory for traditions. And yet the Poetry Project's young writers were far more diversified than first seems to be so. Names like Lewis Warsh and Anne Waldman come readily to mind when writing about the early days of the Poetry Project, and yet the Poetry Project also consisted of poets like Bradford Stark, Elaine Schwager, and Henry Weinfield and prose writers like George Cain, a black novelist and author of *Blueschild Baby* (1970). Ross Feld knew the work of Baudelaire, Mallarmé, and Apollinaire as well as any second-generation New York School poet at the Poetry Project. His interests in art were as avid as any follower of Frank O'Hara or John Ashbery; in fact, he would later write art criticism on a par with these poets. In his memoir of Philip Guston, Feld reminisces:

> I wandered through the two great adjoining museums of Fifty-third Street, the Museum of Modern Art and the Whitney, precisely during the years when the sovereign, gorgeous Abstract Expressionist paintings were pushing their way into those collections. . . . By the mid-sixties

a more personal connection to these paintings happened to be forged for me. Riding the last wave of the twenties-through-sixties Village bohemianism, the pedigree that runs from Edmund Wilson through Dawn Powell to Franz Kline, I took a literary apprenticeship that located itself not in college writing-programs but in downtown bars like Max's Kansas City and the Cedar Tavern, the Metro, the Lion's Head, the Ninth Circle, the St. Adrian's Company; or at jazz clubs: the Five-Spot, the Half-Note, Slugs, the Dom; or at uptown art galleries, or at the Poet's Theatre on Fourth Street, or in slum apartments. (*Guston in Time* 39-40)

Young writers associated with Saint Mark's Poetry Project developed into mature writers who were far more complicated than labels such as Black Mountain, New York School, or Language poetry suggest. Even their politics were far more complicated than terms like Left and Right imply. In his novel *Years Out*, two of Feld's characters, David Abrams and Joyce Cecere, are drawn to each other as university students—it would seem to be City College in Harlem—after "three weeks of before- and after-class time was spent talking about their mutual distaste for the peace movement (on strictly nonideological grounds) and their mutual taste for French literature" (76).

The African American poet Tom Weatherly, whose first book of poems was *Mau-Mau American Cantos* (1970), was an ex-Marine, and a registered Republican, and perhaps one of the most loyal attendees of the workshops at the Poetry Project in its earliest days. Far from being an *Umbra* poet—the radical black magazine that shaped much of the literary image of African American unrest in the mid-1960s—Weatherly eventually converted to orthodox Judaism, and became a clerk at the Strand Bookshop on Broadway at West 12th Street.[12] One young writer in Seymour Krim's prose-writing workshop regularly wrote pieces sympathetic to a Neo-Nazi agenda, though to be sure this was more the exception than the rule at the radical premises known as the Poetry Project. The feminist writer and scholar Shulamith Firestone, author of *The Dialectics of Sex* (1970), was a member of the prose workshops, and so was Bill Amidon, an habitué of Max's and the other bars on the Lower East Side. So was Clark Welton, a writer for the *Village Voice*, as was the future semiologist Marshall Blonsky, and so was the novelist John Bart Gerald. The Olympia Press author Jerry Joth (formerly Jerry Roth) also attended these workshops regularly.[13]

What is true is that *The World*, the mimeo monthly that was connected to the Poetry Project, did not reflect this diversity because it rarely published prose. The poets in *The World* were predominantly second- and third-generation New York School of Poetry writers, with an occasional bone thrown to the young writers in Joel Oppenheimer's workshops, including Tom Weatherly, Scott Cohen, Elaine

Schwager, Ron Edson, and Jerrold Greenberg.[14] Mostly, though, *The World* was a showcase for Anne Waldman's and Lewis Warsh's coterie of friends who emanated outward from allegiances with Ted Berrigan and other New York School writers (Kane 156).

The only prose published at that time were prose poems because the Poetry Project was foremost a venue for poets. It was not the Prose Project. Its reputation was based on its poetry, the same poetry from which Ross Feld began his career. Yet Feld's poetry is still a good route through which to approach his fiction. Throughout his career, Feld was misread by critics, who saw only the realism in his prose writing, not the poetic elements from which the prose derived. Still, this was a novelist who certainly was more involved with Montale and Apollinaire than he was with F. Scott Fitzgerald and William Faulkner. Put another way, Ross Feld was more into Frank O'Hara than John O'Hara, although his critical and literary essays were primarily about poetry, not fiction writing. Yet it was through his deep readings of poetry that he was able to become such a good prose writer.

Ross Feld's four novels are filled with naming and names, what I take to be the foundations of all poetic impulse, and he loved analogies and metaphors, and his most extreme use of these tropes removed his fiction from the realms of realism and naturalism into the fields of poetry. Susan Sontag, who championed Feld toward the end of his life, observed in her own final book of essays that "the distinctive genius of poetry is naming, that of prose, to show movement, process, time—past, present, and future" (5). Perhaps more to the point is Charles Olson's observation that "the whole world & all experience is, no matter how real, only a system of metaphors for the allegory (Keats called it) a man's life is" (qtd. in Clark dust jacket).

Ross Feld's poetry and the critical writings are roadmaps to the novels, although I am aware that using these critical writings as maps to the fiction lessens Feld's efforts in these other nonfictional forms, and his poems and essays are powerful in their own rights and on their own merits. So, after discussing his novels, I will return to Ross Feld's critical and literary essays, concluding with them, as I think ultimately they are what Ross Feld will be remembered for. Nonetheless, in this first instance, I intend to use the essays—and the poems, to some extent—as a kind of apparatus with which to grasp the fictional works—as a kind of apparatus to unlock meanings, intentions, drifts, and tendencies in the novels.

Also, beyond his penchant for naming (the poet's gift) or the allegory his life was, I associate Ross Feld with the Poetry Project at Saint Mark's Church because, in his way, he is a fusion of Joel Oppenheimer's poetic sensibility, by way, if you will, of Paul Blackburn, Gilbert Sorrentino, and Jack Spicer. Yet Feld also was a bit like Seymour Krim in his essays, both of them sharing an affinity for being intellectual mavericks and gadflies in their essays, stylists but also innovators in their contents as well. Unlike some of the more dogmatic young poets at the Poetry Project who could only toe a Black Mountain or a New York School line, Feld loved a vast array of mentors from Williams to Creeley to Sorrentino, from Joel Oppenheimer to Paul Blackburn. He wrote art criticism as good as any New York School poet did, and he knew Frank O'Hara's work as well as probably someone like Ted Berrigan did, and as Berrigan's sonnets prove—being a collage of O'Hara and Ashbery mostly—Ted knew Frank O'Hara's work brilliantly (Kane 100-22). In fact, there is an instance in Ted Berrigan's correspondence to his first wife in which something he writes reminds me more of Ross Feld than Ted Berrigan. He says: "Personally, I think I can write better than many poets in the book (the Don Allen anthology), but I can't write well enough to satisfy myself yet" (qtd. in Kane 101). Just like Berrigan, too, Feld was indebted to Don Allen's poetry anthology, *The New American Poetry* (1960), more than any other piece of writing in his early years as a fledgling writer. In a talk that Feld gave at Notre Dame University on the Objectivist poets, he said that Don Allen's poetry anthology "was probably the single most shaping force for the poets of my generation whom I spoke with and shared work with" ("Talking about Objectivism").

5

Poetry is where one starts with Ross Feld, the novelist. He began in this realm, and forever would live in a tension in relation to it, either denying it in his prose life or embracing it in his literary essays. *Plum Poems* (1972) pays homage but not lip service to all of Feld's mentors, but mostly to two of them—Jack Spicer and Gilbert Sorrentino. The poems are anti-poetic, talky, jagged, irregular, more correct than beautiful. Like Spicer, Feld wanted to relieve poetry of personality.[15]

> Poetry is calling it a day.
>   Someone else, across
> the grove, calls it real and
> continues to sweat.
>   ("A Hard Day's Night," *Plum Poems* n.p.)

Elsewhere he writes:

> They are playing the
>
> Tennessee Waltz and it's getting to
> me already.
>   ("Hit Parade," *Plum Poems* n.p.)

Feld knew what he liked, and said what he didn't like. He didn't care much for Ezra Pound, though he'd read him thoroughly. He liked Creeley—"a grand master," he called him—and, of course, adored Williams, and though widely read in European literature, from Baudelaire, Mallarmé, and Apollinaire, to Italian masters like Montale, Feld had very little tolerance for the fads and schools at a place like the Poetry Project.

A fiction writer digs his origins, his literary foundations, in poetry. But this is not just any poet. Ross Feld is an anti-poet or, more accurately, an anti-autobiographical poet, one who eschews the author's backstory. Like his hero Jack Spicer, Feld believes in a poem without an author; he believes in poetry itself. All of this reminds me of a sonnet written by Feld's college friend, Henry Weinfield, a sonnet from his book *The Sorrows of Eros* (1999).

> For years I sojourned in the Land of Prose;
> With other sojourners I sojourned there.
> It was a land of plenty, I suppose,
> But in the end I was a sojourner. (22)

Henry attended workshops at the Saint Mark's Poetry Project, but only briefly. As he explained it, regarding his friendship with Ross Feld and Bradford Stark: "The truth is that I am and have always been a latter-day Symbolist—and I wound up at City College among a bunch of American modernists for whom symbolism was anathema. I was reading Yeats and they were reading Williams. Ross and I used to have terrible fights" (E-mail 15 Sept. 2004). Henry was a sojourner in the Land of Prose; but not his friend Ross Feld, who pitched a tent in Prose's field.[16] But his prose was to be informed by a highly evolved and sophisticated poetics, just like that of Jack Spicer about whom Feld wrote: "His project was too grand and quixotic, too self-aware, for vain expectation not to have been a part. Spicer would have liked to do the perhaps impossible: to relieve poetry of *personality*" ("Jack Spicer"). Later in this same essay, Feld refers to Jack Spicer's wish to be relieved of "his own masonic sentimentality." Feld saw Jack Spicer's contradictions this way: the poet's need for a "non-personal art," and yet having a need "for human contact." Both in his poetry and in his prose, Ross Feld was everywhere and nowhere. There was never a voice in his poems which you could point to and say: there he is! There was never a character in his fiction who was a stand-in for the author. Every Chekhov play had a doctor or professional person who seemed to mirror its author's sensibility.[17] Not Ross Feld's fiction. Chekhov is a writer I have often thought of when reading Ross Feld's novels. Illness invades the lives of so many of his characters. Feld had a nearly encyclopedic knowledge of medicine and medical practice, no doubt in part because of his own early bout with cancer and in part because of his long relationship with his wife, Ellen, a doctor herself.[18]

Henry Weinfield stayed in the Land of Rhyme while his friend Ross Feld departed for the Land of Prose. The third person in this literary friendship is Bradford Stark, someone who forever seemed to feel that he was an inferior poet to his friend Ross Feld, with whom he lived and whose anti-poetic style he emulated in his own work. Ultimately, I think that Stark became the better poet. Of course, he would not live to appreciate this fact as he committed suicide in 1980.

> The small constellations where lovers
>   live as both partners and disruptive
>
> agents. Who would believe it and in it?
> Those who promise somebody
>
>   something. Happiness, for
> instance: a process
>
> begging description and rendered
> useless. Take the televisions
> away or make them show us things
>
>   happen. This universe
> run down. (Stark n.p.)

When I asked Henry Weinfield if he believed that both Brad and Ross painted themselves into a corner with this kind of anti-poetry, Henry responded: "I don't think Brad painted himself into a corner (to use your metaphor) with his poetry—though maybe Ross did. Brad suffered from depression, and he was probably addicted to Valium. Our supposition is that he was out of Valium and literally crazed when he killed himself." In those days of the Poetry Project's beginnings (1966), I remember these three young poets almost the way one imagines the three friends of Dante's sublime "Sonetto III (da Il Canzoniere)":

> Guido, vorrei che tu e Lapo ed io
>   Fossimo presi per incantamento,
>   E messi ad un vascel, ch'ad ogni vento
>   Per mare andasse a voler vostro e mio.
>
> (Guido, I wish that you and Lapo and I
>   Were taken by enchantment,
>   And put on a boat, that with each wind
>   Would sail the sea at your will and mine.) (18-19)

Although Henry Weinfield says that his own sonnet (Number Ten) is not about Ross Feld, he told me that "Ross liked my sonnets, and that one in particular" (E-mail 15 Sept. 2005). Eventually the young anti-poet Ross Feld would abandon poetry for prose, and so I cannot help but think of him when I read these lines from Henry's poem:

> How long ago it was I cannot say
> That I departed for the Land of Rhyme;
> But it was long ago and far away,
> And I am finished now with space and time. (10)

Back to the Land of Rhyme for Henry Weinfield. So much for the Land of Prose. But Ross Feld's literary life would take a different trajectory. He loved poetry, knew it and read in it vastly. And yet prose would prove far more appealing to him. Prose was, well, prosaic, ordinary and everyday, and Feld relished the quotidian. I never met anyone who so liked to work, even as a teenager at Time-Life and Grove Press as an associate editor. At the latter institution, he worked with Gilbert Sorrentino, then a senior editor at Grove. Gil was passionate about writers like Jack Spicer, and I presume Feld first read Spicer as a result of his association with Sorrentino. Although this influence would not be evident in Feld's first novel, *Years Out*, it was in abundance in his first book, *Plum Poems*. This influence was also evident—as I've previously noted—in the poetry of Feld's college roommate, Bradford Stark, a regular member of the workshops at Saint Mark's. Stark was very much in the sway of Feld by way of Sorrentino and Spicer.

> Here it is. What he once thought
> he was waiting for. There is a table he finds himself
>
> resting on. It is an impossible table,
> for which men have written long and tormented books
>
> attempting an assertion. (n.p.)

As Feld points out so clearly in his essay on Jack Spicer, this San Francisco poet was really not a poet so much as "an anti-poet." Feld writes how the poet "throws in names, direct addresses to lovers" ("Lowghost"). It was not lovers' names but just names themselves that seem so remarkable in many of Ross Feld's novels. His first and second novels have more or less generic names associated with Jewish literature. Their names are Abrams and Lapin, Richmond and Kornbluh. But in his third novel, *Shapes Mistaken*, names seem to explode from the page: Henry Hing, Sid Telscher (a rabbi calls him Tischbein), Iris Seavy, Monte Vogelsang, Theresa Dellamatraccia (one character calls her Mrs. Gimee-I-Want-It-All-a), Merrit Heu-bsch, Ivan Roitman, Lurtha Meneny, Sister Ranelle, Moishe Pipick, Leona Mackey, Meg Seavy, Teddy Ullivan, Tony and Dallas and the Regensteins, Dr. Franziska, and Diane Occhiogrosso. But it is not just people's names; there are explosions of names about things, too. Charles Shapes owns an electronics store, and the place is filled with names like "Audiobrights, Valsalvas, Cranmer-Lutzs, Woeneckes; speakers, tuners, and decks stacked one and two and three high" (159). Perhaps the only book to equal this one's cornucopia of names is Gilbert Sorrentino's own *Mulligan Stew* (1979), a book filled both with the author's own inventions, plus the lists of characters from other books.

Reading Feld's essays on the poet Spicer, one begins to understand how Feld left poetry for prose-writing. Arguing for collage in poetry, in *After Lorca*, Jack Spicer writes:

> But things decay, reason argues. Real things become garbage. The piece of lemon you shellac to the canvas begins to develop a mold, the newspaper tells of incredibly ancient events in forgotten slang, the boy becomes a grandfather. Yes, but the garbage of the real still reaches out into the current world making its objects, in turn, visible—lemon calls to lemon, newspaper to newspaper, boy to boy. As things decay, they bring their equivalents into being. (qtd. in Feld, "Lowghost" 7)

In his speech at Notre Dame, Feld refers to the Objectivist poets (George Oppen, Carl Rakosi, Louis Zukofsky, et al.) as being "epiphenomenal." "Their marginalism was their freedom; they had access to quiet corners in which to handle the polished instruments of the art." He goes on to say that these poets "are much to the point," but that they also "seem narrowed down *to* a point." At first Feld takes exception with the politics of George Oppen's poetry, calling it "a poetry of alibi and bad faith." Later still in the essay, Feld asks whoever promised that we could be innocent of loneliness? Then he answers himself: "Marx, that's who." He calls Oppen's failures "political and psychological." And because Oppen corresponded with Robert Duncan, Feld includes Duncan in his assessment of the Objectivists, and he says the San Francisco poet's fade-out was "a product of social, political, sexual, and almost masonic deliquescence." Whatever the reason, "the effect on me is to read the poets we call Objectivist or Black Mountain or countertraditional with less and less relish each time. The longer I write novels I seem to suspect something structural's behind my disenchantment, too." He continues: "Yet I, from my perch over in the less pure art—and having made poems myself, and having stopped making them—am much less sure that blockbuilding doesn't describe poetry perfectly."

There are many reasons why anyone chooses one thing over another. Ross Feld chose prose over poetry, as he stated in his lecture at Notre Dame. But there are some things worth noting in that journey from poetry to prose. Feld may cite the Objectivists for what he called their "pietism," and he may also say that his disenchantment with poetry is nothing more than a structural awareness. ("The longer I write novels I seem to suspect something structural's behind my disenchantment, too.") One might say that poetry at Saint Mark's went in a direction completely opposed to Feld's own poetics. But I think his main objection to poetry was what Daniel Kane calls its "performative" nature (Kane 27-56). Feld was a writer of words on the page—a writer of language not speech. "The midcentury Anglo-American personal/subjective poem," he says, "was largely one of *performance* [Feld's emphasis]—a formalist's ruse." He says that the Pound/Olson/ Zukofskian vector, in exposing this ruse, "went too far" ("Talking about Objectivism").

Finally, Ross Feld believed that "the poem's exhaustion is what has become sovereign" ("Jack Spicer").

6

Years Out (1973) is Ross Feld's first novel, published when he was twenty-five years old. Although on its surface, it would appear to be a standard realistic novel, all Ross Feld's novels, like his one book of poetry, were about *language*, just as all of Jack Spicer's poems were about language, too. Here is how Feld put it regarding this mentor, the poet's poet:

> The hortatory, long-strided mode we indistinctly call the Black Mountain movement is eclipsed in subtlety by Spicer ten times over, but he is still of that widened-out mode. Clever, pithy, brilliant, daring as he may be, Spicer was set from the start upon the One Thing, larger-goaled even than Olson and his polis and culture-straddling. Spicer wanted no less than to clear the totals on poetry's machine, to introduce the proper multipliers and dividers. Poem was all; and if so, what we made it from had to be more perdurable, of more lasting and truer clay than we ordinarily contributed. Spicer asked that it only be "objects," real things that the poet, totally subordinate, could "disclose. . . to make a poem that had no sound in it but the pointing of a finger." Ghosts, lemons, seagulls, rocks, diamonds, baseball, God, radio, dead letters: they are recurrently placed into the poems as *figuri*, as markers, as shims—but above all as absolute quiddities, made realer than real by a retrospective turn that Spicer would have both appreciated and half as much rued. ("Lowghost" 6)

Not only did Spicer provide Feld with a self-consciousness about language and how one uses it in a poem, but he allowed a young poet to contemplate "the other." "The 'I—never seen' is tacitly replaced with a 'we,'" Feld observes ("Lowghost" 11). Really, this is a kind of truism of fiction writing. Characters become more important than the author. At least, I believe, Ross Feld took Spicer's desire to remove himself from the poem as a kind of invitation for the young poet to write fiction, to eschew the first person for these other persons, these characterizations. In an essay that Feld wrote about John Hawkes and Scott Spencer, he writes: "Characters are a novelist's children not only by force of original creation but in the strength, too, of their rebellion" ("Braving the Depths").

Thus we have this first novel, *Years Out*. Its plot and characters are rather conventional. In fact, these five characters are no more different than the ones found in a movie like *The Big Chill* (1983), a play like Michael Weller's *Moonchildren* (1971), or even the 1990s television phenomenon, *Friends*. But I don't believe that Feld wrote novels purely about language the way that Jack Spicer wrote poems purely about language. No, he believed in the conventions of fiction writing, and plot and character were two of those conventions. *Years Out* chronicles the lives of five friends in the time immediately after university—the years out. The time is the late Sixties. Yet as a language *field* (using the word in the sense Olson employs it in his essay) constructed out of odd bits of metaphor and analogy, *Years Out* more resembles a narrative poem written in American speech rhythms circa the 1970s. In that sense, Ross Feld was writing *projective* prose.

To be sure, Ross Feld read—and was influenced by—prose writers as diverse as Flaubert and Gombrowicz. But his real literary heroes were poets with names like William Carlos Williams, Robert Creeley, Gilbert Sorrentino, Joel Oppenheimer, Jack Spicer, and Paul Blackburn. His other influences would include Montale and Apollinaire, Mallarmé and Baudelaire. For Ross Feld's strongest language is not narratively driven nor for that matter is it character-laced. It is his use of metaphors and tropes. In *Years Out*, David and Serena engage in pillow-talk after making love. But, like Feld, his characters are fond of language.

> In bed, they exchanged verbal doodles. He told her about the fabled Giants team of his youth: "Young" Goodman Brown on first; "Doc" Rappaccini playing short; Ethan Brand—"a real phenom; went to his right beautifully"—at third; "Dimmes" Dale in left; Willie Mays where else but in center; Roger Chillingworth in right; Johnny Calvin calling the signals behind the plate; and Nat Hawthorne throwing heat from the mound. (204)

Of course, this is a New York baseball team, but with certain literary and intellectual over shadings. The only real baseball player is

Willie Mays, the fabled center fielder for the New York and later the San Francisco Giants. Most of the other "players" are really characters from Nathaniel Hawthorne's novels, and he is the pitcher on the mound. Calvin is the stiff-backed, strait-laced minister who was a kind of subtext to so many of Hawthorne's writings, Calvinism being the bane—and sustenance—of early American settlers' lives. But like everything that Ross Feld did, there are still other layers to explore. There is the faint echo of Jack Spicer's own obsessions with baseball, not to mention Gilbert Sorrentino's. But there is also that tribal and territorial one, the oddness of a Brooklyn native creating a New York Giants team. The Brooklyn Dodgers were the team of Brooklyn, while the Giants resided in uptown Manhattan, north of Harlem, and across the Harlem River from Yankee Stadium in the Bronx.

All of these metaphors and tropes are held together by memory. In the beginning of *Years Out*, the narrative states: "The best way to never forget was to never quite remember" (5), which is more indicative of the 1960s and its ethos than Ross Feld whose own ethos was more like, "You must not forget anything." In an essay that he wrote on Witold Gombrowicz's *Diary*, Feld refers to the Polish writer as thinking of himself "like aspirin," ridding one of excessive cramps ("I Am Like Asprin"). Feld is more like glue, making his often extraordinary and even odd tropes adhere to the narrative structure of his writing.

I came across an observation by V. S. Pritchett on Chekhov which I think is apt for Ross Feld here. Pritchett writes: "If his prose is plain and neutral, it is nevertheless musical in its architecture and its curious response to sounds" (6). It is no coincidence that one of the five characters in *Years Out* is a cellist. Besides being a poet with a passion for language, Ross Feld, despite trying to be an anti-poet, even an unmusical one, was a highly lyrical writer. His passion for classical music runs, like a minor motif, like a musical stream, through all of his novels. At times, Feld's musical ability is so effortless, one might not even notice its being there.

There is a passage in *Years Out* in which Serena, the cellist, has an affair with her music teacher. Her teacher seems to observe that "There were only a limited number of means to gain access to new thought; it's why modernism is a declarative moment and then is lost, only to come back in the world of art to haunt and prod and insinuate until its tenets are almost unconsciously accepted" (145). After they make love, Serena declines dinner in order to practice her Kodaly for the next day. "On Sunday, they went to Orchard Street, then Chinatown, crossed the Brooklyn Bridge and strolled the Promenade in Brooklyn Heights, came back into Manhattan, took the I.R.T. to his house, and slept there together until she had to get up and attend her first class, and he had to get up to teach his: the same one" (147). This urban geography is very reminiscent of some of Paul Blackburn's poems, especially his rhapsodizing on the streets of New York.

> Straight rye whiskey, 100 proof
> you need a better friend?
> Yes.   Myself.
>
> The lights
> the lights
> the lonely   lovely   fucking   lights
> and the bridge on a rainy Tuesday night
> Blue/green double-stars   the line
> that is the drive and on the dark alive
> gleaming river
> Xmas trees of tugs scream and struggle. (120-21)

Feld, the anti-poet, less lyrically than Paul Blackburn, but with an equal measure of invention, introduces what amounts to a found-poem, a poem of its time, very Spicerian in its anti-poetic nuances. It is a list of Beatles' songs.

> "Taxman"
> "Eleanor Rigby"
> "Love You To"
> "Here, There and Everywhere"
> "Yellow Submarine"
> "She Said She Said"
> "Good Day Sunshine"
> "For No One."
> "I Want to Tell You"
> "Got to Get You Into My Life"
> "Tomorrow Never Knows" (150)

Yet what could Feld possibly have meant when he wrote that "the best way to never forget was to never quite remember?" If we return to that italicized paragraph in the preface, which is entitled "Out," we find out that:

The day before, they had all graduated. The actual ceremony was unattended—much too formal and unrelated to whatever they felt—but the behind-the-eyes vision of it stayed. The shuffling forth. The years released like a gay balloon. An amphitheatre carbonated with possibility. Rather than ignore the event, they seemed to have settled on finessing it, coaxing it here, to what turned out to be brilliant calming rooms, and, instead of dispatching it with one great binge of memory and regret, marking it with a cool offhand indelibility. The best way to never forget was to never quite remember. (5)

The years were like "an amphitheatre carbonated with possibility." This is not so much a mixed or garbled metaphor as a very surreal one. Keep in mind that Feld's hero, Jack Spicer, ends one poem with these words: "The poet is a radio. The poet is a liar. The poet is a / counterpunching radio" (*Collected Books*). An amphitheatre carbonated with possibility is a poet's way of putting things—a poet who has read Mallarmé and Apollinaire.

Earlier I referred to Feld's *seemingly* realistic narratives. At least, on the surface, they appear to be realistic, and that is what *seems* to be the case; realism skitters over the surface of his prose like a dragonfly over the surface of a pond. But even a cursory examination of his use of language suggests something more disconcerting, more challenging, and the reader either signs on to this agenda or the ride becomes rocky. An example: take the *New York Times Book Review* assessment of *Years Out* (1973). Michael Mewshaw begins the review as if this were merely a realistic novel. He writes:

> The "Years Out" refers to the years after college when one escapes the limits—and consolations—of school, family and most institutional supports. This first novel wanders in the wake of five young people who are out and who share a common fecklessness, confusion and curious inability to make intelligent choices. Their groping feels genuine, and the author allows us instants of poignant insight into their troubled discoveries. Gradually they seem almost more tellingly representative of the times than the radicals, hashheads and commune dwellers who attracted attention in the late 1960's. (80)

I like that hashhead remark, more telling of the reviewer's suburban ethos than anything Feld might be up to or not. Yet after this first paragraph, which almost seems to promise a fair-minded review, Mewshaw takes a critical U-turn. When the novel turns out not to be a realistic one, the reviewer becomes irritated and disappointed. The next paragraph is blisteringly negative in its assessment of Feld's writing style.

> But because of his garbled prose, Ross Feld never fully succeeds in giving shape and voice to their longing. Instead the reader is often left puzzled by sentences like, "Her frame, thin and hooking, was not up to her voice, a full and lifey *de gustibus non est disputandum*." Or to suppress a chuckle at lines like this description of an orgasm: ". . . Marilyn fell apart—steel and raucous, truncheon and holiday, sparks and saliva." (80)

The third paragraph of Mewshaw's review is not much better. He whinges about the plot, claiming that "the novel is utterly devoid of narrative drive":

> Things happen, but very little relates to what has gone before or is to come. As they move from apartment to apartment, take jobs, shack up, marry, have affairs, split up and break down, the characters are self-absorbed, yet seldom analytical or incisive, and crucial scenes frequently blur to sameness. The drifting, disjointed, episodic structure seems more an indication of authorial indecision than an image of anomie. (80)

The last paragraph, in true *New York Times* book-reviewing fashion, hedges its bets. Mewshaw admits that the novel does "capture the gritty reality of city living." And then he concludes rather scoldingly: "If Mr. Feld is to go on to better work, of which he seems capable, he'll have to dig deeper, and find a way of making his vision as immediate and important to the reader as it is to him" (80).

Mr. Feld was twenty-five years old at the time, and a lesser novelist probably would have packed his fictional suitcases and shuffled off to Buffalo, never to be heard from again. He moved to Ithaca, New York. He had been diagnosed with Hodgkins disease, a lymphatic cancer that was something of a death notice in the 1960s but by the early 1970s was a treatable and even curable illness. Feld became one of the survivors. Of course, cancer patients often say that the very cures that give them life will eventually take their lives years later, and I suspect that Feld's dying of cancer in his early fifties no doubt had something to do with the cancer treatment he received in the early 1970s.[19]

But let me return to that *New York Times* review of *Years Out*. Mewshaw says the novel is devoid of a narrative drive, and yet I think that the novel is one of Feld's most plotted enterprises. To say that nothing happens is to miss the point entirely, I think, as philistine as going to a production of Chekhov's *Three Sisters*, and complaining that nothing happens there.

Perhaps it is time to call in Chekhov, the writer I so often think of when reading Ross Feld's novels. Chekhov wrote: "What happens onstage should be just as complicated and just as simple as things are in real life. People are sitting at a table having dinner, that's all, but at the same time their happiness is being created, or their lives are being torn apart" (qtd. in Schmidt 5). This really is the key to Feld's characters. They are sitting at a dinner table having dinner, and their happiness or their lives being torn apart just happen.

In drama school, I was taught that for a play to be dramatic *something must happen*. But it does not necessarily mean that everything must happen to characters. I take *something happening* to mean that characters are different at the end of an action than they were at its beginning. In the best of these dramatic arcs, something happening is even transformative. In this sense of something happening, I believe that all of Ross Feld's novels are plotted and have strong narrative superstructures despite the superficial evidence to suggest otherwise. Feld said as much in an essay entitled "The Spilled Drop," in which he assayed, among other writers, Eudora Welty. He quotes Welty saying that "great fiction shows us not how to conduct our behavior but how to feel." Feld goes on to say that unlike our own errors and shortcomings, those of a character "tremble" with, to quote Welty, "the possibility that they may indeed reveal everything." One last thing regarding Eudora Welty, Feld also quotes her remark that there is more longing in fiction than in love.

I think this issue of something happening is addressed quite well in Feld's Notre Dame address about the Objectivist poets. In that paper, he refers to Wittgenstein alluding to St. Augustine, and how a child acquires language. From this he returns to his abandoning of poetry for prose. This is where he made that remark about "blockbuilding" describing how one makes a poem. At that point in his talk at Notre Dame, Ross Feld articulates, I believe, one of his key theories of fiction writing.

> But in the novel, stuffed as it is with people—many if not most of whom do not tell the truth—there is also an intra-individual element. A. for instance might ask for a stone he knows B. is too clumsy to manage; B. might make believe he asked for a slab instead of a pillar; they might work so smoothly that they fall in love with their own efficiency and forget to make a doorway. Language in a novel is passed from one fictional person to another—blocked, stymied, reflected, flattened, disbelieved. And there is, Bakhtin reminds us, also the matter of what he calls the *superaddressee*—the one (be it the reader, the author, or just plain common sense and experience of the world) who knows that all of them may be equally hopeless as blockbuilders.

Feld believes that poetry lacks this superaddressee, and he wonders if Ezra Pound, "a terrific reader of prose," did not introduce "swerves of tone, the breaks, the echoes of earlier texts that find their way into the *Cantos*, in order to see if a monoreferential form might be made multireferential like the novel."

In an essay Feld wrote called "Timing and Spacing the As If: Poetic Prose and Prosaic Poetry," he mentioned the Russian Formalist critic

Shklovsky who "saw novels *as* poems" (13). (This is not something that Ross Feld himself subscribed to.) Shklovksy believed that prose could easily be broken down to strophes and meters and recurring tropes, and Feld notes that "the sentimentalist avant garde novel feeds on that presumption" (14). But I mention this essay, not to bolster a theory that parallels Feld's own, but for another reason. Later in it, Feld presents what I think is his own most cogent theory of the novel.

> A man and a woman, parents together of the same child, shop for a toy. Both parents know the toy will break or quickly be consigned to oblivion; but in order to buy the toy in that store on that day and not have to make a return trip, one of the pair must will him or herself to a belief in the toy's temporary magic—magic in *time*—to bring pleasure, boldness, and imaginative relief from the self that even children need. The parents do not stop knowing that the toy is just a toy—but know also the fact that the toy's bringing of joy and imagination and even the lessons of loss to the offspring brings all that to themselves, the parents, too. They consciously know one thing less than fully in order to know another thing more. . . . Are toys (or fairy tales or novels) not *serious* enough? Ask a child. (14)

With *Years Out*, Ross Feld lays the foundation stones for his later work, and this concept of knowing one thing less than fully in order to know another thing more, I believe, is yet another key to understanding his fiction. Is *Years Out* serious enough? Ask the fiction writer, not the critic. Yes, it is a serious novel, and something does happen. Five people leave school, go out into the world, in this instance, the world of New York City. Neither self-absorbed nor unanalytical, his five characters are bright and talented, and sometimes like their author, quick-tongued. They engage the world around them, and sometimes they succeed, and often they fail.

Feld's classmate from the City College, Henry Weinfield, a poet and professor at the University of Notre Dame, has noted that the ending of *Years Out* corresponds with the ending of Flaubert's *Sentimental Journey*.

> Flaubert was one of Ross's models (he agrees with Pound and Joyce), and if you read the end of the Flaubert against the ending of *Years Out* you will see a similar tonality, a similar way in which life is cut off in the middle of things, and a similar sense in which our aspirations and hopes for life never amount to anything. The same is true, by the way, of Ross's book, *Only Shorter*, in which the heroine dies at the end—but in a way that fulfills the truth of the book's epigraph from Beckett. (E-mail 15 Sept. 2004)

7

"to recognize the good in the bad, the bad in the worst,
and so grow gently old all down the unchanging days and
die one day like any other day, only shorter."
—Samuel Beckett, *Malone Dies*, as quoted by Feld in the
front matter of *Only Shorter*

In an essay on contemporary fiction, Ross Feld observes that "characters are a novelist's children not only by force of original creation but in the strength, too, of their rebellion" ("Braving the Depths"). In his Spicer essay, Feld said "that ignored poetry, like an ignored child, will go to its room to play hermetic and private games. Its own secrecy, self-congratulatory neatness, compensates for the attention it's not getting—and this it gives up unwillingly if at all" ("Lowghost"). The observation resonates more as an autobiographical instance than a poetics, and yet Feld was an anti-poet, like his hero Jack Spicer, and so perhaps this is an instance of an anti-poetics. In the Notre Dame talk, he mentions a line by the poet Robert Duncan that "love is an answer to a question that has not been askt."[20] In another essay he wrote about contemporary theories of poetry, he calls Charles Bernstein "well-informed, jargony, willful, and impossibly self-important." He also says that Bernstein is prodigious with the moondust ("The Swarming"). Of the poet Michael Palmer, he writes that his "natural lyricism, though, has begun to go spongy under the weight of such Lyotardian 'post-human' gear, rhetorical widgets that make me recall the classic Yiddish definition of the shlemazl, the serious-nik who runs through the streets crying, 'I have a wonderful answer! Quick, someone ask me a question!'" ("The Swarming"). What is love, Feld seems to ask, if Robert Duncan's line is to be considered the answer?

Only Shorter would seem to be the answer to another kind of question that has not been asked. It might even be the shlemazl's answer searching for a question. It is also the closest Ross Feld ever gets to autobiography, to fiction as memoir, to the novel as a roman à clef. Less than a decade after Feld experienced his own lymphatic cancer, he published this book ostensibly about two young people with cancer, one who survives it, the other who almost survives it, but then dies. The latter, oddly enough, is the more accepting, the more decent, the *better* person. The former is not likeable at all. He's a whiner, a malingerer, at times, a nasty bit of business, a snitch, a right-wing dogmatic, a mid-level corporate executive turned landlord, no, slumlord. There is no character who is a stand-in for the author; rather there are narrative events which correspond to the author's experiences, in the first instance, those experiences he had as they relate to having cancer.

Yet if I can make no other point about Ross Feld's writing than this, it would be to say that invariably critics misread his intentions. Because he appeared to be a realistic kind of writer, they wanted him to be just that. But he was not. As I said, all Feld's books are about language, just as his mentors—Gilbert Sorrentino and Jack Spicer—wrote books about this subject, too, language pure and simple or language, to be more exact, impure and complex. But first let me return to the dumbfounded critics.

An unsigned review in *Best Sellers* begins by noting that "it's hard to explain why a novel, obviously written with care and attention to detail, leaves you cold. I ask myself why I admire this author but don't like this book and I think it is because I am thinking about his technique while I read and do not care about the story" (170). The reviewer continues by observing: "The story of two victims of cancer with the prospect of death and desertion of family and friends teems with possibilities, the very stuff of which novels are made. Yet whenever either character heads for a reckoning of his values, the narrative veers away to distracting details, in a tone devoid of sympathy for what it takes to make tragic choices" (170). The reviewer goes on to declare that the novel fails because its characters are not "revealed." Then a big gun is brought in—Tolstoy in *Anna Karenina*—to illustrate the need for revelation. But *Only Shorter*, despite its potential for melodrama or even tragedy, is neither. Its strategy is based on discovery—an almost intellectual kind of white-light experience—rather than revelation. Characters' lives are not stripped away, piece by piece, as they might be in, say, an Ibsen play, but instead arrive at their own epiphanies, not so much through experience, but in spite of the evidence that experience provides. Their discoveries, as I've noted, are intellectual ones, and they usually have to do with something relevatory in their language.

Again, language is everything in Ross Feld's novels.

Joan Silber—herself a subtle fiction writer—wrote more lucidly about *Only Shorter* in the *Village Voice*. Of the two central characters, Jack and Judith, she tells how they meet in a cancer clinic: "They do not fall in love, or anything near it (in fact, in the first scene we see them annoyed with each other and mutually estranged); they have a fitful and weakish affair, as wasteful as if they were regular people" (47). I like that phrase *regular people,* for the fact is that there is nothing regular about cancer, especially when it afflicts young people. Silber later provides an assiduous reading of the novel by noting: "Feld's theme throughout is that no one is ever ready for what always comes as an interruption to things left incomplete." But then she loses the plot.

There is nothing even remotely cloying about this book. It veers instead toward being too distant and crisp (and sometimes over-careful in style). Insisting on the tangle of mundane events, it is at times too loose in its plotting. Often incidents which could provide more information about the characters are merely digressive, and the figures themselves are sketched in lightly, secondary to their own diseases. Still, the novel manages to be impressively truthful in its own hard-headed way. (47)

Silber was one of the regular people on the downtown scene in the days when Ross Feld first began to work at Grove Press and attend workshops at Saint Mark's. I never saw her at the Poetry Project, and I don't think she had much interest in the poetry scene, although she was friends with the poet Harry Lewis, who worked as a bartender at the Saint Adrian's Company bar, an enormous artists' and writers' bar on Broadway in the seam between Greenwich Village and the East Village. Silber was a waitress there for many years. Eventually she began to write herself, and has since published several books of fiction. I note this because one's expectations—and disappointments—reading Feld's novels are in direct proportion to one's exclusive dedication to fiction as a craft or a broader sense of the craft of writing, particularly one that incorporates poetic ideals into notions of prose. In other words, it helps to know Feld's origins in poetry to read his prose. It also helps to have some grounding in the poetry scene of the time—especially the poetry groups at Saint Mark's, including Black Mountain, New York School, and, later, the Language poets.

Ross Feld's trajectory as a novelist is less by way of Flaubert to Joyce to Faulkner and Hemingway and Fitzgerald than it is by way of Baudelaire and Mallarmé, by way of Apollinaire, and then straight to the heart from William Carlos Williams to Robert Creeley, and on to writers like Joel Oppenheimer, Paul Blackburn, and Gilbert Sorrentino. (At the end of his life, he kept reading company with Eugenio Montale, the great contemporary Italian poet.) A writer like Larry Kart, writing in the *Chicago Tribune*, seems to intuit this journey of Feld's writing much better than other critics did. Kart had no trouble delineating the overall arc of *Only Shorter*: "The book's central characters—Jack Richmond, a middle-level corporate executive, and Judith Kornbluh, an assistant curator at an art museum—are suffering from cancer; and in the end we don't know whether either will survive."

Kart clearly sees that characters and plot are only two ways to approach Feld's writing. He shrewdly concludes that *Only Shorter* "is really about paying attention—the sleepy kind of attention we pay each day to ourselves and our worlds, how that attention can shift into a different gear when we know that the next day may be our last and, above all, how this novelist pays attention to the way life and fiction interact." He goes on to note that all fiction asks is who is telling the tale, and *Only Shorter* is no exception. But Feld's narrative voice is told with "such near-invisible grace that it's possible to read through the book without quite realizing what Feld has accomplished." The rest of the review is spent showing and exploring how Feld's subtle narrative voice turns the third person on its ear, making it at times almost painfully autobiographical, the author's voice, and yet never lapsing into an epistolary or a diaristic voice.

The *Tribune* reviewer manages to understand how creating "ordinariness" is one of Feld's chief triumphs. He illustrates with the following sentences from *Only Shorter*: "The man Jack finally got the door open for was neat and chunky—in a golf sweater and light blue slacks. Dark straight hair was combed wet into a just-so sweep and there was a hint of cowlick in the back, like Fred Flintstone's." "The first sentence is Jack's, or at least most of it is. 'He was thinking' tells us that. But the second—though it retains Jack's 'sound' in its awkward, muscular thrust—conveys information that Jack certainly does not possess." In the second, the narrator is speaking, Kart writes. This gives the prose "torque," the reviewer says. "We know Jack and his motives better than he does himself, but the narrator must pull us away from Jack in order to give us this information, as though he were wrenching a man's arm from its socket." Then Kart produces a passage in his brief but uncannily observed review that I think illustrates what I have been saying all along:

> Undercutting the assumptions we make when we read realistic fiction—our willingness to accept or ignore the narrator's presence—Feld has produced a quietly original book that forces us to pay attention both to the "real" lives he has invented and to the fictional brush strokes that create these vivid illusions.

Put another way, Feld is a writer of realistic details as well as the brush strokes of fiction, a more self-conscious writing, one that is reflexive, one that is involved with issues of language itself.

Critics have noted that Feld wrote without sentimental urges, particularly in this novel about cancer. Feld's friend and literary executor, Josh Rubins, writing in *Kirkus Reviews*, where he'd been a co-editor from 1978 to 1985, drew attention to *Only Shorter*, where the author wrote of terminal illness with "an almost breathtaking . . . lack of sentimentality" (1). Rubins acknowledges that Feld introduced poetry reviews into *Kirkus*. "New sections were added to embrace his expertise with Montale and Mandelstam as well as with Americans of every school" (1). Ross Feld was especially good with Montale. Like the great Italian poet about whom Feld said his dubiousness and pessimism were constitutional ("Montale"), Feld himself shaped his own unsentimental prose around a constitutional pessimism and dubiousness. As Feld notes in this lyrical and elegiac essay, Montale's themes often were about illness and family, particularly in later life.

> As in all the Motets, the poet isn't demolished by separation. He's astonished by it. The widest gulf is the one opened not by a lover's flightiness but by the recognition of the dark personal fixations surrounding each of us like pelts: illness (Motet II), for instance, or family (Motet IV). Always Montale is writing less to the lover, Clizia, than to her privacies: *Altro era il tuo stampo*; Something else was your mark (Motet IX).

In his essay "Relievers," Ross Feld notes that Stanley Cavell in one of his own essays observes "that human life is constrained to the life of the human body, to what Emerson called the giant I always take with me. The law of the body is the law." Feld qualifies this by noting that "bodies are somethings, in other words (the sick body a something in error, maybe)." I have always been puzzled by the opening paragraph of *Only Shorter* until I came across this Cavell essay by Ross Feld. The sick body is a *something* in error. Now listen to that opening paragraph in his second novel:

> He hates that she came along. It's even in the way he's grabbing at, angrily yanking, the stickshift. They fly down the slanted streets of the student section; and once, when he makes an unnecessarily sharp turn, she wonders if he doesn't mean to see whether she can be flung off, like a fat pulled drop of something. (3)

Like a fat pulled drop of *something* sounds almost incomplete, not for the character thinking this thought, but the writer writing it. At least that is what I always thought until I came upon that passage by Stanley Cavell and Feld's own interpretation of it. Then I saw how this passage is about *something* in error, and that *something* is the human body.[21] In this case, it is Judith Kornbluh's body, her cancer-ridden body. There is another essay I am drawn to by Ross Feld to illustrate the themes in his second novel. That is a piece he wrote on Primo Levi, the Italian chemist from Turin, the Auschwitz survivor. "Death after death," Feld writes, "is one definition of shame, and as a detective of shame Levi is wholly Célan's equal as a great artist. Levi writes of shame as a kind of nesting of destructions" ("Taking Time" 13).

Finally, despite so many critics still not understanding what Feld was doing with his special kind of realism, I want to note, as in any great piece of writing, there are often passages that don't necessarily add to the narrative thrust or reveal a character into a particular light or even create a further mood, and yet they stand out as exemplary in their execution and observation of detail. *Only Shorter* addresses the subject of cancer in just this way. Afterward, you find yourself thinking back on a certain passage, re-reading, and pausing to think about what the author has done. Chapter 5 of *Only Shorter* does that for me. Jack Richmond finds himself at a business meeting with town leaders. "Just at that moment, something must have bitten Jack—right above the collarbone. A hardy winter mosquito? A flea from the couch? He rubbed at the itch through his shirt." Then: "Jack's bite had begun to itch savagely now. He slipped two fingers down his collar, encountering a swelling distinct as an egg, and raked it good and hard with his nails" (94). Later:

> Four, five, six times during the night his fingers went to it, checking. The itch was mostly gone but not the swelling. That, if anything had increased, become defined and hard. Before dawn he went into the bathroom, turned on the light over the sink, and looked at it in the mirror. Only when he pressed at it did it redden, buzz against the air faintly; he painted the entire area generously with calamine lotion. Hours later, when he drove to work, it was tieless. (95)

Eventually, Jack loses his denial about it being an insect bite and sees a doctor. The doctor's fingers go to the lump, "Jack's bite," "as if quickly covering a boiling pot" (97). Jack is twenty-seven years old. He had a lymphadenopathy. What? Jack asks. "A swollen node" (97). Jack returns to his insect bite theory. But the doctor contradicts him. It is not an insect bite. The doctor thinks it too hard for mono. Then he tells Jack: "it could be Hodgkin's disease" (99).

8

Shapes Mistaken (1989) may well be Ross Feld's finest novel. It holds all the themes of his earlier work, plus it unfolds all his obsessions in the most felicitous way. All of Feld's writings remind me, in their way, of Chekhov's writing, and *Shapes Mistaken* reminds me of the later Chekhov, when the great Russian writer gets beyond the melodrama of *Ivanov* and the arty concerns of *The Seagull* for the quiet tragicomedy of *The Cherry Orchard* and *Three Sisters*. Related to this subtle progression of time in Chekhov's plays, Feld writes of the tick of the clock being a kind of plot.

Frank Kermode, in his useful (and it seems to me never more pertinent) 1967 book about fiction, *The Sense of an Ending*—said that the clock's *tick-tock* is itself a plot, "an organization that humanizes time by giving it form." ("I love History because I hate time and all Time contains," declares Kohler—whose clock, recall, goes *tip tip tip* instead.)[22] Kermode contrasts *chronos*—passing time—with *kairos*—a season, "a point in time filled with significance, charged with meaning derived from its relation to the end." Gass would say (with what Kermode would call the "skepticism of the clerisy") that this shows us as naive: that to expect an end in art means to expect a sum, a sermon, a moral. ("Timing and Spacing" 27)

Nothing seems to happen in *Shapes Mistaken*, and yet in fact everything is happening. Something happens, at least, because the characters are not the same at the end of the action as they were at the beginning of it. There are not so much plot points of recognition as there are character points of awareness, of cognition, of knowing what they have to do with what was and maybe even with what will be. *Shapes Mistaken* begins in what is almost a Lenny Bruce routine.[23]

Before proceeding to Sid's affair, Shapes first drove across the river in weak afternoon light to the restaurant in the D-Lux Motel, where he planned to stuff himself on lion's head and that way be sure to get at least one decent meal for the day. He'd phoned ahead from the store so the Hings would be ready: Aahs of welcome, a little bit of talk about the premature heat, then Henry Hing sweeping an arm through the room, offering any deep-backed seat in the house. Followed by ice water, hot tea, and ultimately Frankie—chef and eldest son—marching out with the burly meatballs, his mother shyly hanging back behind. (5)

If you get Feld's humor, you laugh immediately. A giant meatball called lion's head? A nervous Jewish businessman entering an empty Chinese restaurant to eat a meal that might better serve a family. Even their names. Shapes. Hing. Frankie, the eldest son, bringing out the giant meatballs ceremoniously, and his mother lingering shyly behind. Personally, I find it priceless, and vintage Ross Feld, not to mention classic New York Jewish culture, some of the best Chinese restaurants in New York not being found in Chinatown but rather in Jewish neighborhoods, not the ghettos of one's parents and grandparents, but the affluent places of the Upper West Side. (I am reminded of Saul Bellow's short, lyrical novel, *Seize the Day* (1956).)

The novel is a chronicle of Charles Shapes's seemingly uneventful life, although, again, I return to that operative word to describe all of Feld's novels—*seemingly*. Shapes's life is really too eventful: his chest pains, thus his pangs of regret for his newly deceased wife; his pangs of regret over the poor relationship he has with his daughter; the pangs of inarticulateness and lack of action taken with his partner and old friend, Sid Telscher; the regret he feels even toward an employee who clearly is ripping him off for thousands of dollars in stolen electronics equipment. Shapes's dilemma is summed up even before he finishes his meal: his is a life "spent being nice—and never in the process having to be good" (11). Charles Shapes is a man who wants to do good and be good instead of being Mr. Nice. Being Mr. Nice has gotten him walked over and stepped on by everyone from his wife to his daughter to his business partner to his employees, including his son-in-law. People literally are stealing Shapes blind. Nothing seems to be happening, and yet everything happens to him.

Charles Shapes is a quiet, decent, sophisticated fellow. He owns an electronics store, in partnership with his more successful lifelong friend, Sidney Telscher. A Russian émigré he is trying to help is ripping him off. His daughter thinks him a *shmuck*.[24] While driving in his car, Shapes and his daughter get into an argument over—of all things!—the direction of their route. The direction of their route! It is not about their feelings of love and conflict; about the death of a wife and a mother. It is an argument about the direction they are taking in the car.

In the essay entitled "Relievers," Feld writes smartly and affectionately about the writers Stanley Cavell and Adam Phillips. In one of his own more autobiographical pieces, Stanley Cavell refers to his own parents' bickering and fighting, as a "devastation of spirit in their quarrels." This idea of the detection of voice, Ross Feld points out, has to do with Cavell's "mother's musical grace and sight-reading ability, his father's jokes and their particular flavor of Jewish moral pertinence, his parents' disappointments together and their bitter fights," all bring the philosopher to an unpolemical juncture in his work. That angst that Cavell experiences with his bickering parents I find illustrated vividly by Feld's own description of Shapes and his daughter Amy in the car.

> "You said left."
> "That *was* left."
> "That was *straight*," Amy said.
> "It wasn't—it angled off. Didn't you see it angling off?"
> "THEN THAT'S NOT LEFT. ANGLING OFF IS STRAIGHT. IT CAN MAKE AS MANY CURVES AS IT WANTS—IT'S STILL THE SAME ROAD, STRAIGHT AHEAD."
> "I disagree."

"I know you—I KNOW YOU DO. AND YOU'RE WRONG."
"I can hear you, you don't have to scream." (118-19)

9

Zwilling's Dream (1999) was Ross Feld's most successful book, commercially and critically. Unlike any of his other works, it went into a second printing, and finally critics were beginning to understand that this was realism with a twist. "All fiction offers escape, some from thought, some into it," wrote Cynthia Shearer in the *Hungry Mind Review*. "Ross Feld's third novel *Zwilling's Dream* is of the blessed second type. A trenchant and funny novel about a film that never gets made, it uncovers one of America's little secrets: some of the finest minds of our generation instinctively choose to walk away from the spectacle of what the American art tribe might call 'success'" (36). Well, it was his fourth novel. But no matter. Shearer is right about Feld's novels being an escape *into* thought. That's the important point to be made about in the review. The next sentence she writes could describe Ross Feld; in fact, substitute his name for his character Joel Zwilling, and you have instant biography of the author. "The one who has walked away in this case is Joel Zwilling, a middle-aged writer living quietly in Cincinnati" (36).

For the last twenty years of his life, Brooklyn-born Ross Feld lived in Cincinnati, Ohio, the New Yorker choosing to live in a quiet, out-of-the-way backwater of the American Midwest. His wife Ellen came to this city by way of her medical practice. But, of course, Cincinnati isn't really a "backwater" at all. Poets such as Richard Howard and Kenneth Koch came from Cincinnati. Frank O'Hara, the quintessential hip New York poet and art critic, even included a poem about Cincinnati in *Lunch Poems* (1964):

> I was walking along the street
> of Cincinnati
> and I met Kenneth Koch's mother
> fresh from the Istanbul Hilton
> she liked me and I liked her
> we both like Istanbul. (60)

That other Cincinnati denizen Joel Zwilling has repudiated everything he ever wrote except for a story called "Prague Spring," which turns out to be the first chapter of Feld's last novel. Eventually Hollywood gets wind of this story, wants to buy it, and resuscitate the dead art of Joel Zwilling. Enter Zwilling Junior, a filmmaker, a man-about-town, everything his father is not. The rest of the novel is a trajectory of these two miscast relations, a father and son team devoid of emotional as well as intellectual connections.

Curiously, Ross Feld was a significant enough writer to get an obituary in the *New York Times*. But almost thirty years after the newspaper trashed—and grossly misread—his first novel, *Years Out*, the same lack of understanding was brought to bear with his final novel. Erica Sanders calls *Zwilling's Dream* a "cluttered, melancholic fable about survivor guilt." It is worth reprinting the entire review here to show how profoundly the book has been misread.

> Joel Zwilling, a middle-aged writer, had gained notoriety at a young age after writing an autobiographical novel about growing up in New York as the child of Holocaust survivors. After his wife and daughter die in a car accident, however, he stops writing. While teaching at a small college in Cincinnati, Joel raises his son, Nate, who also grows up to be a writer. Their lives become filled with turmoil when a film director decides to make a movie based on Joel's early work. The director, Brian Horkow, and Selva Tashjian, his producer, descend on the Zwillings and Cincinnnati. The locals are predictably, amusingly wowed by the duo's big-spending ways. But Feld has made a puzzling choice to assemble such a psychically scarred roster: the Zwillings are defeated, the annoying Horkow is a manic-depressive and Tashjian is, tragically, delaying major surgery. No matter, the real story here is the tension between Joel, who thinks of the movie as "foolishness," and his son, who has agreed to write the screenplay. In Joel's mind, his fate is to mourn the family he has lost, while Nate despises him for it—it's an excuse not to write, an unforgivable cowardice. As with other conflicts Feld has set in motion, he neglects to resolve this most central one. With so much going on, one wonders if Feld simply ran out of answers. (25)

Of course, Feld did not run out of answers. Remember that wonderful Yiddish joke he told in one of his essays about the man running around with wonderful answers, asking for anyone to ask him a question. Besides, Ross Feld was more a writer of questions than answers. No, what Ross Feld ran out of was time. Simply put, his time was up. He had come to the end of his mortal coil. But his last novel is not one of exhaustion. Instead, it is a book of life-affirming exuberance. Really it is a stick in the eye of critics like Erica Sanders who quite simply don't get his prose, and frankly never will. Ross Feld will never be everyone's cup of tea, and yet look at the writers who did get him: Richard Howard, Susan Sontag, Philip Roth, Wendell Berry, and when they both were younger, Gilbert Sorrentino.

After Wendell Berry read *Zwilling's Dream*, he said that "I need to think about realism more carefully than before." Berry seemed to sense the end for Feld in this novel because he goes on to say: "What interests me most about the novel is the sense it persistently conveys of the finality of human life." Berry asks:

> How does Ross do this? I don't know. I can't figure it out. Is it a feat
> of style? Is it a quality of attention? What can it be? I don't doubt that
> Ross has a masterful literary intelligence. I have thought so for a long
> time. When you first find a master whose mastery you can understand,
> you are assuredly glad, but you need not be long detained. When you
> find a master whose mastery you can't understand, you have found a
> mentor. A mentor is somebody who has got your attention. . . . Ross
> Feld is a writer I am paying attention to.

As I said, Feld's last novel was the one that was best received critically and commercially. Besides the encomiums from writers like
Wendell Berry, he received a good review of the book in the *Washington Post*. Andrea Gollin, a Miami-based writer and editor, concluded her thoughtful review by observing that "it's not happy ever
after, but there is, finally, some measure of hope" (7). Writing in the
Boston Review, James Hynes assayed the novel, saying, "The book
is a diffident but beguiling performance, obliquely told and gently
ironic, sustained not so much by storytelling as by vividly precise
characterization and artfully colloquial prose." The caption for Peter
Trachtenberg's review of the novel in *Forward* says it all: HOLLY-
WOOD GLITZ MEETS MIDWESTERN GLOOM.

10

I have made the assertion that Ross Feld's novels remind me of Chekhov's writings, particularly in how characters' lives are transformed
in the midst of doing the most ordinary things like driving a car or
eating dinner. In that sense, *Zwilling's Dream* is more *The Seagull*
than *Three Sisters*, *The Cherry Orchard*, or *Uncle Vanya*. It is about
art and writing, subjects that usually put one to sleep rather than
rouse them to character self-assessment. But like Trigorin in *The
Seagull*, Joel Zwilling is a writer. Even the opening of *The Seagull*
could be lifted out of context and the words placed in the mouths of
Ross Feld's characters.

> MEDVEDENKO: Why do you always wear black?
> MASHA: Because I'm in mourning for my life. I'm not happy. (111)

Virtually any character in *Zwilling's Dream* could utter those lines,
particularly, "I'm in mourning for my life." *In mourning for one's
life* is how Joel Zwilling finds himself, but so does his counterpart
in the Hollywood film director Brian Horkow, but also the other
characters like the director's personal assistant, Selva Tashjian, or
Joel's son, Nate. Who is not in mourning for their lives, not just in
Zwilling's world, but in Charles Shapes's world from Feld's previous
novel, and even the one before *Shapes Mistaken*, Feld's cancer novel,

Only Shorter? Being in mourning for one's life is the condition of nearly everyone in all four of the novels.

But that is not the only Chekhovian detail I find in Ross Feld's writings and his life. In fact, Feld's essays remind me that there is more to life than tragedy, and his memoir of Philip Guston is as life-affirming as the essays are, too. No, when I think of Ross Feld reminding me of Chekhov, it is really one bolt of insight that the Russian writer provides in one of his letters. The theatre critic Richard Gilman, in his study, *Chekhov's Plays: An Opening into Eternity*, builds the entire structure for his book around this excerpt: "My holy of holies is the human body, health, intelligence, talent, inspiration, love, and the most absolute freedom imaginable—freedom from violence and lies no matter what form they take" (9). That Ross Feld would die two years after his novel was published tells me how profoundly aware he was of this condition Chekhov writes about, and how, at the end of the day, this is all we have, our bodies, our health—or lack thereof, in the case of both Chekhov and Feld—intelligence, talent, inspiration, and love.

Unlike so many books by my contemporaries, no one in Feld's novels gets punched in the nose or thrown down stairs. No one has a gun pulled on them. People argue, true; they live in constant tension between their ideals and the actions of their lives, ever aware of the irreparable qualities of those lives. Ross Feld lived free of violence and lies, and nearly all of his protagonists do too, though invariably their lives become entangled with people, if not violent in their natures, then often out and out liars, like the Hollywood duo who descend upon Cincinnati, Ohio, to produce a Holocaust movie based on Joel Zwilling's story. These details come out in subtle ways, as for instance a father appraising his annoying son: "His son suddenly was sixteen all over again, a sharp pain in the intellectual ass, goading his father while simultaneously asking for his framework of approval" (81). Even the oily Brian Horkow had his redeeming moments.

> Two things only do I wish for in this life, he thought. That the children not die too soon (meaning not before me, meaning not *ever*) and that I myself be tapped in somehow to authenticity. Not originality, not novelty—just a good center-cut portion of the real. With one sabotaged child plus two adopted ones, do I want to pass down *anything* that is intrinsic to myself and my crummy genes? So why is Shelley bringing up my gums? . . . No, all that he wished for his children was what he wished for himself: to not be so goddamned pure! Let them *blunder* onto reality. And the real, in this instance, would be that an Oreo now and then— *even every afternoon, with milk!*—was not going to peel the enamel off their little teeth. If it did, at least it would happen much later, and first would have come deep pleasure, plus a simultaneous introduction to the manifold ambiguity of the world. Wasn't pleasure *usually* dangerous?

Wasn't everything? *Life* was dangerous. In fact it was a *sugar*: brittle, lacy, quickly surging, only later doing its damage. (43)

Although Ross Feld sedulously avoided being autobiographical in his writings, invariably instances of the autobiographical had to creep in. Joel Zwilling might offer the most fertile ground in this pursuit, although, like Feld, I'm reluctant to ascribe out and out instances of the personal here. Still, this novel would appear to be Feld's farewell address, his swan song, as a writer, and so one can't help over-interpreting moments where the author, not a narrator, is addressing the reader. For instance, Zwilling sits quietly, and then the narrator writes: "To say now that nearly anything he ever said was cribbed from reading would not be advisable" (80). In writing about Feld's gargantuan reading habits, I can't but wonder if he were leaving clues for us to decipher. Then I catch myself up, and say that I am over-reaching, over-reacting.

In my own autobiographical instance, I have to say that all of us became so busy and drifted away from one another. The letters I used to get and send to writers like Ross Feld practically stopped in the 1990s. A character speaking to Zwilling sums it up so beautifully: "We all get so busy, so lousy busy, and people drift out of mind" (214). I think of this because I did lose touch with Ross Feld in the nineties. Then I found myself living in London, pre- and post-9/11. Around Christmas of 2002, I was browsing in a Waterstone's bookstore in Hampstead, and I came across a book of interviews with Philip Roth in which he quotes my old friend Ross Feld in one of these pieces.

Immediately I wrote Ross a letter, thinking that maybe this book was only published in England, and so he would not know that Roth had alluded to him. A month or so later, I received a telephone call from Dr. Ellen Feld, telling me that Ross had died in May of 2001. When Seymour Krim died, I remember attending—and reading at—a memorial service for him at Columbia University, and when Joel Oppeheimer died, I attended—and spoke at—a memorial for him at Saint Mark's Poetry Project. But my old literary friend Ross had been dead almost two years when I found out. It was the first occasion when I felt the profound sense of disjunction that one experiences living abroad, how your life is so different from the lives back home in America.

11

In Bernhard Schlink's novel *The Reader* (1997), the narrator mentions a book he read by a Holocaust survivor, but how the book remains opaque as he reads it in English, not German, his native language. He read it thoroughly, he says, but could not "make it one's own." He goes on to say, "It remained alien, in the way that language is alien" (117). That is how I have always read Ross Feld's novels: *in the way that language remains alien.* Seemingly realistic on the surface, nonetheless, this is really a ruse, for all his novels are like Jack Spicer's book *The Heads of the Town up to the Aether* (1962). Ross Feld's novels really are as odd as Apollinaire's or Mallarmé's poetry. Perhaps *odd* is not the right word, and yet I think maybe it is: unusual or unexpected, strange. But it also means occasional and spare. Language becomes alien—foreign, unfamiliar, or unacceptable—when it brings attention to itself, taking us away from the storyline, the characters, the mood of a piece of writing. Yet this is exactly what all the great modernist writers have done—to have it both ways. They are storytellers and poets of language, and this is true from Joyce to Faulkner, from Virginia Woolf to Gertrude Stein; they make us stand outside their narratives to admire or to experience consternation or wonderment about their language. Poets play this game better than anyone. They make us self-consciously aware of their language, particularly those poets whom Ross Feld admired—Apollinaire, Mallarmé, and Baudelaire. But the contemporary poets whom Feld liked also possessed this self-conscious manner in their poetry writing as witness Jack Spicer or Gilbert Sorrentino. Or even Feld's later poet of choice—Eugenio Montale.

Montale believed that memory was a literary genre before writing, and of this idea, Feld observes:

> There's little of the sands-running-out ruefulness to these observations. Sad they are, but the lack of regret, which some have read as posture, I read as a sort of welcome weightlessness that floats the poet toward heretofore unreachable conclusions. Such as: if time is nothing but something presentness, memory can be valued as much for its inefficiency as its efficiency: *you can sometimes forget to forget.* ("Montale")

Feld ends these observations on Montale by quoting from the poem, "Domande senza riposta":

> Non ho avuto purtroppo che la parola,
> qualche cosa che approssima ma non tocca
>
> All I have had unfortunately is the word,
> something which comes close but doesn't touch

I have used Ross Feld's essays in a way they do not deserve. They have been employed as a kind of torch to illuminate his novels. In fact, I have used his poems in the same way. Though I liked his poems enormously when we both were young and at the Poetry Project, and I have enjoyed revisiting them more than thirty years later, I really have used them to elucidate the novels, which are so much richer and more complex than the poems, not to mention being more original. But the essays are another matter entirely. I have reservations about deconstructing his literary and critical essays to illustrate the fiction because the essays finally are what I see as Feld's finest achievement. In our generation, Ross Feld was not so much conscience as he was our intelligence, the one who read and knew everything, the one whose opinions were not so much beautiful as they were correct. Even when I disagreed with Feld—and the fact is I didn't often disagree with his essays or ideas—I ultimately see his point-of-view as being valid, as representing a kind of thorough-goingness, unearthing, in his way, everything that needs such discovery and exposure.

So many writers from the Poetry Project could have been nothing but poets. Ross Feld could have been anything he wanted, including a doctor or a lawyer, a businessman or even a rabbi. He chose to be a writer. That he was an amazing prose writer, I have no doubt. That his novels are very good, I also do not doubt, once they are understood as being the realism of a poet, and finally are books about language as much as they are about university friends, cancer patients, and middle-aged Jewish men. The essays, on the other hand, operate on several important levels. They are propelled by Feld's intelligence, his sensibility; and by his prose gifts—fluid, graceful, even lyrical at times. Robert Creeley is not merely a great poet, he is "a voice, a choice, a poet" ("Fate" 113). Montale was not simply the greatest contemporary Italian poet, he was an "eelish maestro," and he was "object-oriented . . . even at the heights of his most trance-like purifications" ("Montale"). About Baudelaire, Feld wrote: " '*Un Voyage a Cythere*' (A Voyage to Cythera): a Great Pyramid of literary history which, recalled in memory, seems firmly enough built of black marble—and in re-encounter turns out to be of packed volcanic sand" ("Egress and Regress" 41).

Because Feld was first and foremost a poet, he constantly reverted to the tricks that poets employed, particularly metaphors and tropes. The most complicated ideas were made understandable when Feld reduced them to some metaphoric turn.

Once again, I return to Charles Olson, alluding to Keats's "proposition that a man's life . . . is an allegory" (qtd. in Clark 254).

Ross Feld possessed a poet's gift for metaphor and allegroy. He also had a poet's concision, and nowhere was this more evident than in an essay he wrote on Apollinaire. In this piece, he reduces Apollinaire's complex life into one astonishing, Jamesian sentence. "Language and culture were continually beckoning him into the tightest jams: Monte Carlo (where, as a boy, the Polish-Italian bastard born in Rome learns French—and life-as-risk?); La Sante prison (six days, accused falsely of complicity in the theft of the *Mona Lisa*); the war-time trenches of the Champagne" ("Headless, with Flares").

Tropes and metaphors are one thing; so is a poet's concision in Feld's prose. But Feld is a twofold writer, not just dazzling us with his language, he also impresses with his thoughts. Often he braids both of these angles of pursuit into one manifesto. In that same Apollinaire essay I encountered the following observation by Feld.

A poem like *"Les Colchiques"* could employ the blunted mood, the spoiling modifier, with which French poetry and painting had been quite merrily objectifying self-pity for fifty years:

> De pre est eneneux mais joli en automne
> Le vaches y paissant
> Lentement s'empoisonnent
> Le colchique couleur de cerne et de lilas
> Y fleurit tes yeux sont comme cette fleur-la
> Violatres comme leur cerne et comme cet automne
> Et ma vie pour tes yeux lentement s'empoisonne

William Meredith's translation:

> In fall the fields are poisonous but fair
> Where slowly poisoning the cattle graze.
> The meadow saffron, *colchicum*, thrives there,
> Color of lilacs and the circles under eyes.
> My life pastures so on the autumn hue
> Of your eyes and slowly poisons itself too.

—while the next or previous poem might be *"Le Pont Mirabeau"* or *"Les Spins"* or *"Automne"* or *"Signe"*: crooned lyrics (Apollinaire insisted he composed much of his work to wandering little melodies of his own creation; friends bore out the assertion, as would anyone with half an ear who reads the French aloud) which hug as close to the conditions of pure affectionless song as any of Villon, Nerval, Verlaine; the uncookedness of some of the feelings expressed startles us to this day.

There are many reasons to be impressed by this writing, not the least of which is its observation and its inherent intelligence and breadth of literacy and feeling. Metaphors and tropes abound, although in this instance, concision is thrown to the wind. Instead, a brilliantly snaking sentence unravels itself, Jamesian or Proustian in its intent. I marvel at the fact that all of this passage is literally *one long sentence*. I had said earlier in this final section on Ross Feld's life and work that his essays operate on several important levels, one of them being his gift for writing itself, its grace and fluidity. But his second gift is no less remarkable, and that is the gravity of his prose, a weight given all that he writes by the sheer force of the intelligence behind the observations, the engine behind the metaphors and the tropes and the concision.

In Ross Feld's essays, form and content merge in that projective field that Charles Olson wrote about. Breath and syllable form a coherency in Feld's essays. In Charles Olson's "Projective Verse," the poet writes that "FORM IS NEVER MORE THAN AN EXTENSION OF CONTENT" (240). Yet Ross Feld's essays show that the best writing merges form and content into a coherent whole, a totality bonded by significance and substance. In writing about my dear old friend Ross Feld that is what I now come away with: his lyrical intelligence was equal to anyone's poetry or intelligence. But his rudimentary, everyday intelligence was equal to no one's because it was on a plane by itself. This was the literary intelligence of my generation, and his literary and intellectual brilliance was unparalleled.

Yet saying that, I can hear Ross Feld answering, "Well, that is what I do." Of course, he would not merely be making a statement of fact. He would be alluding to a great philosopher, for Feld liked to quote Wittgenstein in this matter. The great Austrian philosopher observed: "This is simply what I do" ("Talking about Objectivism").

Notes

[1] These biograxphical details were supplied to me by Feld's widow, Ellen and by his childhood friends, including Larry Merrill and Archie Rand.

[2] Both Lyman Gilmore's biography of Joel Oppenheimer and Daniel Kane's chronicle of the 1960s downtown poetry scene amply detail these two artists' and writers' hangouts.

[3] Endorsement on the jacket copy of *Guston in Time*.

[4] I am indebted to Feld's widow, Ellen, and his childhood friend, Larry Merrill, for this and other personal information about Ross Feld.

[5] Herbert Leibowitz, editor of *Parnassus,* provided me with most of the essays that Ross Feld published in his magazine as well as other ones which he had in his possession. I often quote from the unedited manuscript throughout this piece, not the published essay, though, as Feld was preparing this manuscript for publication before he died, and in that case, it is more up to date than, say, an essay that was published in *Parnassus* many years earlier.

[6] Larry Merrill, Feld's best friend from childhood onward, provided me with this information in interviews at his home in Rochester, New York, 16-18 October 2004. Merrill also provided me with Feld's last CV, which contained his employment information.

[7] Although I always presumed that Guy Lewis was a pastiche of several characters, ostensibly the poet Harry Lewis, who in turn was reprised in the character of Lou Henry, too, this kind of detective work invariably is fruitless and invariably incorrect. Now I see that the name Guy Lewis is a kind of play on words which Sorrentino employed regarding Fielding Dawson, Black Mountain alumnus, visual artist and writer. When Fee, as Dawson usually

was called, died in 2002, all the obituaries I read gave his complete name as Guy Fielding Lewis Dawson, i.e., Fielding Dawson equals Guy Lewis.

[8] Mednick was a playwright who, along with Sam Shepard, often had his plays produced at Theater Genesis at St. Mark's Church.

[9] People usually thought Leo was based on Joel Oppenheimer, and Oppenheimer believed this so much that, although he and Sorrentino were close friends and both eventually lived in Westbeth, the artists' and writers' coop in Greenwich Village, Joel never spoke to Sorrentino again. In Oppenheimer's vitriolic dedication to his book, *the wrong season* (1973), about the New York Mets baseball team, he writes:

> this book is for
> walter o'malley
> and
> gilbert sorrentino

—a reference to the fact that Walter O'Malley, who owned the Brooklyn Dodgers, unforgivably took the team from Brooklyn and moved them, quite successfully, to Los Angeles. The implication is that Sorrentino was a turncoat like O'Malley, untrustworthy and never to be forgiven. Sadly, Oppenheimer carried this vendetta with him to the grave, and as far as I know Sorrentino has never softened his excoriating appraisal of Oppenheimer as a failed drunk of great initial poetic promise. I have often thought of writing a play about these two warring poets, and like Lucky and Pozzo showing up in *Waiting for Godot*, intercut their feud with one between two writers like Walter Abish, the eye-patch-wearing experimental prose writer, and someone like Marvin Cohen, another experimentalist, who was nearly completely deaf.

[10] I would refer the reader to a delightful correspondence with this world of Max's Kansas City. The Andy Warhol Museum in Pittsburgh has a room that replicates the upstairs backroom at Max's. You may also take one of those sequential photographs from a booth in a basement of the museum, something so tacky and so right. I went to this museum with the writer Richard Elman and his wife Alice during a break in the Associated Writing Programs' conference in 1995. It is also worth noting that Chamberlain's sponge sculpture, whether intentionally or not, eventually was picked into nonexistence by the bar's customers.

[11] According to Larry Merrill, "Ross had scoliosis as a teen, and he was in a body cast for a long time. That's when he began his reading and writing and listening to music. When he got out of the cast, he began to play a banjo in Washington Square Park." In conversation, 17 October 2004, Rochester, New York.

[12] The author spoke with Tom Weatherly about this information (1999) at the Strand Bookstore on 12th Street and Broadway in Manhattan where Weatherly worked for many years

[13] I am indebted to Jerry Joth for many of these names.

[14] *The World* was edited by various poets during its history, but initially edited by Joel Sloman, then by Joel Oppenheimer, Anne Waldman, and Lewis Warsh, and finally by the last two poets exclusively.

[15] From Feld's "Jack Spicer: The Apostle's Grudge at the Persistence

of Poetry," part of a manuscript tentatively entitled *The Spilled Drop*, a collection of essays that RF was putting together at his death (inedited).

[16] The "field" of course is the one Charles Olson alludes to in his essay, "Projective Verse." "First, some simplicities that a man learns, if he works in OPEN, or what can also be called COMPOSITION BY FIELD, as opposed to inherited line, stanza, over-all form, what is the 'old' base of the non-projective" (239).

[17] In *Ivanov*, we encounter Yevgeny Lvov, a young local doctor. There is Yevgeny Sergeyevich Dorn, the local doctor, in *The Seagull*. And in *Uncle Vanya*, we find Mikhail Lvovich Astrov, a doctor. The army doctor, Chebutykin, inhabits *The Three Sisters* drama. These are not central characters to the storyline. But they are central to the lives of the other characters. In an odd way, they resemble the Greek chorus, the voice of the citizenry, the voice of the golden mean.

[18] In a 23 March 1978 letter to the author, Feld writes: "We've got a nice piece of hotcha news ourselves: Ellen got into medical school, right here at Downstate in Brooklyn."

[19] Henry Weinfield has told me that Feld died of pneumonia after cancer treatments lowered his immune system's tolerance (Letter 25 Oct. 2004).

[20] Robert Duncan, like Charles Olson and Ezra Pound, often used phonetic spellings such as "askt" instead of "asked."

[21] The word "something" has probably not worked so hard since Joe Cocker sang the Beatles' song, "Something."

[22] In a book I wrote on digital time (*Circles End*), I tried to show that the pulse of quartz, highly exact, and unvarying, is always Be-Be-Be-Be . . .

[23] Lenny Bruce often did a routine in a Chinese restaurant in which the waiter tells him how beautiful his showgirl wife is. "Mama, so beautiful!" Then Bruce gets divorced, and goes into the restaurant for dinner. "Where's mama? She so beautiful!" The Chinese waiter goes on and on with his praise of Bruce's ex-wife until the comedian finally says, "We're divorced." Without losing a beat, the waiter says, "Oh, you betta off."

[24] Leo Rosten in *The Joys of Yiddish* (1968) defines a shmuck as an ornament or (obscenely) a penis. But in everyday New York City parlance—even outside the purlieus of the Jewish world—it has come to mean "a dope, a jerk, a boob; a clumsy, bumbling fellow." Charles Shapes is that: a clumsy bumbling fellow.

Works Cited

Babel, Isaac. *You Must Know Everything*. New York: Dell, 1970.

Berry, Wendell. Unpublished manuscript.

Blackburn, Paul. *The Collected Poems of Paul Blackburn*. Ed. Edith Jarolim. New York: Persea, 1985.

Chekhov, Anton. *The Plays of Anton Chekhov*. Trans. Paul Schmidt. New York: HarperFlamingo, 1997.

Clark, Tom. *Charles Olson: The Allegory of a Poet's Life*. New York: Norton, 1991.

Creeley, Robert. *Selected Poems*. Berkeley: U of California P, 1991.

Dante. "Sonetto III (da Il Canzoniere)." *Italian Poetry: An Anthology.* Ed. and trans. Arturo Vivante. Wellfleet: Delphinium Press, 1996. 18-19.

Feld, Ross. "Braving the Depths as Man and Boy: Two Novels of the Seventies." Unpublished manuscript.

—. "Egress and Regress." *Parnassus* 11.2 (1983-1984): 39-40.

—. "The Fate of Doing Nothing Right." *Parnassus* 12.1 (1984): 95-122.

—. *Guston in Time.* New York: Counterpoint, 2003.

—. "Headless, with Flares." Unpublished manuscript.

—. "I Am Like Aspirin." Unpublished manuscript.

—. "Jack Spicer: The Apostle's Grudge at the Persistence of Poetry." Unpublished manuscript.

—. Letter to M. G. Stephens. 23 March 1978.

—. Letter to M. G. Stephens. 25 June 1982.

—. Letter to M. G. Stephens. 12 Aug. 1983.

—. "Lowghost to Lowghost." *Parnassus* 4.2 (1976): 5-30.

—. "Montale." Unpublished Manuscript.

—. *Only Shorter.* San Francisco: North Point Press, 1982.

—. "Oz Is Home." http://www.counterpointpress.com.

—. *Plum Poems.* Highlands: Jargon Society, 1972.

—. "Relievers." Unpublished manuscript.

—. *Shapes Mistaken.* San Francisco: North Point Press, 1989.

—. "The Spilled Drop." Unpublished manuscript.

—. "The Swarming, the Pure." *Parnassus* 23.1-2 (1998): 51-62.

—. "Taking Time." *Parnassus* 15 (1990): 7-15.

—. "Talking about Objectivism at Notre Dame." Unpublished manuscript.

—. "Timing and Spacing the As If: Poetic Prose and Prosaic Poetry." *Parnassus* 20.1-2 (1995): 11-31.

—. *Years Out.* New York: Knopf, 1973.

—. *Zwilling's Dream.* New York: Counterpoint, 1999.

Gilman, Richard. *Chekhov's Plays: An Opening into Eternity.* New Have: Yale UP, 1995.

Gilmore, Lyman. *Don't Touch the Poet: The Life and Times of Joel Oppenheimer.* Jersey City: Talisman House, 1998.

Gollin, Andrea. Rev. of *Zwilling's Dream*, by Ross Feld. *Washington Post* 7 Nov. 1999: 7.

Howard, Richard. Introduction. *Guston in Time.* New York: Counterpoint, 2003. 1-5.

Hynes, James. Rev. of *Zwilling's Dream*, by Ross Feld. *Boston Review* 1999-2000.

Kane, Daniel. *All Poets Welcome: The Lower East Side Poetry Scene in the 1960s.* Berkeley: U of California P, 2003.

Kart, Larry. Rev. of *Only Shorter*, by Ross Feld. *Chicago Tribune* 29 Sept. 1982.

Kott, Jan. *Shakespeare Our Contemporary.* Trans. Boleslaw Taborski. Garden City: Doubleday, 1964.

Mewshaw, Michael. Rev. of *Years Out,* by Ross Feld. *New York Times Book Review* 4 Nov. 1973: 80.

O'Hara, Frank. *Lunch Poems.* San Francisco: City Lights, 1964.

Olson, Charles. "Projective Verse." *Collected Prose / Charles Olson.* Ed. Donald Allen and Benjamin Friedlander. Berkeley: U of California P, 1997. 239-49.

Oppenheimer, Joel. *the wrong season.* Indianapolis: Bobbs-Merrill, 1973.

Pritchett, V. S. *Chekhov: A Spirit Set Free.* New York: Vintage, 1988.

Rev. of *Only Shorter,* by Ross Feld. *Best Sellers* Aug. 1982: 170.

Roth, Philip. *Shop Talk: A Writer and His Colleagues and Their Work.* London: Vintage, 2000.

Rubins, Josh. Rev. of *Only Shorter,* by Ross Feld. *Kirkus Reviews* 15 June 2001: 1.

Sanders, Erica. Rev. of *Zwilling's Dream,* by Ross Feld. *New York Times Book Review* 14 Nov. 1999: 25.

Schlink, Bernhard. *The Reader.* London: Phoenix, 1997.

Schmidt, Paul. Introduction. *The Plays of Anton Chekhov.* Trans. Paul Schmidt. New York: HarperFlamingo, 1997.

Shearer, Cynthia. Rev. of *Zwilling's Dream,* by Ross Feld. *Hungry Mind Review* Fall 1999: 36.

Silber, Joan. Rev. of *Only Shorter,* by Ross Feld. *Village Voice* 22 June 1982: 47.

Sorrentino, Gilbert. *Imaginative Qualities of Actual Things.* 1971. Elmwood Park, IL: Dalkey Archive Press, 1991.

Sontag, Susan. *Where the Stress Falls.* London: Vintage, 2003.

Spicer, Jack. *A Controversy of Poets.* Ed. Paris Leary and Robert Kelly. Garden City: Doubleday, 1965.

—. *The Collected Books of Jack Spicer.* Ed. Robin Blaser. Los Angeles: Black Sparrow, 1975.

Stark, Bradford. *An Unlikely but Noble Kingdom.* New York: Rainbow Press, 1974.

Stephens, Michael. *Circles End.* New York: Spuyten Duyvil, 1982.

Trachtenberg, Peter. Rev. of *Zwilling's Dream,* by Ross Feld. *Forward* 1999.

Weinfield, Henry. E-mail to M. G. Stephens. 15 Sept. 2004.

—. Letter to M. G. Stephens. 25 Oct. 2004.

—. *The Sorrows of Eros and Other Poems.* Notre Dame: U of Notre Dame P, 1999.

Williams, William Carlos. *Selected Poems.* New York: New Directions, 1969.

A Ross Feld Checklist

Plum Poems. Highlands: Jargon Society, 1972.
Years Out. New York: Knopf, 1973.
Only Shorter. San Francisco: North Point Press, 1982.
Shapes Mistaken. San Francisco: North Point Press, 1989.
Zwilling's Dream. New York: Counterpoint, 1999.
Guston in Time. New York: Counterpoint, 2003.

Ross Feld
(Photograph by Larry Merrill)

Book Reviews

Gilbert Sorrentino. *Lunar Follies*. Coffee House Press, 2005. 143 pp. Paper: $14.00.

Sorrentino is a master, but a particular specialty of his has always been illustrating the "eight million ways to step off the cliff"—or lose one's soul—in the pursuit of art. No one is better at showing us how sentiment and self-importance go wrong, or at illuminating the real tragedy behind the sham art he excoriates with such precision: namely, that the desperation we all have to find some kind of aesthetic unity in our unhappy lives—and our concomitant desire for self-expression—has filled the world with so much mind-numbing *garbage*. One would also have to look back to Pope to find Sorrentino's equal as far as making poetry out of the "wooden language" of critical discourse ("disarmingly irreverent sophistication," etc.). But though *Lunar Follies* is, in this sense, a return to familiar ground, Sorrentino's not after big game. Unlike the coruscating mediocrities and almost-rans that populate earlier works, the fifty-three fictional artists and gallery shows cataloged here (each named for locations on the lunar surface and arranged alphabetically) are, for the most part, lost causes from the get-go, hermetically absurd and viewed obliquely, as though in passing—postcards from the moon. Their work is not too much more fantastic than the realities of conceptual art (I wonder has Sorrentino heard about the performance artist Shishaldin petitioning the French government for permission to posthumously marry Lautréamont?), and that the artists themselves are letches admired more for their fame than their accomplishments can come as no surprise. While the satire in *Lunar Follies* is the easiest element to engage, what's most affecting about the book are the views it gives of an arid but magical world, unique to Sorrentino, where Kafka's Odradek is put on display in a museum ("preserved in . . . a solution of equal parts hydrogen peroxide, lemon juice, and triple-distilled 160-proof Ukrainian vodka"), where lost lovers can wander through a limpid collage equal parts Ernst and Joseph Cornell, and where—despite the cruelty and vapidity of the art world and world-at-large—our need for beauty can wind up requited even in the schlock of tin pigs and terrible songs. [Jeremy M. Davies]

Boris Vian. *Autumn in Peking*. Trans. Paul Knobloch. TamTam Books, 2005. 283 pp. Paper: $18.00.

Virtually unknown to the English-speaking world, Boris Vian's fiction remains highly popular in his native France. *L'Automne à Pékin* is his fourth novel, and it was originally published in 1947. Contrary to what the title indicates, it takes place in an imaginary desert land called Exopotamie, where the sun emits black rays and an ill-matched collection of eccentric characters is trying to build a railroad. Whether this project is eventually accomplished is a matter of indifference to both the novel's characters and its narrator. As in his third novel *Foam of the Daze* (1947), Vian's absurdist humor highlights the pointless and demoralizing effects of modern work. It also serves as a tonal counterpoint to the tragic love triangle that comprises the other main plot thread. What's most characteristic of this novel are its nonsensical events, its unpredictable dialogues and interactions, and the random and careless acts of violence that its characters both suffer and commit. Neither shocking nor even darkly humorous, Vian's scenes of violence have a hilarious effect. It's not unusual for a character who has had his hip broken in five places to exclaim, "If you only knew how happy I am! . . ." Although these characters certainly feel pain, they don't seem to resent being poisoned, or getting maimed by uncooperative vehicles, or having their limbs sawn off. With a slapstick exuberance reminiscent of the Marx Brothers, this novel is much more fun to read than countless other modern experiments in narrative form. At its end, all that's left are ruined romances, several dead or vanished characters, and a renewed plan to start up the railroad project again with a different set of workers. It's all completely devoid of purpose, but Vian provides exactly the kind of pleasurable and surprising purposelessness that art is supposed to offer. [Thomas Hove]

Ian McEwan. *Saturday*. Nan A. Talese/Doubleday, 2005. 294 pp. $26.00.

As if to verify W. H. Auden's claim that "Poetry makes nothing happen," a poem keeps a thug from doing something dreadful to the family whose house he has invaded. The fact that neither Baxter, the would-be rapist and murderer, nor Henry Perowne, a leading neurosurgeon, recognizes the mesmerizing verse as "Dover Beach" when Perowne's daughter, Daisy, recites it also illustrates the closing of the English mind. A circadian novel that confines itself to one eventful twenty-four-hour cycle, *Saturday* begins before dawn on 15 February 2003, as Perowne awakens to what seems a terrorist attack from the skies above London. On his way to a fierce squash match against a medical colleague, Perowne drives past a massive demonstration against the war in Iraq and into a confrontation with the odious owner of a car that grazes his. After visiting his mother, though she has lost the ability to recognize him, Perowne returns home for dinner with his wife, two grown children, and his father-in-law, a famous poet. Unlike *Atonement*, a metafiction about a novelist's attempt to rewrite history, *Saturday* is less postmodern than post-9/11, an evocation of a perilous world in which ignorant armies clash by night and day. In McEwan's previous novel, an early manuscript by his character Briony Tallis is rejected because it "owed a little too much to the technique of Mrs. Woolf," and *Saturday* appears indebted to *Mrs. Dalloway* for its premise. Yet McEwan has claimed Saul Bellow as Muse, and this book is more akin to *Seize the Day* as well as those Bellovian fictions in which nasty urban realities intrude on an urbane man's privileged existence. It is veritably Zolaesque in the way McEwan absorbs and flaunts his research into neurosurgery to make credible Perowne's professional labors and his meditations on how mind meets brain. But it is the melancholy ghost of Matthew Arnold who haunts *Saturday*, which concludes its diurnal dash through a day lacking certitude, peace, and help for pain with the solace of two lovers, Perowne in bed with his wife, Rosalind: "There's always this, is one of his remaining thoughts. And then: there's only this." [Steven G. Kellman]

Javier Marías. *Your Face Tomorrow, Volume 1: Fever and Spear*. Trans. Margaret Jull Costa. New Directions, 2005. 387 pp. $24.95.

Jacques Deza, the narrator of Javier Marías's newly translated *Fever and Spear*, is languishing personally and professionally. Estranged from his wife and family, Deza works for the BBC in London. His real talent is for espionage or, as Deza himself puts it, the interpretation "of people: of their behaviour and reactions, of their inclinations and characters and powers of endurance." Deza gets a chance to exercise his spying skills after he is recruited by a mysterious surveillance organization. But these familiar spy novel elements are only the beginning; they are not part of the novel's plot so much as a frame for Marías's far-ranging meditations on history, memory, and identity. The narrative is organized around several engrossing set-pieces told out of chronological order; these include the dinner party where Deza is recruited, the Spanish civil war, World War II, and a chase scene in which the narrator may or may not be pursued by a woman walking her dog. Spying becomes an extended metaphor for the human desire to impose order, however false, on events without an inherent pattern. "Life is not recountable," muses Sir Peter Wheeler, a former colleague of Deza's at Oxford, "and it seems extraordinary that men have spent all the centuries we know anything about devoted to doing just that, determined to tell what cannot be told." The overall effect recalls the cerebral play of Borges, the dark humor of Pynchon, and the meditative lyricism of Proust. *Fever and Spear* is the first volume of *Your Face Tomorrow*. With the second volume, *Dance and Dream*, slated for publication from New Directions next year, Marias promises to make a substantial contribution to the growing body of philosophical genre novels. [Pedro Ponce]

Julio Cortázar. *The Diary of Andreas Fava*. Trans. Anne McLean. Archipelago Books, 2005. Paper: $14.00.

Granted, *The Diary of Andres Fava* isn't *Hopscotch*. Nor is it *62: A Model Kit*. Yet for fans of Cortázar it's a reason to celebrate, since it's the first new work of his to appear in English since 2000 when New Directions brought out *Final Exam*, Cortázar's first novel, and our introduction to his character Andres Fava. In fact, *The Diary* was originally written as part of *Final Exam*, but was pulled from the novel and saved for separate publication. Basically, this book is what its title suggests: a diary of Andres Fava's reflections on his reading, his dreams, conversations with his friends, music. There's no real plot, but that's beside the point. What's interesting about this book is the way it constructs a character behind these diverse observations and sentiments. In a way it's odd; the varied tone and similar elements make it seem as if this were Cortázar's diary, which in a way demonstrates the effectiveness of the writing. This "diary" serves as a sort of playground for the developing Cortázar. It's in this informal element that he's able to toy around with language and ideas for stories. Sometimes the writing falls short and is a bit immature—as in one bit about how power corrupts—but there are some brilliant passages, like the "list of received ideas that circulate in my family," which include "Americans are abnormal, sickly beings because they only eat canned food," and "Children speak when hens piss. (My great-grandmother's phrase.)" Even more telling of the purposes for which Cortázar uses this "diary" is the inclusion of a passage describing a story written by Andres Fava that, years later, will become Cortázar's famous "Continuity of Parks." Although occasionally uneven, this is still a valuable book for the way in which the reader is privy to the development of one of the twentieth century's greatest authors. [Chad W. Post]

Bilge Karasu. *The Garden of Departed Cats*. Trans. Aron Aji. New Directions, 2003. 256 pp. Paper. $18.95.

Nameless characters move about a cryptic text-scape, an elusive environment constructed from the lyric energy of language, a symbolic-world coaxed into depth, plots unhinged from causality, rent by intrusive absurdities—these are disquieting fables that are breathtakingly enthralling. The twelve tales of Bilge Karasu, the late Turkish writer, compel by their elusiveness. More Kafakesque fables, they suggest defining human compulsions—compassion, guilt, dependence, hope, humiliation, joy—by reconfiguring those compelling energies into character-creatures within enigmatic tales rendered with an indefinable urgency (the translation is superb, the lines sing, emphatic and graceful). A fisherman's prize catch slowly gnaws its way up his arm. A medieval monk conceals a carnivorous creature within the folds of his traveling tunic that tears his flesh. A young acrobat can see an insidiously expanding mole on the face of those marked for imminent death. The potent leaf of a rare flower renders its consumer incapable of lying. Without resorting to the tiresome standby of traditional storytelling, Karasu constructs form-intensive texts that calibrate the force of his profound (and indignant) moral imagination. In narrative counterargument, Karasu intercuts quasi-realistic vignettes of a traveler-writer intrigued by a handsome stranger he chances to see while visiting an ancient city somewhere in the Mediterranean basin. This sustained narrative of sublimated eroticism is enhanced when both men participate in a living chess game that the city ritualistically stages every ten years—the game itself is ringed with anxiety as the players are armed even as the moves foretell horrific violence. The subtle shuttling between the growing anxieties of the traveler and the cycle of dream-parables creates a resonance, an anatomy of obsession and heightened emotionalism, that illuminates—as such texts have since Borges—the enchanting human energies that narrative cannot tidy into explanation. [Joseph Dewey]

Steve Erickson. *Our Ecstatic Days*. Simon & Schuster, 2005. 317 pp. $24.00.

Linked to Erickson's *The Sea Came in at Midnight* (1999), *Our Ecstatic Days* continues the story of Kristin, following her through several shifts in identity and into becoming a mother. As is often the case with Erickson's connected books, the world of the previous novels has gone through unexpected shifts, with a strange lake welling up in the middle of Los Angeles and swallowing the city, a lake Kristin comes increasingly to feel has come after her child. In an attempt to neutralize the threat she dives in but, when she resurfaces, finds her boy has disappeared. In fact what has occurred is a moment where two realities, equally strange, seem to have leaked into one another, something it takes Kristin herself years (or minutes, depending what reality one is in) to figure out. As the novel progresses, the characters split and shift identities, a boy takes on the characteristics of an owl, people addicted to their past begin indulging in "lapsinthe" trying to bring on memory lapses. Point of view shifts constantly, a political upheaval occurs, buildings appear out of nowhere, and a small toy takes on enormous significance. The narrative splits too, a single long sentence slipping through the last two-thirds of the book, cutting a wake through the other story. The typography of the text itself, as in Mark Danielewski's *House of Leaves*, becomes palpable, inflected (and infected) by the narrative it recounts. Except for the typographical gestures, these are all things that readers of Erickson will recognize, but in *Our Ecstatic Days* they approach a complexity and expansion that goes beyond Erickson's previous work. Despite his real interest in experimentation and innovation, there's a human core to the book, which circles around how humans cope with loss, particularly the loss of a child. Indeed, *Our Ecstatic Days* is a visionary work, full of stylistic risk, but with a concomitant emotional payoff that very few books, experimental or otherwise, ever manage to achieve. [Brian Evenson]

Robert Majzels. *Apikoros Sleuth*. The Mercury Press, 2005. 55 (folio) pp. Paper: $15.95.

If Dashiell Hammett had written the stream-of-consciousness detective novel he once claimed he would like to, and that manuscript had been passed on to Edmond Jabès for severe line editing, then stolen by early-career Samuel Beckett to be dosed with bursts of hot humor and jaunty textures, then revisited by late-career Samuel Beckett for cooling and quieting, then borrowed by the late poet Jackson Mac Low to undergo various destabilizing textual operations, we might, if we could lay our hands on the resultant hybrid wonder, have some sense of the baffling, polymorphic territory limned in Robert Majzels stunning antinovel, *Apikoros Sleuth*. As the publisher describes it, *Sleuth* is "a murder mystery in the form of a Talmudic Inquiry," and there is no question that it is in negotiating the interwoven modes of inquiry (quotation, commentary, elaboration, aside, negation, blood stain, palimpsest, broken form, etc.) that the reader glimpses the mysterious, murderous architecture of Majzel's gesture, in which language is both victim and description of victimization, and in which standard narrative has been put in a compressor and squeezed into more interesting ways of thinking. "Shall we solve this death or that one? Having failed to solve, or represent, or think those millions. This cannot enter your mind. Death is become a problem of degrees. How shall we dispose of it? The question, the difficulty, returned to its place. Where is a qualitative leap? Qu'est-ce qu'un simple meurtre?" Majzel's novel offers up its intriguing verbal conundrums on page after visually stunning page (the book designer at Mercury Press must be resourceful indeed), their individual uniqueness underscoring the emphatic sui generis nature of the project. The reader won't encounter another book like this one anytime soon. [Laird Hunt]

Roberto Calasso. *K.* Trans. Geoffrey Brock. Knopf, 2005. 327 pp. $25.00.

This extended commentary on Franz Kafka's fiction is the fourth installment in a brilliant and highly original series of works that render the distinction between literature and scholarship meaningless. The three other works in Calasso's series are *The Ruin of Kasch* (1983), *The Marriage of Cadmus and Harmony* (1988), and *Ka* (1996). As in his earlier explorations of Greek and Hindu mythology, Calasso interweaves interpretive commentary with his own retellings of Kafka's stories. Instead of attempting to formulate an "all-encompassing interpretation," Calasso's aim is to sustain and enrich "the torment of endless commentary" that Kafka's fiction calls forth. At the center of this study are the literal and metaphorical predicaments of K. from *The Castle* and Joseph K. from *The Trial*. Treating the two novels as counterparts and extensions of each other, Calasso explains how they blend detailed realism and inscrutable myth. He pays special attention to the thematic significance of K.'s and Joseph K.'s "elections" by a mysterious power: "*The Trial* and *The Castle* share a premise: that election and condemnation are *almost* indistinguishable. . . . The elect and the condemned are the chosen, those who are singled out among the many, among everyone." This theme reflects Calasso's own interest in locating the veiled presence of the divine in modern literary experience. He's particularly eloquent when writing about the uncanny effects of Kafka's minimalist style: "behind the formulas of common speech a space suddenly opens where words reverberate and sprout meanings, acquiring an intensity that at times is paralyzing." Calasso assumes that readers will already be familiar with most of Kafka's fiction. But since his retellings of Kafka's tales are so detailed and suggestive, *K.* can also serve as a helpful guide to those who know little about Kafka but need an erudite commentator to open up its complex aesthetic and philosophical dimensions. [Thomas Hove]

William T. Vollmann. *Europe Central.* Viking, 2005. 811 pp. $39.95.

Sixteen months after the initial shock of William T. Vollmann's three thousand-plus page nonfiction opus, *Rising Up and Rising Down*, just as the literary community begins to pick itself up off the canvas, he floors us again, this time with a book of fiction that may be the longest single-author collection of new short stories ever published. Impressive, surely, but given his prodigious output, readers having a hard time keeping pace might be justified in wondering whether he's offering anything other than sheer volume. *Europe Central* emphatically affirms that he is. These thirty-seven stories—arranged, except for the first, in thematic pairs—employ artists, apparatchiks, soldiers, and scientists to explore the competing militaristic societies of mid-twentieth-century Germany and the USSR as they prepare to, and eventually do, tear each other apart in war. The broad outline and public face of history are only suggested (ardent researcher Vollmann flatteringly assumes we've done as much homework as he has) but the personal motivations that drive characters to embrace or reject their cultures of death are lovingly detailed. In this, these stories are of a piece with the rest of Vollmann's oeuvre. His collected works form an investigation of all that is normally considered immoral, most notably prostitution and violence, and here he continues to examine all the varieties of human experience in an attempt to judge what morality truly is. The scale of this latest incarnation of his ongoing project defies critical analysis, especially in such a short review, so one note about the diversity of techniques on display will have to suffice. The point of view is ever-shifting, sometimes a first-person "I" that lives a story, sometimes a third-person eye that floats above, and occasionally, most seductively, a collective "we" that's simultaneously inviting and indicting, just like *Europe Central.* Read it. It stands with Vollmann's best work, and his best work can stand with anyone's. [James Crossley]

Christopher Sorrentino. *Trance.* Farrar, Straus & Giroux, 2005. 516 pp. $26.00.

A little more than twenty years after the fact, the abduction of Patricia Hearst by the Symbionese Liberation Army is an event whose assumption into the realm of docudrama is so complete as to preclude us any imaginative access to the event—a not-uncommon end for many misfortunes since the advent of television, but in this case aided by the already mythical status of the Hearst family and the media-minded tactics of Patty's kidnappers-cum-comrades. It must have been a blow: what wrongheaded Papa

Hearst fought so hard to keep Orson Welles from doing—fictionalizing his life—the world did to his grand daughter with a vengeance, and apparently with her cooperation. (Future generations, finding her in all those John Waters films—subsumed entirely into entertainment—will assume that her ordeal, rebirth, and punishment were all one long audition—as has already been suggested by *Network*.) Now, ten years after his debut novel *Sound on Sound*, Christopher Sorrentino gives us *Trance*, a beautifully successful—indeed, heroic—attempt to restore to us what is surely one of the great American folk stories of the twentieth century. Where his previous book's structure aped the process of recording and mixing a rock song, *Trance*, less obviously, is a full-blown opera—an epic documentary fiction, a post-Coover *In Cold Blood*—presenting a harmony of hundreds of points of view (both protagonists and bystanders get their say), all winningly imperfect, often outright comic: a revolutionary vaudeville starring the SLA and the "fascist insects" of seventies America. *Trance* pokes gentle (and occasionally not-so-gentle) fun at these middle- and upper-class guerrillas—and the culture of continual reinvention and personal empowerment that they've taken to heart even while making "war" on it—all the time affirming that, loony, confused, and ineffective as his rebels may be, "revolutions are acts of supreme creativity," and are thus—however ridiculous, however hopeless, and however tragic—always necessary. [Jeremy M. Davies]

David Ohle. *The Age of Sinatra*. Soft Skull, 2004. 168 pp. Paper: $11.95.

David Ohle's new book begins on "the Sinatra-age pleasure ship *Titanic*," and so establishes from the start an anachronistic universe that looks both backward with empty nostalgia and forward toward an inevitable, disastrous end. The wandering plot follows the character Moldenke through French sewers, on bus rides to see an organ doctor famous for using "French pig," and, well, all over. From bizarre episode to bizarre episode, we are introduced to a world that is a nihilistic parody of our own, an existentialist grotesque ("'Nothing matters,' he says, with an emphasis on the nothing. It's a recurring theme"). And nothing *does* matter here, if only because cultural and individual memory are constantly clean-slated by a form of mass amnesia called "Forgettings." Rumored to be brought about by government-sanctioned media broadcasts, these Forgettings are nonetheless accepted (at times embraced) by the citizenry, in keeping with a theme of negation—more specifically, of hunger for negation, desire for emptiness—that runs through the book. Similarly, we meet human characters only sexually attracted to "neuts," sentient creatures who have "no frame of reference, no cultural traditions." We watch humans snack on green neut glands called "flocculi," and Ohle gives us such satirically suggestive lines as "My flocculus, it's fruiting. Why don't you Americans have a taste of green." The satire here is systematic and at times surprisingly direct. Ohle's humor carries strong whiffs of Burroughs or Pynchon (the comedy of random smothering bureaucracy, names like "Ophelia Balls") but is also deeply entrenched in what Bakhtin calls "the lower bodily stratum." Eating shit is not a figure of speech in this world, nor is it the most disturbing culinary experience a person might have. Not to worry, though. All will soon be forgotten. [Martin Riker]

———————

Yuri Olesha. *Envy*. Trans. Marian Schwartz. Intro. Ken Kalfus. New York Review Books, 2004. 152 pp. Paper: $12.95.

This is a new English translation of a novella by Yuri Olesha (1899-1960) originally published in Russian in 1927. A welcome addition to the admirable NYRB Classics series, it looks at early Soviet society through the bleary eyes of one Nikolai Kavalerov, a young, sozzled dropout, who is rescued from the gutter by a middle-aged functionary, Andrei Babichev, Director of the Food Industry Trust. Babichev, who personifies the purblind utopianism of the communist regime, cuts a truly grotesque figure as the votary of social planning, epitomized in his quest for the perfect mass-produced sausage. Kavalerov, the jaundiced narrator, finds the regime and its activities monstrous: "A piece of lousy sausage was directing my movements, my will. I didn't want that!" Yet Kavalerov is himself an object of satire: like Dostoyevsky's Underground Man, he seems in danger of choking on his own spleen. This odd little book weighs collective ideology against individualism, caricaturing both. We can add Olesha to the long list of Russian writers who have investigated problems of freedom and conformism without offering prescriptions. The ramshackle idiom of *Envy* recalls Mikhail Bulgakov's sublime *Master and Margarita*, although Olesha's approach is more narrowly satirical. In the 1920s, Bulgakov and Olesha both wrote for *Gudok* (The Whistle), a newspaper for railway workers, which also published the young Isaak Babel. The decade that followed saw Olesha's output reviled by the Stalinist establishment and he disappeared from view as a prose writer, although he lived until 1960, working for the Soviet film industry and as a translator. Readers interested in the exuberant literary culture that challenged the Soviet system in the twenties will find *Envy* worth their attention. [Philip Landon]

———————

Sándor Márai. *Casanova in Bolzano*. Trans. by George Szirtes. Knopf, 2004. 204 pp. $22.00.

In Márai's striking incarnation, the legendary lover appears as a sleeping wonder whose mere presence frightens and bewitches the village of Bolzano. Being Casanova is no mean feat, yet as the awakening hero erupts with laughter, scaring some prying servant wenches half to death, he becomes larger than life, worthy of his name. Freshly escaped from the Inquisition in Venice, Casanova and Balbi, his factotum, lay over in Bolzano en route to Munich. Casanova's appeal to an old patron wins enough credit to outfit him for a new start. A winsome chambermaid at his inn will join the duo. But the town belongs to the duke of Parma, to whom Casanova lost the duel that landed him in prison, the duel over Francesca, whom both men coveted but the duke took as his own. After intercepting a message from his wife to her old lover requesting a meeting, Parma makes a surprise call on his rival to gloss the letter's insinuations, a nonpareil of sustained critical exegesis. His vehemence nearly persuades Casanova to accept his terms when another unexpected caller, Francesca herself, puts to shame her husband's interpretation of her desire. Still, this tryst is not to be. Even the chambermaid demurs; she will no longer fly. Momentarily taken aback, Casanova at length resumes his way, for his is the path of destiny. Overcoming the temptation to return his antagonist into the hands of the Inquisition, the aged Duke's duel of wits with Casanova displays the force of the notorious rake's attraction. Yet this Casanova cannot love, at least not in the romantic manner of popular sentiment, depending instead on presence of mind, wit, and supreme confidence to sway ordinary mortals. Written in the 1940s, Márai's stunning portrait of a celebrity confronting his bubble of reputation is a tour-de-force not to be missed. [Michael Pinker]

Blaise Cendrars. *Gold: The Marvellous History of General John Augustus Sutter*. Trans. Nina Rootes. Peter Owen, 2003. 128 pp. Paper: $18.95. (Reprint)

Gold is Blaise Cendrars's leanest novel, written mainly in brief lines and compact imagery, a lesson in economy and precision that minimalists would envy. It is also a masterly act of mythologizing. Cendrars transforms the historical Sutter, on whose California property was found the gold that launched the Gold Rush of 1848, into a larger-than-life character whose ambition, drive, and bloody-mindedness encounter the similar ambition and greed of those who want to wrest money out of his land. Sutter left the Old World to make his name and a fortune in the New, and invents paradise using productive farmland, thereby creating a self-sustaining fiefdom, an idyllic place for everyone except the slaves and Indians. "And after having ventured all, risked all, dared all and created for himself a way of life, he is ruined by the discovery of gold-mines on his lands," as Cendrars laconically puts it. Sutter's political maneuvering with Mexican and Washington politicians, as well as the brutal assault on his property and family by "stampeding mobs of people," are crisply set down in this mix of morality play, Greek tragedy, and reportage. Published originally in 1925, translated into over a dozen languages, and rarely out of print, this was Cendrars's first novel, written after he decided that poetry, to which he had devoted himself since 1911, held no more challenge. He would go on to write four other novels by 1930. Aside from its sheer readability, this "marvellous history" is an essential work in discovering how Cendrars combined the terseness of his poetry with his idea of what the novel form could do. "Hinge" novels are often of historical interest only; *Gold* is of interest for its own sake. [Jeff Bursey]

Antoine Volodine. *Minor Angels*. Trans. and preface Jordan Stump. Univ. of Nebraska Press, 2004. 166 pp. $25.00.

The Young Marble Giants song "Final Day" could serve as *Minor Angels*'s soundtrack: a single sci-fi theremin note hovers over a quavering organ, muted, downpicked guitar, and a plain but lovely female voice that sings about the final day, the world lighting up for the last time only to fall into endless night "for the people who never had a say." The song ends all too soon, and the theremin drops off as if snuffed. It's the sound of the world ending not with a bang or whimper but a resigned sigh, both harrowing and gorgeous. Similarly, *Minor Angels* documents the end of a world gone desolate and rotting, "not only the human species but even the meaning of language was dying away," yet still shot through with streaks of hope and beauty. The book comprises forty-nine "narracts," unstable chapters describing an unstable world, one that sometimes seems well-populated and sometimes contains only thirty-five living people; one where cities on opposite points of our globe seem to be within walking distance of one another; a world where time has gone strange, where uneventful executions drag on for years and brief pauses in conversation can last days. Encircling the narrative is a group of immortal grandmothers who literally stitch together Will Scheidmann, a patchwork savior, only to lose him when he's sent out to overthrow the vestiges of the old corrupted system but instead resurrects "the cruel chaos of capitalism." Volodine's characters struggle against humankind's demise, managing to cling to their full names and little else, and in the process they reveal their compelling histories and strange presents, all of them concerned that their stories be told as they ride out the last days of a world "ill-equipped to go on living but not knowing how to die." [Tim Feeney]

Igor Klekh. *A Land the Size of Binoculars*. Trans. Michael M. Naydan and Slava I. Yastremski. Intro. Andrei Bitov. Northwestern Univ. Press, 2004. 216 pp. Paper: $18.95.

A Land the Size of Binoculars is the first batch of Igor Klekh's fiction to be translated into English, and with this collection the Ukranian author squarely positions himself as a disciple of Nikolai Gogol. Klekh doesn't emulate Gogol's wit or gift for satire; rather, he shares with his icon an inborn obligation to give voice to the complex cultural history of the Ukraine. Gogol, himself Ukranian, was obsessed with his homeland—he wrote an unpublished, eight-volume history of the Ukraine—and he strove his entire life to establish the rightful place of "Little Russia" in the world order. Klekh isn't quite that ambitious, but he clearly sees himself as a literary chronicler of his native land. Translators Naydan and Yastremski aptly compare Klekh's style to Gabriel García Márquez in their introduction; Klekh's prose is a little more descriptive and a little less mystical, but at its best, it's just as rich and poetic. He is a polished stylist, and his themes and narrative structures are intriguing. "Kallimakh's Wake," the novella that opens this collection, depicts a 13th century scholar and political figure, but the narration is periodically interrupted by the story's author—presumably Klekh himself—who in turn doubts and chastises himself for writing about something he supposedly knows little about. Unfortunately, Klekh's ideas aren't always so well executed, and his writing is, on a few occasions, a bit simplistic and self-absorbed. Gems like "The Foreigner," a darkly brilliant and masterfully efficient piece, are often followed by less mature stories like "The Way Home," where the central character quickly transforms from a hazed, troubled souse to a sentimental father figure. Think of it as an album with a few hit singles and a handful of forgettable songs. But do think of it, and keep an eye on Mr. Klekh, as the best writing in this collection shows real talent. [Chris Paddock]

Blaise Cendrars. *The Astonished Man*. Trans. Nina Rootes. Peter Owen, 2004. 260 pp. Paper: $22.95. (Reprint)

The modernist memoir is compulsively prone to fabrication, but in this respect Cendrars is in a class of his own. *The Astonished Man* is the first of four autobiographical volumes Cendrars wrote between 1943-49 and is a fine example of his characteristic mannerisms and concerns. There is little effort to create a rounded life narrative or a discernable sequence or thematic interrelation between the various episodes, although clearly the opening account of Cendrars's experiences with the French Foreign Legion during WWI offers an explanation of sorts for the anarchistic and outsider perspective that permeates throughout, a disdain for all manifestations of conventional shibboleths. Each major section has a home-base, a site in and around which the author situates himself, often with the intention of writing, while his memories ramble off on his famous worldwide peregrinations—one running theme is car travel, a subject Cendrars fears is underappreciated in literature. Cendrars, as he presents himself, prefers associating with social rejects and the oppressed on the one hand and wealthy women on the other, while the more usual fare of modernist autobiography, fellow famous writers and artists, makes only fleeting, usually unflattering appearances, which invariably offer the author an opportunity to assert his anticliquish, indeed, anti-aesthetic perspective. The only sustained portrait of an artist is of the prolific pulp writer Gustave Lerouge, whom Cendrars presents as a true but unrecognized literary giant. But most compelling is what Cendrars calls "the demon of writing," which takes the autobiographical as a space where not only can we be abruptly transported to another continent without knowing just how we got there but allows a seamless movement between normally segregated modes of writing: from meticulous realistic description and Whitmanesque catalogs to quasi-philosophic or sociological meditations to surrealistic or lyrical passages that at times rise to the rhapsodic. Although Cendrars presents himself as a man of aplomb in the face of all manner of odd situations and characters, the astonishment is manifest in this demonic writing that re-creates or simply creates a sense of life experienced as a perpetual force of mutation, and it is the mutants who have Cendrars's allegiance. [Jeffrey Twitchell-Waas]

––––––––––––

Witold Gombrowicz. *A Guide to Philosophy in Six Hours and Fifteen Minutes.* Trans. by Bill Johnston. Yale Univ. Press, 2004. 128 pp. $22.00; *Polish Memories.* Trans. by Bill Johnston. Yale Univ. Press, 2004. 208 pp. $24.00.

These two short volumes augment the overdue English translation of the complete works of one of the twentieth century's most original writers. Witold Gombrowicz was writing a primer on the course of Western philosophy from Kant to existentialism for his young wife shortly before he died in 1969 in France. His unvarnished remarks resemble written-up lecture notes, talking points set down in short, snappy phrases, concise expositions of complex issues informed by serious reading and plenty of strong opinions. While apparently having a great deal of fun doing it, Gombrowicz deftly assesses the European tradition after Descartes as he draws out the arguments that permanently changed the nature of rational thought. Chapters are chronologically organized, each rising genius armed with his magnum opus standing on his predecessors' shoulders as, in Gombrowicz's view, he reduces the range and conduct of rational inquiry, transforming the intellectual basis of contemporary life. Such an informal account, betraying no pretensions to having the last word, may well prove intriguing to those who do not ordinarily read philosophy for diversion, yet may be curious about the point of view of the author of *Ferdydurke*. For while devoting the greater part of his discussion to the existentialists, Gombrowicz himself remains largely neutral, despite his evident sympathy, as he works through the philosophical classics of continental Europe. The clarity and mordant wit of his treatment, along with its occasional lacunae and unforeseen suspension, defer any final judgment.

Polish Memories is equally entertaining, albeit in a different vein, scanning the years before Gombrowicz arrived in Argentina on a cruise and World War II broke out, leaving him stranded. The writer's irreverent detachment lends a touch of absurdity to what fired his imagination while growing up, depicting scenes of furtive pleasure and embarrassment that evoke the insouciance and particular joy in confounding conventions characteristic of his fiction and plays. Written in the early 1960s for broadcast on Radio Free Europe, these sketches recount episodes from school and university days, habits and friendships of early adulthood, the discovery of a vocation by a rather privileged, epicurean, unambitious idler who decided to take up his pen for a living during the brief Polish independence between the world wars. Here in the context of a wryly retrospective perusal emerge the major themes informing his literary works: the concept of form, deliberate reversal of expectations, immaturity vs. maturity, dreams, sybaritism, and, especially, the vexed problem of being Polish in an insecure cultural backwater. Those familiar with the *Diaries* will recall a voice brilliantly querulous and provocative, while a new reader will discover an inspired raconteur charmed by the spell of his own language.

The two books taken together help to illuminate Gombrowicz's sardonic perspective on his early life and ripened learning, for in his ironic scrutiny both are viewed with detachment, mockery, and panache, as might be expected. Considerable interest lurks in these byways for every reader of Gombrowicz, a few more pieces to the puzzle of one whose style resists easy classification. [Michael Pinker]

Uwe Johnson. *A Trip to Klagenfurt: In the Footsteps of Ingeborg Bachmann.* Trans. Damion Searls. Northwestern Univ. Press, 2004. 92 pp. Paper: $19.95

Days after Ingeborg Bachmann's death, Uwe Johnson travels to her gravesite in her hometown of Klagenfurt. If this be pilgrimage—and it is—it is also intervention. Bachmann left Klagenfurt never to return—"above all," she writes, "one cannot . . . come back"—living in New York, Zurich, and, most recently, Rome, at the time of her death. Johnson's account of his trip explains why Bachmann had to leave and could not return, although suggesting an interpretation Johnson himself resists. "I need say nothing. Only show," Walter Benjamin says of his method in his unfinished *The Arcades Project*. "The rags, the refuse . . . not to make an inventory of these things, but to allow them, in the only possible way, to fulfill their existence." Johnson's method in *A Trip to Klagenfurt* is a layering—an accretion, if you will—of newspapers, histories, lists, state documents, statistics, interviews, tourist information, culture, geography, talk, observation, schedules, letters from Bachmann, quotations from her fiction, which allow the material to speak for itself. "There was one specific moment that shattered my childhood," Bachmann comments in an interview. "The march of Hitler's troops into Klagenfurt [in 1938 when she was 12] . . . that was the first time I felt the terror of death." The war never ended for Bachmann ("The assassins are still with us") and fascism did not die when the guns stopped ("the first element in the relationship between a man and a woman"). Johnson's assemblage pieces together a Klagenfurt of the past, the one Bachmann lived in as a teenager during war, the one standing today as a footnote to her judgment. He gives the first words of his book to Bachmann, in a letter she writes him: "every obituary is necessarily an indiscretion." The indiscretions writers commit to keep obituaries from being last words. Searls's new, more powerful, translation of Bachmann's story, "Youth in an Austrian Town," included here, parallels Johnson's document and presents her own version of why she had to leave. [Robert Buckeye]

Thomas DePietro, ed. *Conversations with Don DeLillo.* Univ. Press of Mississippi, 2004. xiv + 183 pp. Cloth: $50.00; Paper $20.00.

This latest volume in the Mississippi Literary Conversations series collects seventeen interviews with Don DeLillo from 1982 through 2001. The series policy is always to present the full texts of interviews so inevitably there is some repetition, but this only reflects DeLillo's priorities. Having adopted Joyce's "silence, exile, cunning" as a personal slogan, DeLillo avoids personal issues and comments instead on his writings and on the position of the novelist in American culture. "The writer is the person who stands outside society," he declares; and this explains his fascination in *Libra* with Lee Harvey Oswald, the "outsider who wants to belong." DeLillo emerges from these interviews as a supreme craftsman, constructing his sentences with the care of a poet even in these interviews. His New York background has given him an ongoing fascination with the different speech registers of that city, hence his use of dialogue as a recurring means to construct his characters. To balance that interest, he acknowledges repeatedly that his fascination with sixties film—particularly with Godard, Antonioni and others—helped to shape his narrative methods. They suggested ways of finding mystery in the commonplace and offered a method of visual analysis: "film allows us to examine ourselves in ways earlier societies could not." DeLillo's chosen stance as cultural observer enables him to comment on the symbolic importance of the Kennedy assassination and the circulation of violent images. The novel offers a "balance and rhythm" found neither in real life nor in history, but the result is an induced engagement, not escapism. [David Seed]

Books Received

Ali, Tariq. *A Sultan in Palermo*. Verso Books, 2005. $24.00. (F)

Allemand, Roger-Michel and Christian Milat. *Le Nouveau Roman en Questions 5: Une "Nouvelle Autobiographie"?* Lettres Modernes Minard, 2004. Paper: €25.00. (NF)

Andrukhovych, Yuri. *Perverzion*. Trans. and intro. Michael M. Naydan. Northwestern Univ. Press, 2005. Paper: $25.95. (F)

Aslam, Nadeem. *Maps for Lost Lovers*. Knopf, 2005. $25.00. (F)

Auslander, Shalom. *Beware of God*. Simon & Schuster, 2005. $19.95. (F)

Averill, Thomas Fox. *Ordinary Genius*. Univ. of Nebraska Press, 2005. $22.00. (F)

Badaracco, Claire H., ed. *Quoting God: How the Media Shape Ideas about Religion and Culture*. Baylor Univ. Press, 2005. Paper: $29.95. (NF)

Baingana, Doreen. *Tropical Fish*. Univ. of Massachusetts Press, 2005. $24.95. (F)

Balsamo, Gian. *Joyce's Messianism*. Univ. of South Carolina Press, 2004. $34.95. (NF)

Bamberger, W. C. *The Master Tanner Heads West*. Livingston Press, 2005. Paper: $14.95. (F)

Barash, David P., and Nanelle R. *Madame Bovary's Ovaries*. Delacorte Press, 2005. $24.00. (NF)

Barnes, Dick. *A Word like Fire*. Other Press, 2005. Paper: $17.00. (P)

Belli, Gioconda. *The Inhabited Woman*. Trans. Kathleen March. Univ. of Wisconsin Press, 2005. Paper: $19.95. (F)

Bernard, Kenneth. *The Man in the Stretcher*. Starcherone Books, 2005. Paper: $18.00. (F)

Bloland, Sue Erikson. *In the Shadow of Fame: A Memoir by the Daughter of Erik H. Erikson*. Viking, 2005. 24.95. (NF)

Bollas, Christopher. *I Have Heard the Mermaids Singing*. Free Association Books, 2005. $22.99. (F)

Bouazza, Hafid. *Paravion*. Prometheus, 2004. €15.00. (F)

Boydon, Joseph. *Three Day Road*. Viking, 2005. $23.95. (F)

Brady, Joan. *Bleedout*. Touchstone, 2005. $25.00. (F)

Brennan, Karen. *The Garden in which I Walk*. FC2, 2005. Paper: $14.95. (F)

Broder, Gloria Kurian. *Their Magician*. Other Press, 2005. $20.00. (F)

Brossard, Nicole. *Yesterday, at the Hotel Clarendon*. Trans. Susanne De Lotbiniere-Harwood. Coach House, 2005. $19.95. (F)

Bruns, Gerald L. *The Material of Poetry*. Univ. of Georgia Press, 2005. $24.95. (NF)

Bryce Echenique, Alfredo. *A World for Julius*. Univ. of Wisconsin Press, 2005. Paper: $19.95. (F)

Burdett, John. *Bangkok Tattoo*. Knopf, 2005. $24. (F)

Buzura, Augustin. *Requiem for Fools and Beasts*. Trans. Liviu Bleoca. Eastern European Monographs, 2004. $30.00. (F)

Carruthers, Gerald, David Goldie, and Alastair Renfrew, eds. *Beyond Scotland: New Contexts for Twentieth-Century Scottish Literature*. Editions Rodopi B.V., 2004. Paper: $70.00. (NF)

Casanova, Pascale. *The World Republic of Letters*. Trans. M. B. DeBevoise. Harvard Univ. Press, 2004. $35.00. (NF)

Charun-Illescas, Lucia. *Malambo*. Trans. Emmanuel Harris II. Univ. of Chicago Press, 2005. $28.00. (F)

Ciuraru, Carmela, ed. Motherhood: *Poems about Mothers*. Knopf, 2005. $12.50. (Anthology)

Coake, Christopher. *We're in Trouble*. Harcourt, 2005. $23.00. (F)

Coe, Jonathan. *Like a Fiery Elephant: The Story of B. S. Johnson*. Continuum, 2005. $29.95. (NF)

Cokal, Susann. *Breath and Bones*. Unbridled Books, 2005. $23.95. (F)

Corrigan, Michael. *The Irish Connection*. Publish America, 2004. Paper: $21.95. (F)

Crasnaru, Daniela. *The Grand Prize and Other Stories*. Northwestern Univ. Press, 2005. Paper: $14.95. (F)

Cronin, Gloria L., and Ben Siegel, eds. *Conversations with Robert Penn Warren*. Univ. Press of Mississippi, 2005. Paper: $20.00. (NF)

Cruz, Angie. *Let it Rain Coffee*. Simon & Schuster, 2005. $23.00. (F)

Currey, Richard. *Lost Highway*. Vandalia Press, 2005. Paper: $16.50. (F)

Dasgupta, Rana. *Tokyo Cancelled*. Grove, 2005. Paper: $13.00. (F)

Davies, Lewis, ed. *Urban Welsh*. Dufour Editions / Parthian, 2005. Paper: $19.95. (F)

De Luca, Erri. *Three Horses*. Trans. Michael F. Moore. Other Press, 2005. Paper: $11.95. (F)

Deblanco, Andrew. *Melville*. Knopf, 2005. $30.00. (NF)

Deloria, Vine Jr., ed. *A Sender of Words: Essays in Memory of John G. Neihardt*. Univ. of Nebraska Press, 2005. Paper: $14.95. (NF)

Dery, Tibor. *Love and Other Stories*. Trans. various. New Directions, 2005. Paper: $17.95. (F)

Edwards, Martin, ed. *Crime on the Move*. Foreword Michael Jecks. Dufour Editions / Do-Not Press, 2005. Paper: $18.95. (F)

Ellis, Bret Easton Ellis. *Lunar Park*. Knopf, 2005. $25.00. (F)

Erickson, Steve. *Days between Stations*. Simon & Schuster, 2005. $24.00. (F)

Erickson, Steve. *Tours of the Black Clock*. Simon & Schuster, 2005. $24.00. (F)

Eshleman, Clayton. *My Devotion*. David R. Godine / Black Sparrow, 2004. Paper: $16.95. (P)

Falco, Edward. *Sabbath Night in the Church of the Piranha*. Unbridled, 2005. Paper: $13.95. (F)

Federman, Raymond. *My Body in Nine Parts*. Starcherone Books, 2005. Paper: $16.00. (F)

Fischer, Detlev. *Secret Ballet*. Salon Verlag, 2004. Paper: $15.00. (F)

Foos, Laurie. *Before Elvis There Was Nothing*. Coffee House Press, 2005. Paper: $14.00. (F)

Fowles, John. *The Journals, Volume One: 1949-1965*. Ed. and intro. Charles Drazin. Knopf, 2005. $35.00. (NF)

Fried, Golda. *Nellcott Is My Darling*. Coach House, 2005. Paper: $14.95. (F)

Furman, Andrew. *Alligators May Be Present*. Univ. of Wisconsin Press, 2005. $24.95. (F)

Gaige, Amity. *O My Darling*. Other Press, 2005. $22.00. (F)

Gaustad, Edwin S. *Faith of the Founders*. Baylor University Press, 2005. Paper: $24.95. (NF)

Gifford, Barry. *Do the Blind Dream?* Seven Stories, 2004. $21.95. (F)

Gilliland, Norman. *Sand Mansions*. University of Wisconsin Press, 2005. $24.95. (F)

Giono, Jean. *The Serpent of Stars*. Trans. Jody Gladding. Archipelago Books, 2004. Paper: $15. (F)

Glaister, Lesley, ed. *Are You She?* Dufour Editions / Tindal Street Press, 2005. Paper: $16.95. (F)

Glatt, Lisa. *The Apple's Bruise*. Simon & Schuster, 2005. Paper: $12.00. (F)

Glatt, Lisa. *A Girl Becomes a Comma like That*. Simon & Schuster, 2004. Paper: $12.00. (F)

Gonzalez, Jose Luis. *Ballad of Another Time*. Trans Asa Zatz. Intro. Irene Vilar. Univ. of Wisconsin Press, 2005. Paper: $17.95. (F)

Grassian, Daniel. *Understanding Sherman Alexie*. Univ. of South Carolina Press, 2005. $34.95. (NF)

Hamill, Sam. *Almost Paradise*. Shambhala Publications, 2005. Paper: $15.95. (P)

Hauser, Marianne. *The Collected Short Fiction of Marianne Hauser*. FC2, 2005. Paper: $17.95. (F)

Henning, Barbara. *You, Me, and the Insects*. Spuyten Duyvil, 2005. Paper: $14.95. (F)

Heuler, Karen. *Journey to Bom Goody*. Livingston Press, 2005. Paper: $14.95. (F)

Hickey, Patricia. *Green Poppies*. Dufour Editions, 2005. Paper: $16.95. (F)

Hooper, Brad. *The Fiction of Ellen Gilchrist*. Greenwood, 2005. $39.95. (NF)

Irwin, John T., and Jean McGarry, eds. *So the Story Goes: Twenty-Five Years of the Johns Hopkins Short Fiction Series*. Foreword John Barth. Johns Hopkins Univ. Press, 2005. Paper: $18.95. (F)

Jablonsky, William. *The Indestructible Man*. Livingston Press, 2005. Paper: $14.95. (F)

Jaffe, Harold. *Terror-Dot-Gov*. Raw Dog Screaming, 2005. Paper: $13.95. (F)

Kadushin, Rapael, ed. *Barnstorm*. Univ. of Wisconsin Press, 2005. Paper: $19.95. (F)

Kahn, Robert S. *An Honest Thief*. Livingston Press, 2005. Paper: $14.95. (F)

Kaukonen, Scott A. *Ordination*. Ohio State Univ. Press, 2005. $29.95. (F)

Kelly, Robert. *Lapis*. David R. Godine / Black Sparrow, 2005. Paper: $18.95. (P)

Kettmann, Steve. *One Day at Fenway*. Atria, 2004. $25. (NF)

Klimontovich, Nikolai. *The Road to Home*. Trans. Frank Williams. Northwestern Univ. Press, 2004. $17.95. (F)

Laughlin, James. *Byways*. Ed. Peter Glassgold. New Directions, 2005. 35.00. (NF)

Le, Doan. *The Cemetery of the Chua Village*. Trans. Rosemary Nguyen, Duong Tuong, and Wayne Karlin. Curbstone Press, 2005. Paper: $14.95. (F)

Lesser, Wendy. *The Pagoda in the Garden*. Other Press, 2005. $23.95. (F)

Lester, David. *The Gruesome Acts of Capitalism*. Intro. Jean Smith. Arbeiter Ring, 2005. Paper: $9.95. (NF)

Link, Kelly. *Magic for Beginners*. Illus. Shelley Jackson. Small Beer Press, 2005. $24.00. (F)

Lopez, Alejandro. *Die Lady Die*. Aliform Publishing, 2005. Paper: $12.95. (F)

Lucas, Tim. *The Book of Renfield*. Touchstone, 2005. Paper: $14. (F)

Macaulay, Ronald K. S. *Extremely Common Eloquence*. Editions Rodopi, 2005. Paper: $34.00. (NF)

Mandelman, Avner. *Talking to the Enemy*. Seven Stories, 2005. $20.00. (F)

Mann, Thomas. *Joseph and His Brothers*. Trans. John E. Woods Knopf, 2005. $35.00. (F)

Marias, Javier. *Your Face Tomorrow*. Trans. Margaret Jull Costa. New Directions, 2005. $24.95. (F)

Martin, Lee. *The Bright Forever.* Crown Publishing, 2005. $23.00. (F)

Marzan, J. A. *The Bonjour Gene.* Univ. of Wisconsin Press, 2005. $26.95. (F)

Mazza, Chris. *Disability.* FC2, 2005. Paper: $13.95. (F)

McCall Smith, Alexander. *In the Company of Cheerful Ladies.* Pantheon Books, 2005. $19.95. (F)

McCann, Richard. *Mother of Sorrows.* Pantheon Books, 2005. $20.00. (F)

McCarthy, Cormac. *No Country for Old Men.* Knopf, 2005. $24.95. (F)

McClennen, Sophia A. *The Dialectics of Exile.* Purdue Univ. Press, 2004. Paper: $32.95. (NF)

McClennen, Sophia A. and Earl E. Fitz, eds. *Comparative Cultural Studies and Latin America.* Purdue Univ. Press, 2004. Paper: $32.95. (NF)

McCune, Adam, and Keith. *The Rats of Hamelin.* Moody Publishers, 2005. Paper: $12.99. (F)

McHugh, Maureen F. *Mothers and Other Monsters.* Small Beer Press, 2005. $24.00. (F)

McLaverty, Michael. *Lost Fields.* Dufour Editions, 2005. Paper: $16.95. (F)

Mejia, Michael. *Forgetfulness.* FC2, 2005. Paper: $15.95. (F)

Millet, Richard. *The Glory of the Pythres.* Trans. John Cumming. Northwestern Univ. Press, 2005. Paper: $19.95. (F)

Modiano, Patrick. *Missing Person.* Trans. Daniel Weissbort. David R. Godine, 2005. Paper: $16.95. (F)

Monson, Ander. *Other Electricities.* Sarabande Books, 2005. Paper: $14.95. (F)

Montale, Eugenia. *Montale in English.* Trans. various. Other Press, 2005. Paper: $17.00. (P)

Murray, Francis. *Satirical Americana.* Xlibris, 2004. Paper: $20.99. (F)

Nathan, Micah. *Gods of Aberdeen.* Simon and Schuster, 2005. $24.00. (F)

Paglia, Camille. *Break Blow Burn.* Pantheon Books, 2005. $20.00. (NF)

Palyi, Andras. *Out of Oneself.* Trans. Imre Goldstein. Twisted Spoon, 2005. Paper: $13.50. (F)

Payne, Jack. *Six Hours Past Thursday.* Impact, 2004. Paper: $16.95. (F)

Pearlman, Edith. *How to Fall.* Sarabande Books, 2005. Paper: $14.95. (F)

Pearson, T.R. *Glad News of the Natural World.* Simon & Schuster, 2005. $24.00. (F)

Pekic, Borislac. *How to Quiet a Vampire*. Trans. Stephen M. Dickey and Bogdan Rakic. Northwestern Univ. Press, 2005. Paper: $18.95. (F)

Perez, Benjamin L. *The Evil Queen: A Pornolexicology*. Spuyten Duyvil, 2005. Paper: $13.00. (F)

Perez, Richard. *The Loser's Club: Complete Restored Edition*. Ludlow Press, 2005. Paper: $13.95. (F)

Perova, Natasha, ed. *Strange Soviet Practices*. Northwestern Univ. Press, 2004. Paper: $17.95. (F, NF)

Plascencia, Salvador. *The People of Paper*. McSweeney's, 2005. $22.00. (F)

Powers, Alice Leccese, ed. *Tuscany in Mind*. Vintage Books, 2005. Paper: $14.00. (F, NF, P)

Prior, Amy, ed. *Lost on Purpose*. Seal Press, 2005. Paper: $13.95. (F)

Rabassa, Gregory. *If This Be Treason*. New Directions, 2005. $21.95. (NF)

Rathwell, Richard. *The Bush: Hank the Aid Detective*. Blue Orange Publishing, 2004. Paper: $18.67. (F)

Rayfiel, Thomas. *Eve in the City*. Ballantine Books, 2005. Paper: $13.95. (F)

Reeve, F. D. *My Sister Life*. Other Press, 2005. $23.95. (F)

Richardson, Peter. *Building Jewish in the Roman East*. Baylor Univ. Press, 2004. Paper: $39.95. (NF)

Rimington, Stella. *At Risk*. Knopf, 2005. $24.95. (F)

Ripper, Jo. *Moments in Time*. Dufour Editions, 2005. Paper: $19.95. (F)

Rogers, Thomas. *At the Shores*. Other Press, 2005. Paper: $14.00. (F)

Ruskin, John. *Praeterita*. Intro. Tim Hilton. Knopf, 2005. $23.00. (NF)

Salter, James. *Last Night*. Knopf, 2005. $20.00. (F)

Sankaran, Lavanya. *The Red Carpet: Bangalore Stories*. The Dial Press, 2005. $23.00. (F)

Schor, Lynda. *The Body Parts Shop*. FC2, 2005. Paper: $14.95. (F)

Seitz, Cristopher. *Word without End*. Baylor Univ. Press, 2005. Paper: $24.95. (NF)

Sijie, Dai. *Mr. Muo's Travelling Couch*. Trans. Ina Rilke. Knopf, 2005. $22.00. (F)

Sirias, Silvio. *Bernardo and the Virgin*. Northwestern Univ. Press, 2005. $26.95. (F)

Spiegelman, Peter. *Death's Little Helpers*. Knopf, 2005. $22.95. (F)

Steen, Thorvald. *Don Carlos and Giovanni*. Trans. James Anderson. Green Integer, 2005. Paper: $13.95. (F)

Stenberg, Peter, ed. *Contemporary Jewish Writing in Sweden: An Anthology*. Univ. of Nebraska Press, 2004. $60.00. (F)

Stern, Richard. *Natural Shocks*. Foreword James Schiffer. Triquarterly, 2004. Paper: $15.95. (F)

Stern, Richard. *Other Men's Daughters*. Foreword Wendy Doniger. Triquarterly, 2004. Paper: $15.95. (F)

Stern, Richard. *Stitch*. Foreword Ingrid D. Rowland. Triquarterly, 2004. Paper: $15.95. (F)

Stern, Richard. *Almonds to Zhoof: Collected Stories*. Triquarterly, 2005. $29.95. (F)

Stern, Steve. *The Angel of Forgetfulness*. Viking, 2005. $24.95. (F)

Stiks, Igor. *A Castle in Romagna*. Trans. Tomislac Kuzmanovic and Russell Scott Valentino. Autumn Hill, 2005. Paper: $12.95. (F)

Stolls, Amy. *Palms to the Ground*. Farrar Straus & Giroux, 2005. $17.00. (F)

Strand, Ginger. *Flight*. Simon & Schuster, 2005. $23.00. (F)

Suprynowicz, Vin. *The Black Arrow*. Mountain Media, 2005. $24.95. (F)

Syrotinski, Michael, ed. *The Power of Rhetoric, The Rhetotic of Power: Jean Paulhan's Fiction, Criticism, and Editorial Activity*. Yale French Studies: Yale Univ. Press, 2005. Paper: $20.00. (NF)

Tabucchi, Antonio. *The Missing Head*. Trans. J. C. Patrick. New Directions, 2005. Paper: $14.95. (F)

Taylor, Joe. *The World's Thinnest Fat Man: Scenes from a Life in Fugue*. Swallow's Tale, 2005. Paper: $14.95. (F)

Thomson, Rupert. *Divided Kingdom*. Knopf, 2005. $25.95. (F)

Tinti, Hannah. *Animal Crackers*. Delta Books, 2005. Paper: $12.00. (F)

Todd, Loreto. *A Fire in His Head*. Univ. of Wisconsin Press, 2005. Paper: $19.95. (F)

Tomasula, Steve. *VAS: An Opera in Flatland*. Art and design by Stephen Farrell. Univ. of Chicago Press, 2004. Paper: $18.00. (F)

Trakl, Georg. *Poems and Prose*. Intro., trans., and notes Alexander Stillmark. Northwestern Univ. Press, 2005. Paper: $17.95. (P)

Tropper, Jonathan. *Everything Changes*. Delacorte Press, 2005. $20.00. (F)

Valladres, Michelle Yasmine. *Nortada, the North Wind*. Global City Press, 2005. Paper: $12.00. (P)

Vaught, Carl G. *Metaphor, Analogy, and the Place of Places*. Baylor Univ. Press, 2005. $29.95. (NF)

Verissimo, Luis. *Borges and the Eternal Orangutans*. Trans. Margaret Jull Costa. New Directions, 2005. Paper: $13.95. (F)

Wakoski, Diane. *Emerald Ice*. David R. Godine / Black Sparrow, 2005. Paper: $18.95. (P)

Weatherby, H. L. and George Core, eds. *Place in American Fiction*. Univ. of Missouri Press, 2005. $42.50. (NF)

Weber, Myles. *Consuming Silences: How We Read Authors Who Don't Publish*. Univ. of Georgia Press, 2005. Paper: $19.95. (NF)

Weiss, Ben. *The ACAC Conspiracy*. Vantage Press, 2005. $22.95. (F)

White, Edmund. *Arts and Letters*. Cleis Press, 2004. $24.95. (NF)

Winslow, Don. *The Power of the Dog*. Knopf, 2005. $25.95. (F)

Wolf, Christa. *In the Flesh*. Trans. John S. Barrett. David R. Godine, 2005. $24.95. (F)

Woo, David. *The Eclipses*. BOA Editions, 2005. Paper: $14.95. (P)

Contributors

STAN FOGEL, Professor of English at St. Jerome's University/ University of Waterloo, has an honorary degree from Instituto Superior de Arte, Havana, Cuba. He is the author of, among other works, *A Tale of Two Countries*, *The Postmodern University*, and *Gringo Star*, a travel book.

JAMES REIDEL is the author of *Vanished Act: The Life and Art of Weldon Kees* (University of Nebraska Press, 2003). An independent scholar, Reidel's interests are in writers whose disrupted careers or neglected work need a presence in the canon. He is also a poet, having published in the *New Yorker*, *Paris Review*, *TriQuarterly*, *New Criterion*, *Verse*, *Poets Lore*, *Ploughshares*, and in such online journals as *Cortland Review*, *Pierian Springs*, *Web-Conjunctions*, the *Adirondack Review*, and *Slope*. Black Lawrence Press will publish his first collection, *My Window Seat for Arlena Twigg*, in Spring 2006. Also forthcoming is his rendering of two of Thomas Bernhard's poetry cycles from the German, *In Hora Mortis* and *Under the Iron of the Moon*, published by Princeton University Press as a single volume. Reidel plans to edit a selected critical edition of Lowry's fiction. He is also currently writing a piece about the photography of Weldon Kees for the *Ephemera*.

M. G. STEPHENS is the author of eighteen books, including *Season at Coole* and *The Brooklyn Book of the Dead*, both of which were published by Dalkey Archive. *The Brooklyn Book* was later published in Ireland by New Island Books in 1999, and in Germany by Achilla Presse in 2002. He recently finished a book of sonnets, *One for Nought*, and a novel, *Kid Coole*, parts of which have appeared in *Ontario Review* and *Witness*. His other published work includes the memoir *Where the Sky Ends*, the travel memoir *Lost in Seoul*, and the play *Our Father*, which was revived in London in 2004. He is a Senior Lecturer and Director of the M.A. in Creative Writing at Kingston University in London. The Ross Feld essay is part of a doctoral thesis he is completing at the University of Essex, Colchester, England, on the Saint Mark's in the Bowery Poetry Project and its influences.

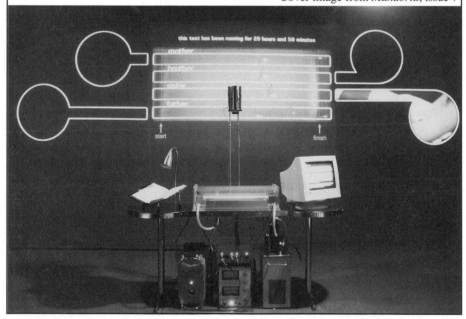

CONJUNCTIONS:44

An Anatomy of Roads: The Quest Issue

Leaving home is a dangerous business. Whether it's to walk across the street or travel to another continent, one never returns the same. This issue explores in fiction and poetry the complex process of defamiliarization as the ultimate path to knowing oneself. Includes new work by John Barth, Elizabeth Hand, Jonathan Carroll, Rikki Ducornet, Susan Steinberg, Joshua Furst, Robert Antoni, Joyce Carol Oates, Forrest Gander, Jon McGregor, Robert Coover, Joanna Scott, Paul West, and many others. The issue also features a portfolio of fiction and poems by writers including William H. Gass, Elizabeth Willis, John Taggart, Martine Bellen, Rachel Blau DuPlessis, Richard Meier, and others. 404 pages.

CONJUNCTIONS
Edited by Bradford Morrow
Published by Bard College
Annandale-on-Hudson, NY 12504

To order, phone 845-758-1539,
or visit www.conjunctions.com

Golden Handcuffs Review

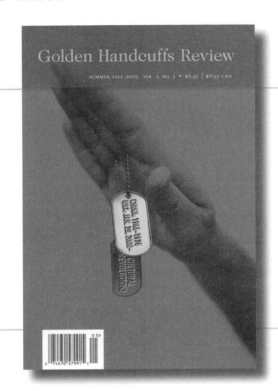

In letters, there is nothing like Golden Handcuffs, and nothing better.

−Harry Mathews

THE HUDSON REVIEW

684 PARK AVENUE • NEW YORK, NY 10021

In the Summer 2005 issue

"Flaubert in 1848," an essay by Frederick Brown

"Periodicity in English Verse," an essay by Emily Grosholz

"Betjeman's Way," a review by William H. Pritchard

"Pritchett Unselfing Himself," a review by Dean Flower

Brooke Allen on Alexander the Great

Poems by Daniel Hoffman, Annie Boutelle, Peter Makuck,
    Brooks Haxton, and Jon Mooallem

"One of the most prestigious literary journals in the
country. The list of those who began their careers in
the journal includes some of the most formidable
writers and poets in the second half of the 20th
Century."   —*The New York Times*

Start a future of good reading...

[ ] ONE YEAR (FOUR ISSUES): $32 / $36 FOREIGN
[ ] TWO YEARS (EIGHT ISSUES): $56 / $64 FOREIGN
[ ] THREE YEARS (TWELVE ISSUES): $80 / $92 FOREIGN

NAME _____

ADDRESS _____

CITY _____ STATE ____ ZIP _____

Please return with check or money order.

www.hudsonreview.com

Joseph Conrad
The Short Fiction.

Edited by Daphna Erdinast-Vulcan,
Allan H. Simmons, and J.H. Stape

Amsterdam/New York, NY 2004. X, 156 pp.
(The Conradian 28:2)

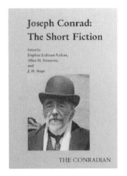

Joseph Conrad:
The Short Fiction

Edited by
Daphna Erdinast-Vulcan,
Allan H. Simmons,
and
J. H. Stape

THE CONRADIAN

ISBN: 90-420-0960-8   € 34,-/US $ 44.-

Joseph Conrad: The Short Fiction offers a wide range of perspectives on Conrad's short stories. Nine essays, by established and emerging scholars, deal with early and classic stories as well as the relatively neglected works of Conrad's later career.
The essays explore in depth the historical and publishing contexts of individual stories and provide insights into Conrad's practice as a writer of short fiction. These new readings, based on contemporary theoretical and interpretive perspectives, will appeal not only to specialists of literary Modernism but also to the advanced student and the general reader.

Rodopi

USA/Canada: 906 Madison Avenue, UNION, NJ 07083, USA
Call toll-free (USA only)1-800-225-3998, Tel. 908 206 1166, Fax 908-206-0820
All other countries: Tijnmuiden 7, 1046 AK Amsterdam, The Netherlands.
Tel. ++ 31 (0)20 611 48 21, Fax ++ 31 (0)20 447 29 79
Orders-queries@rodopi.nl   www.rodopi.nl
Please note that the exchange rate is subject to fluctuations

Dalkey Archive Press announces a call
for submissions to the

DALKEY ARCHIVE SCHOLARLY SERIES

(expanding opportunities for
specialized scholarly research)

AREAS OF INTEREST:

.... **monographs** on authors from throughout the
world in the aesthetic tradition represented
by Dalkey Archive Press's list

.... **encyclopedic companions** to contemporary
fiction from around the world

.... **literary history** and **theory**

.... **cultural studies**

.... **collections of interviews**

.... **aesthetics**

.... **bibliographies** of contemporary novelists

For further details related to submission, please visit
www.dalkeyarchive.com

DALKEY ARCHIVE PRESS

Dalkey Archive Press

NEW RELEASES

Voices from Chernobyl
SVETLANA ALEXIEVICH

My Life in CIA
HARRY MATHEWS

Europeana
PATRIK OUŘEDNÍK

Hobson's Island
STEFAN THEMERSON

On April 26, 1986, the worst nuclear reactor accident in history occurred in Chernobyl. *Voices from Chernobyl* presents first-hand accounts of what happened to the people of Belarus and the fear, anger, and uncertainty that they lived through. From innocent citizens to firefighters called in to clean up the disaster, this is a crucial document of what happened and how people reacted to it. Svetlana Alexievich presents these interviews in monologue form, giving a harrowing inside view of the affected people and leaving us with the life-shattering pain of living through such an event and its aftermath.

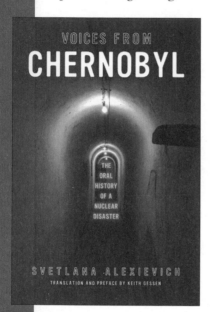

Voices from Chernobyl

Svetlana Alexievich
Translation and Preface by
Keith Gessen

Russian Literature Series
World History
$22.95 / cloth
ISBN: 1-56478-401-0

"*Voices from Chernobyl* builds to the tragic power of a Greek chorus and it is unlikely that we will soon again read such a chronicle of agony and stupidity, heroism and loss."
—*London Times*

"Svetlana Alexievich has devoted her career to capturing eyewitness accounts of communism's extremes—its ability to inspire and command loyalty, and its clumsiness, hypocrisy and contempt for human life."
—*Moscow Times*

Through a series of improbable coincidences in the early 1970s, Harry Mathews was commonly reputed to be a CIA agent. With growing frustration at his inability to make anyone believe his denials, Mathews decided to act the part. *My Life in CIA* documents Mathews's experiences as a would-be spy during 1973, where amid charged world events he found himself engaged in a game that took sinister twists as various foreign agencies decided he was a presence that should be eliminated. Mathews has turned these strange events into a spellbinding thriller that relentlessly blurs the line between fact and fiction.

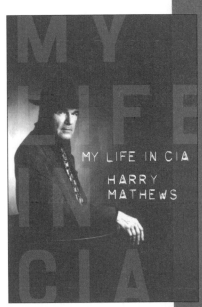

My Life in CIA

Harry Mathews

American Literature Series
Autobiographical Novel
$13.95 / paper
ISBN: 1-56478-392-8

"It's outrageous that an educated man and a gifted writer like Mr. Mathews could make such a public confession of such shameful activities."

—Q. Kuhlmann, author of *The Eye of Anguish: Subversive Activity in the German Democratic Republic*

"This is an honest account by someone (he seems at the time to have been a bit of a ne'er-do-well) who tried to play spy without knowing what the word meant and landed himself in boiling-hot water. The book, which is as exciting as any novel, proves a useful moral: leave this business to the pros."

—Colonel Raymond Russell (ret.),
Counterintelligence Corps, U.S. Army

Told in an informal, mesmerizing voice, *Europeana* represents the twentieth century in all of its contradictions and grand illusions, demonstrating that nothing substantial has changed between 1900 and 1999—humanity is still hopeful for the future and still mired in age-old conflicts. As he demonstrates that nothing can be reduced to a single, "true" viewpoint, Ouředník mixes hard facts and idiosyncratic observations, highlighting the horror and absurdity of the twentieth century and the further absurdity of attempting to narrate this history.

Europeana:
A Brief History of the Twentieth Century

PATRIK OUŘEDNÍK
TRANSLATION BY GERALD TURNER

Eastern European Literature Series
A Novel
$12.50 / paper
ISBN: 1-56478-382-0

"Touching on subjects and events as disparate as the invention of the bra, Barbie dolls, Scientology, eugenics, the Internet, war, genocide and concentration camps, it unspools in a relentless monotone that becomes unexpectedly engaging, even frightening."

—*New York Times Book Review*

"*Europeana* reads like a frenzied encyclopedic compression of thousands of history books; it's cleverly constructed and more subjective than it first appears. . . . Laughs guaranteed, uneasiness probable, impressions strong: in short a great book."

—*Chronic'art*

Hobson's Island enjoyed decades of isolation in the Atlantic Ocean. For years, the caretakers lived there peacefully, with only a cow for company and an empty house to care for. But all is suddenly disrupted when a wave of unusual visitors arrive. In typical Themerson fashion, the comic is wound up with the serious and let go to devastating effect. A clever and apt parody of Cold War power plays and twisted science, *Hobson's Island* is a strangely touching, sympathetic, and emotional account of the families and individuals brought together and broken up by Hobson's Island.

Hobson's Island

STEFAN THEMERSON
PREFACE BY BARBARA WRIGHT

British Literature Series
A Novel
$13.95 / paper
ISBN: 1-56478-417-7

"Themerson's neo-surrealist style enables him felicitously to interweave incongruities, ludic exercises, shrewd observations, jokes, lightly worn learning, *cris de couer*, and parables."
—*Times Literary Supplement*

"When all is said and done, Themerson is of the company of Carroll and Queneau, a master of controlled inconsequence, God's spy with no one to give reports to, a fine flea in the ear of the modern novel."
—*Guardian*

ORDER FORM

Individuals may use this form to subscribe to the *Review of Contemporary Fiction* or to order back issues of the *Review* and Dalkey Archive titles at a discount (see below for details).

Title	ISBN	Quantity	Price

Subtotal _____

Less Discount _____
(10% for one book, 20% for two or more books)

Subtotal _____

Plus Postage _____
($4 domestic, $5 foreign)

1 Year Individual Subscription to the **Review** _____
($17 domestic, $20.50 foreign)

Total _____

Mailing Address _____

_____

_____

_____

xxv/2

Credit card payment   ☐ Visa   ☐ Mastercard

Acct # _____   Exp. Date _____

Name on card _____   Phone Number _____

Please make checks (in U.S. dollars only) payable to *Dalkey Archive Press*

mail or fax this form to: Dalkey Archive Press, ISU Campus Box 8905, Normal, IL 61790-8905; *fax:* 309.438.7422; *tel:* 309.438.7555